SHADOWS OF LELA

LELA TRILOGY BOOK ONE

TESSONJA ODETTE

NORUN
TOMAS
RISA
Kero
RIDINE CASTLE
Sele
DERMAINE PALACE
VERLOT PALACE
Mena
LELA

1

EXILE

Coralaine

I felt her screams before they left her mouth.

A pain that was not my own invaded my body, flooding my senses with ripples of terror. I sat upright in my bed and rubbed sleep from my eyes, trying to separate myself from the intrusion. The sharpness in my abdomen and pressure between my thighs were not the sensations a ten-year-old girl like myself should have.

Linette! The realization sent me running from my bed. *No. Please no. It's too early for the baby.*

Another scream reverberated through my mind, so much louder and clearer than before. I fell to my knees and put my hands over my ears in an impossible attempt to drown out the sound. I took a deep breath and forced the sound to recede until I was left with nothing more than a sharp ache behind my eyes. My vision blurred as I stood and fled, half-blind and nearly naked in my shift, down the hall.

I ignored the next scream yet couldn't help but double over with the rekindled fire in my abdomen. I bit my lip, and tears pricked my eyes. Still I forced myself onward, stumbling through the empty corridors of Ridine Castle until I found myself in Linette's room. Empty. I knew where to go next.

The pain grew stronger as I neared the birthing chamber, and I had no doubt I would find her there. My heart sank.

I opened the door to a scene of grim-faced queens-maids surrounding the birthing bed. Linette's pain still burned inside me, yet I managed to keep my composure as I pushed my way past the melancholy women to my sister's side.

"What's wrong?" I demanded of the queensmaids, ashamed of how small my voice sounded.

"You shouldn't be here, sweet princess," said one of the maids, laying a sympathetic hand on my shoulder. "This is no place for a young lady. You should return to your bed."

I shot her a defiant stare, and not another word of reproach was made.

I turned my attention to Linette, quivering and pale upon the bed, auburn hair soaked with sweat, head lolling from side to side as she mumbled and moaned. Her frail, white hands twisted in the bloodstained sheets as she gripped them with all her strength. The midwives were in an anxious flurry at the foot of the bed. This was much worse than last time.

I clutched my abdomen, the pain almost impossible to endure. I wanted to run away. I wanted to free myself from her agony. Yet I remained at her side, still as stone, feeling each spasm as if it were my own.

My eyelids fluttered as waves of pain rose and subsided, over and over, tearing through us both for an endless time. Hours passed. Or was it days? I knew nothing but agony.

Until finally, the torture was over.

Linette lay still. I touched her lightly on the shoulder and she slowly opened her eyes, blinking into the light of the room. She took in the faces around her. When her eyes locked on mine, she pulled her lips into a small smile. I tried to mirror her but could manage no more than pressing my lips into a tight line. No matter what I told myself, I couldn't shake the nagging fear that the danger was yet to pass.

"My little sister," Linette whispered and reached a trembling hand toward mine.

A sob escaped my throat as I grasped her cold fingers. "Sister."

Linette may not have been of my blood, but she was my sister in every other significance of the word. In the five years since she had married my brother, we'd grown close—close enough for her to fill a portion of the hole in my heart left by my parents' deaths. How could I bear it if she left me too?

"My baby?" Linette's brows furrowed as she lifted her head and tried to look over my shoulder.

I turned to the downcast midwives. They shook their heads, confirming what I already knew. Tears streamed down my face as I delivered the news with a solemn shake of my head.

My heart broke alongside Linette's as I watched the

anguish pass over her face. Helpless, I could do nothing but witness the storm of her emotions flooding my consciousness. *What use is this curse of mine if I can't help anyone with it?*

I prayed for her emotional turmoil to subside so I could be free from it myself, but when it finally did, I realized it could only mean one thing; her fight was over. She was slipping away.

Linette's hand fell limp from my grasp. "Get the king!" I shouted at the sobbing maids. "Now!"

A flurry of commotion erupted behind me. It took only a few moments to summon a red-eyed King Dimetreus. His face was slack as he entered the room, and a moan escaped his throat as he fell to his knees at his queen's side.

I quickly backed out of the room, gasping for air as I choked on the suffocating emotions. I took flight down the hallway, stopping only when I felt like I could breathe freely again.

I fell to my knees and shouted into my hands. My anguish dissipated into a wail as I pounded my fists on the stone floor beneath me. I cried for the loss of my mother and father. I cried for Linette and the three children she'd tried so hard to bring into this world. I cried for the burden I carried, knowing all of this was happening, and being helpless to stop any of it.

"Now, now, child, that's enough of that," said a voice behind me, startling me from my grief.

I turned and glared into the pale, long, scowling face of my enemy. My sorrow hardened into hate. "What are you doing here, Morkai?"

"You act as if I don't live here too." He looked down at me with a satisfied grin.

I stood and faced Morkai with balled fists. "How dare you come near Linette's birthing chamber? I know you are responsible for this."

"Coralaine!" came my brother's shout from down the hall. "How could you say such a thing?"

I could barely meet his eyes as I faced him. The pain on his face was enough for me to know Linette was gone. I hung my head and muttered a tearful apology.

"Come now, Dimetreus, she is just upset. I take no offense."

I clenched my teeth, hearing the double effect of Morkai's voice. The voice my brother heard was genuine and caring, but I could hear his true voice and it was full of mocking and malice.

"He has no right to be here," I whispered.

"He has every right. Morkai is one of the most powerful mages in all of Lela. Whom else would I want here at a time like this?"

My head snapped up, and I stared at my brother with wide eyes. "You invited him here? To Linette's birthing chambers?"

"He was trying to save her, Coralaine."

"It's true. I gave her a healing tonic and placed every protective spell around her that I know. I'm sorry I couldn't do more." Morkai rested his hand on my brother's shoulder in what appeared to be a comforting gesture. But I recognized the influence of control flowing from his palm.

Heat flooded my body, a fire I could not ignore. My muscles tensed, quivering from my shoulders to my toes.

"Was it the same tonic you'd been slipping Linette in her drink every night?"

"That was for fertility," Dimetreus said, "to bring us a son."

I ignored my brother, my eyes locked on Morkai. "Or was it the same tonic you put into my parents' cups every night before they died?"

Dimetreus' shadow fell over me as he took a forbidding step between me and Morkai. "I don't like what you are implying. If I hear another word of disrespect from you, I will throw you out of this castle forever."

"But he murdered our parents!"

"That's a lie."

"He's killed every child you've ever conceived!"

"Enough." Dimetreus' face began to redden. That should have been enough to quiet me, yet the fire still burned within.

"He murdered your wife, and you invited him here!"

"Not another word, Coralaine."

"You might as well have just killed her yourself!"

Dimetreus raised his hand and sent it hard across my face.

After a moment of stunned silence, I placed a palm on my cheek and glared at my brother through a pool of tears. I knew I had crossed the line, but I never expected Dimetreus would strike me.

"You will get out. You will never return here." Dimetreus' voice held a cold, sharp, unfamiliar edge. His eyes were hard and black; I could barely make out the green that used to shine so brightly.

"Dimi," I whispered.

"You have disrespected me, and I am not only your

brother but your king. You have disgraced the name of our deceased parents with your lies. The queen is just moments dead, and already you speak evil of her."

"Please, Dimi. I'm sorry."

"I don't ever want to hear another word from your mouth. Get out and don't come back. You are hereby banished from Ridine Castle, stripped of your name. You are no longer Princess Coralaine of Kero. You are nobody. You are dead to me. Your memory will be buried with the queen."

I stood frozen, staring at my brother, looking at the face that had become a stranger's. *My brother is dead to me too.*

Morkai grinned at me over my brother's shoulder, jubilant with triumph. A shiver ran down my spine as I understood the full strength of his powers. I'd underestimated him. Tears stung my eyes, my hands clenched into fists. I didn't know whether to scream, cry, run, or plead.

I chose to run.

2

POEMS

Teryn

My hands were sweating.

I kept them busy behind my back, folding and unfolding the small piece of paper within them. The paper bore the most important words I would ever say, words that would bring about an avalanche of events that would change my life forever. Who knew a simple poem could hold such power?

But that's not why I was sweating. At that moment, I had no idea where my poem would ultimately lead me. It was simply a declaration of love to the most beautiful woman in all of Lela. Considering the large number of other princes surrounding me with the same intentions as my own, I had every right to be sweating.

It was the spring festival at Verlot Palace, where Princess Mareleau of Sele would be presented to a public audience for the first time in two years. She was now sixteen and ready to marry. Her portrait had been sent far and wide, along with invitations to compete for her hand at the festival. Here I was, preparing to do just that.

I closed my eyes and went over the poem in my head one more time. I let out a heavy sigh as I finished with every word intact and in perfect order. *I just have to read it once, that's all.* But if my voice shook as much as my hands did, I was in deep trouble.

It didn't help that I would be first to present my poem. If I was terrible—or even plain good—I would get lost and forgotten after the numerous poems that followed. But if my poem was great—or if I was lucky, amazing— no other poem would compare.

But amazing? My poem? I didn't think so. I could only hope the close friendship between Mareleau's family and my own would be enough to give me an advantage.

I stared at Mareleau's empty balcony, lit by the morning sun like a beacon. It was well after third bell, and I felt the crisp, spring air beginning to warm—an unwelcome sensation, considering my current temperature.

I took a cooling breath and turned my attention to King Verdian. The King of Sele stood below Mareleau's balcony on a raised dais upon the lawn, droning on and on in a long and boring speech that would be a challenge to enjoy on even my least anxious day. My eyes blurred, and my mind wandered once again until I heard, "I would now like to present my daughter!"

Just like that, my interest returned. The men around me straightened to full attention as King Verdian contin- ued, "It is a great honor to have you witness the beautiful rose that has blossomed right before my eyes. From a tiny, young bud—"

For the love of Lela, just bring her out already.

"—I am pleased to see so many young princes here today, eager to win her hand and her love—"

My heart raced.

"I now present to you, Princess Mareleau!"

Complete silence followed as the crowd stared wide-eyed at Mareleau's empty balcony. Nothing happened.

"Princess Mareleau!" Verdian repeated. His face turned red as silent moments passed and the balcony doors remained closed. He opened his mouth to speak again but was saved from further embarrassment by the slow swing of the double doors.

The princess stepped out onto the balcony with slow, swaying steps. She was tall and slender with long, willowy limbs and a petite waist. Round, seductive hips and an ivory swell of breasts above her tight bodice added an enticing softness to her frame. Her hair cascaded past her graceful neck down to her waist in rivulets of gold adorned with intricate braids, pearls, and little white rosebuds. She wore a gown of silver and white brocade hemmed with dark blue velvet. Her eyes sparkled like blue sapphires in a porcelain oval of a face. She was perfect in every way.

Except one.

Mareleau stood before the balcony rail, arms crossed, hip popped to one side, nose turned up—the epitome of smug. This should have turned me off, I know, but instead I was fascinated. I found her charming and bold, and imagined her yielding that stubborn demeanor just for me. The thought filled me with warmth, a sense of home and romance and everything I'd ever imagined I would want with my future queen. This was the woman I was going to marry. I was sure of it.

I realized I was being watched, which pulled me from my pleasant thoughts. I turned and met the hard gaze of my twin brother, Larylis. His eyes were pleading; I could almost hear him begging me not to want her. As much as I loved my brother, I knew—we both knew—his desires were useless. I was Prince Teryn, heir to our father's throne as ruler of Mena. Larylis was born too late, too small, and too sickly to be named heir. He was not worthy of Mareleau. I was. And I was willing to do anything to have her.

∼

Larylis

If only I had been born first. If only I had been born strong and healthy. If only I had been chosen as our father's heir. If only Teryn wasn't so damn ambitious. If only he didn't want Mareleau. If only I could accept my fate and let her go.

So many *if only's*, yet if anything had been any other way, if I had been born first, if I had been born healthy, I never would have loved *her*.

And I wouldn't give that up for the world.

Teryn stared like a man enchanted, eyes fixated on Mareleau standing silently on her balcony. I had hoped beyond hope that he wouldn't want her. I knew he would find her beautiful; it was impossible not to. But I didn't want him to *desire* her. As I studied Teryn's awe-stricken face, desire was all I saw. He would call it love, I was sure, but he didn't know what love was. I did.

"Please, Teryn."

Teryn put his hand on my shoulder. His lips were drawn into a frown but there was an excitement behind his eyes. "I'm sorry, brother, but I must."

"You *must*?" My words were drowned by King Verdian's booming voice.

"It is now time for the reading of the poems! First to present his poem is Prince Teryn of Mena, Son of King Arlous and Queen Bethaeny."

Teryn's face turned white as his jaw fell open. The hand he'd placed on my shoulder tightened in an iron grip. For a wonderful, selfish moment, I imagined Teryn would remain frozen in fear. But after only a brief hesitation, he took a deep breath, flashed me an apologetic smile, and stepped forward to read his poem.

> "Oh, what beauty shines from my love fair!
> 'Tis greater and beyond any to compare,
> Her eyes, they glisten like the sea so blue,
> She is as sweet as my love is true,
> Her lips are rosebuds, her skin like a dove,
> Her smile is what my dreams are made of,
> Her voice rings like bells so sweet,
> I ask one thing; will you be my queen?"

Please let her hate it. I held my breath and looked up at Mareleau. She simply continued to stare off into the distance, completely unmoved by the activity below her balcony. *Excellent.*

"Very good, Prince Teryn!" Verdian clapped his hands and created a wave of applause.

My brother's shoulders relaxed as he stepped back into the crowd of princes, wearing a broad smile. I glared at him, but he wouldn't meet my eyes.

"Thank you, Teryn, Prince of Mena. Next we have—"

"Teryn is not the only prince of Mena." I stepped forward, hearing a ripple of gasps around me.

"What are you doing?" Teryn whispered, tugging at my sleeve.

I shrugged from my brother's hold. "I have a poem to read as well, Your Majesty."

Verdian cleared his throat. "I'm sorry, Prince Larylis, but you were not invited to participate in this competition."

"Yet, I have every right to. I love Mareleau more than any man here, and I am just as much a prince as my brother is."

"I'm sure you are familiar with the requirements. Only a crown prince will marry my daughter." Verdian puffed his chest, yet the flush in his cheeks betrayed his composure.

"You care more about making her a queen than giving her a life of love?"

"Silence!" Verdian stepped off the dais and strode toward me, his face now fully crimson. He lowered his voice just above a whisper. "Just because I have known you since you were a boy does not mean you can speak out in such a manner. If you will not honor the rules of this competition, I will have you removed from palace grounds for the remainder of the festival."

Two of the Royal Guard stepped forward, hands on the hilts of their swords as they flanked the king.

"No need," I said through clenched teeth. "I'll remove myself." My shoulders slumped. I turned around, head hanging low as I walked through the sea of staring, smirking, whispering faces. I had lost. Mareleau was lost. How could this be? Doesn't love conquer all? *Not unless you are crown prince, apparently.* I continued through the crowd, muttering to myself and grinding my teeth.

Wait, is this how a man fights for the woman he loves?

I darted back to Mareleau's balcony, once again interrupting Verdian before he could finish announcing the next contestant. "I love you, Mareleau! You can pretend you don't remember me all you want but I see through you! You are still the same beautiful, caring, loving, smiling girl you were when we were kids."

Mareleau's eyes met mine, and in that moment I was entranced, wanting nothing more than to fall into those blue pools forevermore. What did they hold in their sparkling depths? Recognition? Love? Her lips parted, and I was sure I saw tenderness in her eyes. Before my hope could swell for another heartbeat, something else crossed her face. Something like pain. Or was it irritation? She snapped her head to the side. "Take him away."

My heart felt as if it was torn from my body. My mind was numb. Not even my arms would obey when I told them to resist the guards who grabbed me. Instead I surrendered, keeping my eyes on Mareleau as I was dragged through the crowd. She never gave me a second glance.

3

THE QUEST

Mareleau

"You choose Teryn?" I stared open-mouthed at my father. "But why? His poem wasn't even that good. And it's...Teryn! It would be like marrying a brother."

"Teryn comes from a fine family, a family we have been loyal to for generations. It would be wise to join the two of you. And it would be wise for you to change your tone about him." Father put his hands on his hips and stepped toward me in a way that was meant to be intimidating.

Unfortunately for him, it was he who I had learned my own powers of dominance from. I crossed my arms and took a bold step forward, bringing us nearly eye to eye. Standing this close, I could see every crease and wrinkle on his face, every wiry, silver hair sprouting from his brows and beneath his crown. His dull, gray eyes held a desperation where there used to be fierce, terrifying power. I felt almost guilty for bullying him so. "You know I don't want to marry him."

We glared at each other for silent moments, neither of us daring to move or blink.

Before long, my mother came and placed a hand on each of our shoulders. "My darlings, don't be silly. There's no need to get worked up."

"Then you talk some sense into her, Helena! She doesn't know what's for her own good. She doesn't want to marry Teryn. She doesn't want to marry King Dimetreus—"

"Oh, don't get me started on old King Dimetreus again!" I said.

Father threw his hands in the air. "Old? *Old*? He's only eleven years your senior and may be younger than most of the princes here today."

"But he's a widower!"

"Of six years! He's an ideal prospect. If you married him, you'd already be queen, but no! You refuse—"

"Enough, enough," Mother said softly as she took a graceful step between us. "This is old news. We all know King Dimetreus never responded to our offer of marriage, so there is nothing more to be done." She turned her nose to the air and pursed her lips.

"King Dimetreus never responds to anything," Father said under his breath.

"Darling, why don't you get some air?"

Father held my gaze for a few moments, the redness in his face starting to recede. Then, without another word, he turned and stomped out the doors of my chambers.

Mother took my hand and led me to the window

overlooking the palace gardens. I looked below at the revelry of the spring festival, still in full bloom. Many anxious faces flickered up to my empty balcony, likely wondering how much longer until the winners of the poetry contest would be announced. I sighed and turned away from the window.

"Don't worry, Mareleau. Just because your father chose Teryn, doesn't mean Teryn will win the Quest. I still have my choice to make and you have yours. After that, we let love decide."

I rolled my eyes and went to my lounge, sulking into the pillows beneath me. "A stupid poetry contest and a ridiculous quest are supposed to prove true love?"

My mother stood over me, frowning as she narrowed her crystal blue eyes. "Isn't this what you wanted? You do remember it was *you* who came up with these terms, don't you? And after all that we've been through, after all the allowances we've given you, you're still not satisfied?"

I leaned back further, covered my eyes with my hands, and let out an agitated moan.

"Now look here, Mareleau!" I peeked through my fingers at Mother shaking a forefinger at me. "You are not going to ruin this! You have managed—who knows how —to destroy every single engagement opportunity you have had. We ask what we can do to make you happy, and you say you must marry for love! We let you have your poetry contest and we are letting *you* choose the goal of the Quest. What more do you want?"

I was too annoyed to argue. She wouldn't understand, anyway. The only thing that could make me happy was the very thing I couldn't have. Now I was just buying time. I crossed my arms and pouted at the floor.

Mother sat next to me with a sigh, patting her perfectly coiffed, silver-blonde curls. "I'm sorry, darling. You frustrate me so. But you *need* a good match. You are destined to be queen. I will not let a rose like you go to waste." She reached a hand to brush my cheek as she beamed her goddess-like smile at me. I could feel her maternal powers softening my irritation.

"Fine. Who do you choose, Mother?"

Mother clapped her hands in front of her chest. "Yes, let's talk about that. I choose Prince Helios of Norun. He read a fine poem and was very handsome. And Norun is a wealthy kingdom. He would be perfect for you. How about you, my sweet? Who do you choose?"

I suppressed a laugh, realizing I hadn't given my choice a moment's thought. What did it matter? They were all the same, these strange men from distant lands and kingdoms, all disgustingly desperate to risk anything to win my body for their own enjoyment. I could hardly remember a single name. "Uh, was there a...Thomas?"

Mother eyed me with a squint, then snapped her fingers at her scribe, who handed her a scroll. She and the scribe whispered back and forth, consulting the long list of names. "Ah, yes," Mother said. "There were three. Thomas of Albuin? Thomas of Ermynia? Thomas of Durry? Or it says here there was a Lexington *of* Tomas, but I doubt—"

"Prince Lexington of Tomas, that's the one." It sounded interesting enough.

My mother frowned. "Odd. I don't remember him or his poem."

"Oh, he was terribly handsome."

"And his poem?"

"Exquisite."

"Very well. Are you ready to announce the winners and reveal the Quest?"

My eyes widened. "I have to announce the Quest now?"

"Yes, Mareleau. Don't tell me you haven't decided where to send them!"

My heart raced, and my forehead prickled with sweat. Of course I hadn't decided. I didn't care! But if I wanted this to work, I would have to come up with something good...and fast. "Just give me a moment. I need to perfect my speech."

"You have until fifth bell," Mother said through clenched teeth, then left my room with a slam of the doors.

I spun, looking frantically around me as if I would find my solution in plain sight. Finally, I spotted some inspiration. "Lurel," I called to my young chambermaid.

Her eyes shot up and widened. She took one step forward from where she had been standing by my door, hands clasped. "Yes, princess?"

"Come here, I need help. Can I be any clearer?"

Lurel rushed to me, bowing her dark-blonde head as she sank into a deep curtsy. "What can I do for you, Your Highness?"

"Well, you're not deaf, so you must know the problem I face."

"A lady should never eavesdrop, princess." Lurel's wide, watery, blue eyes remained somewhere near the hem of my dress, her cheeks blazing.

"Don't play coy, this is important. I need to come up with a dangerous goal for the Quest." I began pacing. "I

need to send these princes somewhere in search of something...but what?"

"A rare, magical flower? A potion of everlasting
youth?"

"Is there such a thing? Where would they find it?"

Lurel shook her head. "I'm sorry, highness, I don't
think there is such a thing. I was only thinking of
fairytales."

"It must be something real, something believable. But
also difficult to find. You must hear as much gossip as you
do fairytales. Are there any rumors afloat of anything
incredible? Magical? Something that inspires desire and
jealousy?"

"Your Highness, in my world, the things that inspire
desire and jealousy are things you already have."

I let out a frustrated moan. There must be something!
I couldn't just make it up, or my parents would see
through my ruse and be done with me. I was already
pushing them close enough to the edge. It was only a
matter of time before they forced me into an arranged
marriage. I shuddered at the thought.

"Must it really be something so dangerous, princess?"
Lurel asked. "Wouldn't it be easier to send them to find
you a four-leafed clover or a beautiful songbird? Besides,
what if they are killed doing something dangerous?"

I spat out a cold laugh. "Who cares?"

Lurel gasped and put her hand over her mouth. Her
innocence was annoying me.

"If you can't help me, you are dismissed." I turned my
back to her. My mind was spinning wildly for a solution.
What was I going to do? When I turned back around,
Lurel was still standing in the same place she'd been

before. Her brows were furrowed, and her head was cocked to the side. "What? Do you have something for me or not?"

She slowly met my eyes. "Well...would a unicorn work?"

A unicorn! The very thought sent my heart aflutter. I'd seen a few rare artifacts made from the horn and skin of a unicorn. Each piece was exquisite and priceless. Some pieces were even said to harbor magical properties. Then again, these artifacts were ancient. Everyone knew unicorns didn't exist anymore. My mood turned sour once again. "Can't you give me something useful? I said it needed to be real."

"But they are real." Lurel's eyes bulged as she smiled from ear to ear. "Or so I've heard. There have been rumors for months of unicorn sightings all over northern Kero. All from different sources too, so they must be true!"

I pondered this new idea and grew excited once more. "Have any been caught?"

"Not that I have heard, princess. They are said to be most difficult to find and impossible to capture. It takes enough courage as it is just to travel to the spooky forests of northern Kero."

"Then it's perfect."

I nearly bounced with excitement as I stood between my mother and father on my balcony, overlooking a vast sea of hopeful men. What was it about crushing the dreams of these loveless impostors and sending three of them to their deaths that delighted me so?

"I will now announce the three winners of the poetry contest," Father bellowed over the crowd. Dead silence responded as the young men awaited the delivery of their fates. "First, we have Teryn, Prince of Mena!"

Teryn came forward, bowing low. His smiling eyes met mine. All I wanted to do was stick my tongue out at him. Instead I smiled indulgently, knowing I would be delivering my justice soon enough.

"Encore!" Father shouted, and the crowd echoed him.

Teryn blushed but confidently repeated his poem. I barely listened. Why torture myself a second time?

My father announced the next winner. "Helios, Prince of Norun! Please step forward and present your poem one more time!"

I rolled my eyes as the tall, handsome, muscular Helios pushed his way forward and parted the crowd. Teryn looked alarmed as Helios stood next to him, towering nearly two heads taller. Helios looked at me yet didn't so much as smile. He simply stood, chest puffed, arms stiff at his side. I knew his type just by looking at him—arrogant, aggressive, and fully aware of his power. Men like him had no power over me, though. I ground my teeth and imagined how fun it would be to watch him fail.

I returned my attention to Teryn. He was handsome, I supposed, but in a subtle way next to Helios. Teryn was of lean build with hazel eyes, a fair complexion, and fine, sandy-brown hair cropped short and neatly styled after the modern fashion—unlike his brother, whose hair always seemed a little too long, tousled either from lack of sleep or lack of care. Perhaps both?

Thoughts of Larylis prompted the memory of his

brazen declaration that morning. What had he been thinking standing up to my father like that? My throat felt tight, and I shook my head to clear it, returning to my scrutiny of the two men. My eyes found Helios, who contrasted Teryn with his arms roped with muscle, his skin tanned and leathery. His deep-set eyes were the blackest of browns, and his hair was a thick, dark mass of short curls. His features were hard and angular, as if they were chiseled from stone. He looked to be about ten years my senior while Teryn was seventeen, only a year older than I.

But compare as I might, neither man took my fancy. Helios was just another rich prince who thought his looks were enough to win a woman's heart, and Teryn was nothing more than a boring, slightly taller version of his twin brother. It took everything I had to keep from glowering.

Helios reread his poem, comparing me to some goddess of the sea. His voice was deep and strong—probably the only tolerable quality about him. I could see a handful of simpleminded maidens swooning in the crowd.

When Helios finished his lengthy poem, Father announced the third winner. I was intrigued to find out who I had chosen. "Lexington, Prince of Tomas!"

There was silence. The men in the crowd looked from one to the other, trying to identify the winner. Slowly, from the back of the crowd emerged a short, chubby, young man with ruddy cheeks and messy, blond hair. He looked as thrilled as he'd be at a funeral. *That makes two of us.* I suppressed the giddy laughter that bubbled in my throat.

Mother's head swung toward me. "Are you sure this is the man you intended to choose?"

"Why, yes, of course he is," I said in my sweetest voice. I turned to my other side where Father was gaping at the newcomer. With a nudge, I urged him to continue.

He blinked a few times, cleared his throat, and forced his kingly smile. "Prince Lexington, please grace us with your poem one last time."

Lexington turned bright pink as he fumbled through his pockets, eventually pulling out a crumpled piece of paper. His voice was so quiet I had to strain to hear his mumbling.

> "Your hair is golden like a pint of rich ale.
> Your lips are red like a glass of wine,
> Your eyes are blue like the sea,
> Your skin is pale like fresh milk.
> You are graceful like a deer,
> And smart like a fox,
> If you choose me, I'll make you very
>   happy."

My eyes watered with the effort it took to turn my squeal of mirth into, "Oh, how sweet!" I could see my mother shaking her head beside me. To anger her more, I put my hand to my heart and swooned, eyelids fluttering as I smiled down at my chosen champion.

Father scratched the side of his head. "Congratulations to the...three of you."

Now it was my turn. I stepped forward and my mother and father stepped back. I lifted my chin and my chest, standing tall. "I will now announce the goal of the

Quest. The three of you have been chosen for very special reasons. In two weeks, each of you will embark on a dangerous mission in search of my heart's desire. He who returns first with what I demand will prove he loves me most. What I ask for is rare and will put its seeker in grave danger. You must accomplish the Quest without the aid or accompaniment of your guards. He who has the determination and skill to persevere is the one worth my hand in marriage. Listen carefully to what I ask, for you must bring me exactly what I demand.

"For the Quest, you must find me three unicorns. From the first unicorn, I require a horn. From the second, its pelt. And the third will be my pet. I wish you three the best of luck, and may the worthiest man win." I grinned at the three dumb princes and the stunned and silent crowd. I then grinned at my parents, who were frozen with horror.

I turned on my heel and left the balcony, closing the doors behind me so I could erupt with victorious laughter.

4

SECOND LIFE

Cora

I stood at the edge of a barren cliff. The harsh wind cut my skin as it threatened to throw me off the edge. I looked down at a dark castle which stood in an equally dark valley below me. Red fog swirled about the base. Sharp, black towers jutted out at odd angles and climbed impossible heights above the castle. All the windows were black except one—in the middle of the highest tower glowed one red eye.

From somewhere in the distance, I could hear my name. *Coralaine.* I shuddered. No, that was not my name anymore. *Coralaine,* I heard again. The voice was merely a whisper, yet it felt as if it were pounding in my ears.

A pale face appeared in the red window. A wide, malicious smile revealed sharp, yellow teeth. "Hello, Coralaine."

I opened my eyes but all I could see was black. I fought the arms that pinned down my shoulders.

"Cora, quiet, you're safe."

It took me a moment to realize the screams I heard were my own.

"It's just me," soothed the voice of Maiya.

My body went limp and I resigned to tears and quiet sobs. The arms at my shoulders gently released me.

"It was just another bad dream." Maiya stroked the damp hair away from my forehead.

"I'm sorry," I whispered, and rolled over on my side to bury my face in my blanket. Maiya gave my shoulder a light pat and returned to her cot next to mine. Even in the darkness I could feel her eyes on me.

"Is something wrong?" she asked quietly.

I remained silent. The truth was I had no idea what was wrong with me. This was the third night in a row I had woken screaming from this same, terrifying dream.

Six years had gone by since I was banished from my home at Ridine Castle. I'd given up my name, my title, and my past when the Forest People found me. I'd done my best to forget the life I'd once lived. Why the nightmares now?

"Would you like to tell me about your dream? Perhaps I can help divine its meaning." Maiya tried to sound nonchalant, but her concern was obvious.

I ignored her, breathing slow and deep as if I'd fallen back asleep. Even though I trusted Maiya like a sister, I would not burden her with my dream or my past. I wouldn't allow any of the Forest People to bear the burden of knowing they were harboring an exiled princess.

Before I knew it, I found myself blinking into the warm morning sun diffused through the thick, patterned fabric that made up the tent I shared with Maiya. I stretched my arms and rose. Outside the tent Maiya met my eyes with a weak smile as she hung clothes to dry on a line. "Did you sleep well?"

I nodded, giving her what I hoped to be a convincing grin. Yet, my skin still prickled at the memory of dark turrets, an evil wind, and a voice hissing my name.

I strolled through our camp, nodding and smiling at the familiar faces as I passed. Most of the Forest People looked alike with their tan skin, dark-brown eyes, and thick, dark hair. According to legend, the Forest People descended from the Faeran, the ancient race that was once native to Lela in centuries past. I, with my brown eyes and long, brown hair, fit right in. Of course, not all the Forest People bedded exclusively within our tribe, so there were also a few fair-skinned, golden-haired or bronze-headed youths in our company.

I felt guilty for sleeping in, seeing everyone else already hard at work with their daily tasks of sewing, washing, cooking, hunting, or practicing the Arts. Most everyone in our tribe practiced some form of the Arts, which was our name for what I'd previously known as magic or sorcery. The Arts included many forms of heal- ing, telling, and enchantment. Even those without natural talent for the Arts were useful in collecting herbs, brewing tinctures, and making salves or other concoctions.

As a child, magic had seemed nothing short of evil. Now that I was with the Forest People, the Arts were a way of life, something alive and ever-present in all things. I even learned the truth about what I'd previously only known as my *curse*. Where would I be if the Forest People hadn't found me?

As I reached the common area, the smells of roasting meats, boiling soups, and steeping herbs intoxicated me, making my stomach growl. I walked amongst the cooking fires, investigating the contents of the boiling pots and roasting spits of meat. I helped myself to a heaping bowl of soft-cooked root vegetables and a mug of fragrant tea, then took a seat on one of the logs surrounding the clearing.

We'd been at our camp since the beginning of winter, but I knew we would be moving on soon. One of the first things I had to learn after being taken in by the Forest People was that my home would no longer be defined by a place. We moved often to keep from desecrating the land that nourished us, and to keep us from being pursued by those who wished us ill. Even though we had peaceful exchanges of business with most of the villagers and travelers we encountered, there were still others who feared and even scorned us.

I jumped as the log thumped beside me. It was Maiya.

She smiled, but it didn't reach her eyes—they were busy studying my face. Her shoulders were tense as she folded her hands in her lap.

"I'm fine, Maiya." I elbowed her playfully, making her blush.

"I just worry about you, that's all. You know I would never pry, but I'm here if you ever need to talk."

"I know. I'm fine, though."

"My mother is here for you too. She's an elder. She has more wisdom than anyone."

"I know she does, and I love Salinda, but I won't bother her with my silly nightmares." I turned my attention back to my food, even though I could still feel Maiya staring at me. She opened her mouth to say something else but was interrupted by commotion at the other end of the clearing.

"Roije has returned!" Ciela squealed as she ran over to us. Ciela was a tall, willowy blonde, said to be the bastard daughter of a wealthy lord. Although it was never said exactly *which* wealthy lord, rumor claimed her mother had charmed him with her exotic beauty when she'd visited his land on trade. Rumor also said Ciela was just as charming as her mother in that respect.

"Roije's back?" Maiya began smoothing her tangled, curly, black hair away from her olive-toned face.

"I thought you'd want to know." Ciela winked at Maiya, then pulled us both to standing, forcing me to abandon my food. She linked her arms through ours and dragged us toward the gathering crowd. We pushed our way forward until we were in the middle of the circle, an arm's length away from Roije, who stood at its center.

Roije had grown up with the Forest People, but when his mother took ill and died, he left our tribe for modern society, shocking us all. Even though we were free to come and go as we pleased, few of us ever did. His hunting and tracking skills had been an asset to our tribe, and his presence was missed by many. Now that he was back, I was curious to know why. I clearly wasn't the only one.

Inaudible questions were shouted left and right as he was smothered with hugs, handshakes, and excited greetings. Maiya and I kept our hands to ourselves, admiring

him from where we stood. He had grown into a handsome young man since I'd last seen him, tall and nicely
muscled with short, neatly trimmed curls, dark eyes
under heavy eyebrows, and high cheekbones.

He waited with grace for the crowd to quiet, but the
questions grew and multiplied, drowning out his every
attempt to answer them.

"Where did you go?"

"What did you do?"

"What was it like?"

"How did you find us?"

"Why did you come back?"

Roije remained composed and smiling. He waved a
hand for the crowd to calm so he could finally speak. "All
right, all right. I'll tell you, but just one question at a
time." His voice was rich with laughter.

"Where have you been?" asked a voice from
behind me.

"I went to the village of Kubera to make a living
hunting and trading with the butcher. It was much
different than the life I'd known. It was worth the experience, but after a while I knew I had to come home. I
began tracking you from our old camp...and now here
I am."

"We're so happy you're back." Ciela flashed him her
flirtatious smile.

"I'm happy to be back as well. I truly missed every one
of you." Roije's handsome grin stretched over his face as
he scanned the crowd, his eyes lingering a moment
longer when he saw Maiya. I could almost feel the heat of
her blushing beside me.

"What news do you have from Kubera?" someone asked. "Anything interesting?"

"Interesting, yes, but not in a good way. Things feel strange. The king is recruiting young men to join the Royal Force, and no one knows why. I left Kubera when I heard his recruiters were on their way."

I stiffened. It had been years since I'd heard any word about my brother.

"He's growing his Royal Force?" another voice asked. "Kero has been at peace for as long as anyone remembers. What does the king need such a large army for?"

"Who knows," Roije said. "I've heard all kinds of tales about Ridine Castle. Most of the household staff have either left or been relieved of duty, and no one has had direct contact with the king in years. Ridine holds no court and entertains no festivities. He's the last living member of the royal family. That's strange enough as it is."

My throat felt dry. Did I hear him right? My brother, the last living member of the royal family. Did that mean I was considered...dead? *Roije probably misunderstood.* But something about his words sent a chill down my spine and set my heart racing, reminding me of my haunting nightmare.

Coralaine, whispered the trees around us.

Coralaine, whispered the dark turrets in my mind.

I shook the dream from my head. *No, just breathe. It wasn't real.* But I had already lost control. My vision swam, and my mind flooded with a clamor of voices all at once—thoughts of everyone around me, so loud and disjointed I couldn't make sense of them. I tried to push them back, but it was too much. My lungs felt too small to breathe. I reached out for Maiya's arm just as my legs gave out from beneath me. I was almost grateful when the world faded to black.

5

TURMOIL

Teryn

Where am I going to find a unicorn? I thought for the hundredth time that day. *Three unicorns, for that matter!* I stared into the depths of my dinner plate as if the half-eaten wing of duck would wave me in the right direction.

"To Teryn!" I jumped as the chorus of my name echoed through the great hall of Dermaine Palace. From the seat of honor at the head table, I looked down the hall at the hundreds of guests standing at their tables with their goblets held high. Each pair of eyes was fixed on me as I stood blushing and mumbling my thanks.

This was my celebratory feast, but I didn't feel like celebrating. I was too anxious to enjoy myself and didn't feel like there was anything worth celebrating until I brought the princess home with me as my bride. Despite my many protests, Father insisted I owed it to our people to indulge them with a feast.

I sat back down, expecting my guests to follow suit until I noticed my father had remained standing and was gazing at me with a teary-eyed look of fatherly love. I returned to standing, shoulders hunched in anticipation of a sentimental speech.

"I'm so proud of you, my boy." Father's usual husky voice had turned soft and unsteady. "Bards all over Lela are singing your praises. You have the love and support of not only our kingdom of Mena, but of the whole land of Lela!"

My guests, most of whom I had never seen before, shouted their agreement. I accepted the compliment with a nod and a smile, hoping the praise would end soon so I could hide behind my dinner plate again.

However, my father wanted to torture me. "You and Mareleau are the perfect pair. What could be better than Lela's most beautiful princess married to Lela's most beloved prince?"

While my guests cheered in agreement, I stole a wary glance at Larylis. He paid me no heed, deep as he was in his fourth goblet of ale. Either he didn't notice the slight my father's words had dealt him, or he was too drunk to care. My heart sank. He hadn't said a word to me, much less looked in my direction since we'd returned home from the spring festival.

"It takes a big man to win a woman's heart," my father continued. I could feel my ears growing hot. "But it takes an even bigger man to find *one unicorn horn, one unicorn pelt, and one living unicorn!*"

The hall erupted with laughter.

"I know you will win, my boy! You and Mareleau will be the best king and queen Lela has ever seen!"

My cheeks blazed as my father ended his speech with another raise of goblets, then finally allowed us to return to our seats. I lifted my fork to my mouth but couldn't take a bite. I let it drop to my plate and leaned back in my chair.

I felt sick. I knew my father's faithful words were meant to encourage me, but instead they made me feel as if my guts were being squeezed tight. He seemed so sure of me, so confident I had what it took to win the Quest. However, as soon as I'd heard I was to find a mythological creature—three of them, at that—I'd lost all faith in myself. I was dumbfounded. The Quest began in one week, and I didn't even have a plan.

I was relieved when the feast was over, and I gladly began to ascend the stairs toward my chamber. My feet felt heavier with every step, and my eyes began to droop. I could almost hear my bed calling my name.

Outside my door, my chambermaster greeted me. "Prince Teryn, you have a guest waiting in your study."

My eyes grew wide. I cocked my head and considered if I'd heard him right. "A guest?"

He nodded.

"It's after eighth bell. Can't it wait until morning?"

He raised an eyebrow at me, making my cheeks flush as I realized what a whining child I'd sounded like.

I cleared my throat and straightened my posture. "What I mean is, I have been in attendance of my guests all evening. I'm sure whoever seeks my presence has had enough of me for today."

He took a step forward and lowered his voice to a whisper. "This guest was not an attendant at the feast. It is with utmost secrecy that your guest is meeting with you. I was told not to say this guest's name aloud, so as not to inspire gossip."

My heart skipped a beat. A guest who was not at the feast, asking for a secret rendezvous...could it be Mareleau? I quickly dismissed my chambermaster and all but bounded through the double doors to my rooms.

My jaw dropped, and I paused mid-step. "Prince Lexington?"

The chubby, pink-faced Prince Lexington sat reclining on one of the chairs at my desk, toying with a long quill. His eyes shot up as he saw me. He clumsily dropped the quill, removed himself from the chair, and came to greet me. "Just call me Lex," he grumbled as he gave a short bow. "I hate the name Lexington."

After a moment's hesitation, I remembered to return the bow. It was hard to believe the man before me was a prince. Once the shock abated, the disappointment hit me all at once. If I wasn't going to be meeting with Mareleau, the only other meeting I desired was with my bed. I'd have to sort things out fast if I wanted that desire fulfilled. "What brings you to Dermaine at this hour, Prince...Lex?"

Lex began pacing and running his hands through his unkempt hair. "I have a proposition for you. A favor, perhaps. Well, I want to offer you my assistance. I want to help you win the Quest."

"You want to do *what*? But we're competitors! Why would you want to help me win?"

"Because I don't want to marry Mareleau."

"How could you not want to marry the most beautiful woman in the world?"

Lex stopped pacing and looked at me as if I had

grown two heads. "Are you kidding me? Why would I want to marry such a spoiled, stuck up, mirror gazer? Besides, I have a fine lady back home in Tomas whom I am determined to marry."

"Then why don't you just forfeit the Quest and go home?"

Lex shook his head. "My father would kill me. I cannot bring shame upon my family or my kingdom. I am Crown Prince of Tomas and I must earn the respect of our people and my father. Therefore, my only solution is to make them *think* I am fighting to win so that when *you* win, you can talk about what fierce competition I was."

So that was the catch. He would help me win the Quest in return for bragging rights. It didn't sound like the worst deal. But could I trust him? "Why me? Why not offer your assistance to Helios?"

Lex made a face of disgust. "That man scares me."

I couldn't help but laugh. "I know what you mean, but how do I know you won't betray me? Steal the goods for yourself and leave me behind?"

"Look at me." Lex gave me a crooked smile. "What could I do to betray you? I can barely run for longer than ten breaths, my arms are too short to have any kind of reach with a sword against you, and...I can't even think of any other way I *could* betray you."

He certainly had his charm. Was it worth the risk to ally with him? I looked him up and down, trying to find any reason why I should turn his offer down. "Fine, but we still have a lot of work to do, and I won't be doing it all myself. If you want an alliance, then we work as equals."

"Thank you. I won't let you down." Lex's face brightened as he grabbed my hand in an exuberant handshake.

We made plans for our next secret meeting, then Lex departed. The sound of the door closing behind me was like a lullaby. I sighed and began to make my way toward my sleeping chamber.

Until I heard a knock.

I threw my head back and closed my eyes, grumbling. Perhaps if I didn't answer, whoever was at the door would leave.

Knock, knock, knock.

It couldn't be anything important.

Knock, knock, knock, knock, knock...

I cursed under my breath, stormed to the door, and flung it open.

"Why?" Larylis' voice was like a croak. He stared at me with bloodshot eyes and a goblet in his hand.

"Larylis, what's wrong with you?"

"Why are you doing this to me?"

So, the confrontation was finally here. I lowered my head and stepped aside, allowing Larylis to stumble into my study. I took a seat at my desk and Larylis took one opposite me. "Come on, brother. Let it all out."

Larylis narrowed his eyes at me and repeated his question.

I rubbed my temples and closed my eyes. "Larylis, you are doing this to yourself. You're the one who's been drinking yourself into a stupor every night for the past week."

"You are taking away the woman I love!" Larylis pounded a fist on the desk. "How am I supposed to handle that? How am I supposed to watch you marry her?"

"Do you truly love her?" I asked.

"Yes."

"Then you will want what is best for her. Do you want her to marry me or that ogre, Helios?"

Larylis scowled but didn't answer.

"I can love her, care for her, respect her, and provide her with everything she needs. If she marries me, she can remain in her homeland of Lela. Or she could marry Prince Helios. You didn't get to meet him, but I assure you, he looks about as gentle and loving as a boar."

"What about the third? Prince Lexington?"

"Lexington won't win, I know that much." My eyes met his for a moment, and I felt a pang of guilt for not telling him about the alliance.

Larylis didn't seem to notice my omission. He put his head in his hands. "Why do you want her?"

"Why do *you* want her? You are a good person, Larylis. You are kind and loving. You deserve someone who will love you for all you're worth, not some cold-hearted woman who won't even acknowledge your existence."

Larylis stood and glared down at me. "You know nothing about her. She and I were friends. In the three years I spent at Verlot, she was my *only* friend. You weren't there. Our parents weren't there. You all left me in another kingdom with hardly a visit."

"You act as if we abandoned you! You were sent to Verlot for their healers. It is thanks to them that you are as well as you are today."

"And I am grateful to them every day," Larylis said through clenched teeth. "But I am not grateful for you taking away the woman I love—"

"You loved her when you were six years old!"

"Are you saying a child cannot know love?"

"I'm saying people change. She clearly has. You haven't spoken to her in years. Now I have a chance to find love with her, to start a family, to bring our future queen into our kingdom. Am I to be punished just because I didn't meet her first?"

"Am I to be punished because I wasn't born first? Because I've had to live my life in your glorious shadow? I actually had one thing that you didn't have, and now you're taking that from me too."

My face softened. "I'm sorry you feel that way, Larylis, I truly am. But she doesn't belong to you. She has a right to love whomever she chooses, and she didn't choose you."

Larylis sat back down in his seat, eyes out of focus. He let out a heavy sigh. "You're right. You're completely right. I'm beating myself up over a woman who chose my brother. I'm doing this to myself."

My throat tightened. I didn't expect to feel so guilty about being right.

"It just hurts, you know?" Larylis' voice cracked. "It kills me to think about the two of you together. No matter how she has treated me, I have never stopped loving her. I doubt I ever will." A tear slipped from Larylis' eye, and suddenly he was no longer my brooding, irrational competitor. He was my brother, my best friend, my companion who'd always known me better than anyone else. Could I bear the burden of causing him so much pain?

On the other side of Larylis' pain was a chance for me to find love with the most beautiful woman I'd ever laid eyes on. She would be my lifelong partner, forever by my side. She would fulfill me and make me a king our people would be proud of. I couldn't give that opportunity away.

I ran a palm over my face and leaned back in my chair. "If you honestly, truly love her, you will do what is right for her. I don't want to hurt you, but I can't give her up for nothing. The choice is yours. Let her go, and I promise I will love and cherish her forever. Or say the word and I will forfeit the Quest, and neither of us will have her."

Larylis' eyes went wide and locked on mine. His mouth opened, yet not a sound came out. I held my breath and waited for the words that could put an end to the only thing I'd ever wanted.

6

A DARK PATH

Cora

I nocked an arrow into my bow and pulled it back to my cheek. I released it and heard the beautiful strum of the string snapping forward, followed by the *thud* as the arrow hit the old log. I smiled, but only felt it on the outside. I shot again, bringing the narrow cluster of arrows protruding from the log to a total of seven. Then eight. Then nine.

"Is beating up that poor, old thing really going to make you feel better?" I turned and saw Salinda walking through the trees toward me, arms behind her back as she took one slow step at a time. Her sun-browned face was warm and smiling, creased at the corners of her mouth and eyes. Her petite frame made her look so much younger than she was. She was even tinier than her daughter, Maiya, but with the same dark eyes and dark hair.

I tried to match her smile. "It is making me feel

better," I lied, and walked over to fetch my arrows. I could still feel Salinda's eyes studying me as I yanked the arrow tips from the crumbling bark. When I turned around, her face was full of sympathy.

"Really, I'm fine," I said. "I don't know what everyone is so worried about. I fainted. That was a week ago. It was nothing."

"And the nightmares?"

I sighed, my shoulders drooping. "Maiya told you."

Salinda walked over to me and pressed a soft hand to my cheek. "You can tell me, my dear Cora." Her face was so warm, so gentle. I could feel my walls beginning to crumble around me. "Start with the fainting, if that's easier to explain."

"I just lost control, you know, of my..."

"Of your *power*. You're an empath, don't be ashamed to call it what it is."

I closed my eyes and nodded. "It overwhelmed me."

"That hasn't happened in a long time. What triggered you to lose control?"

My throat tightened. "It was something Roije said. It scared me."

"Did it have to do with what you've been dreaming about?"

"It did."

Salinda remained silent. She would not press me from here. Part of me wanted to take the opportunity to end the conversation and excuse myself, but there was another part of me that begged to open, begged to release the burden I'd been carrying. Maybe Maiya was right. Maybe Salinda could help.

"I've been having these terrible dreams about

my...former home. I can see my...house, and it's different, changed. It looks monstrous. There's nothing but darkness surrounding it—and evil."

Salinda nodded. "Your past is haunting you."

"Yes, and when Roije showed up with his dark tidings regarding my former home, I lost control. It was too much. I couldn't help but worry about what may have befallen my family." My heart was racing now.

"It's natural to worry about your original home and family, no matter how painful your past is."

"But worrying will do me no good, you taught me that. I can never go back. I don't ever *want* to go back, and I wouldn't be of any help if I did. I just want these nightmares to end so I can be free from the ghosts of my past." I sighed. "Can you help me? Can you get rid of these nightmares?"

Salinda studied me for a moment. "I'm not sure if I should do that."

"What do you mean? If you can't do it, I don't know who can."

"I didn't say I *couldn't* do it, I said I wasn't sure if I *should*."

I cocked my head to the side. "What else is there to do about it?"

"Perhaps you should listen to the message. There must be a reason these dreams are speaking to you."

All I could imagine was that glowing, red window in the black tower, and the malicious voice ringing through my mind. I shuddered. "No, my dreams are not speaking to me. They are nothing but fear trying to drive me mad."

"Beyond your fear there may be truth, Cora."

I shook my head. My chest constricted as my

breathing quickened and my hands clenched into fists. Salinda put a comforting hand on my arm, and the tension melted from me like ice under the sun. "Calm, Cora. This dream takes you to a dark place, I can see that, but you must move past it. Let the fear go, let the dark feelings fade. What is left? What are these things telling you?"

I inhaled and exhaled deeply, closed my eyes, and followed her instruction. I calmed the anxiety, the fear, the feelings, letting them drift away a little at a time until I was left with my watchful awareness. "I'm worried. My old home is in trouble." With the words came a calm certainty. I opened my eyes and felt a shiver run down my spine.

"Your path is changing," Salinda said.

"But I don't want anything to change."

"Your purpose is bigger. You are meant for so much more."

"I never asked for a bigger purpose! I never asked for my path to change!"

"Few of us ever do, but when we accept our calling, we can accomplish great things." She gave my shoulder a gentle squeeze. Without another word, she turned and left me alone with my thoughts.

My mind and heart were at war as I reflected on our conversation. My heart felt the wisdom of her words, but my mind couldn't solve what to do about it. *How do I embark on a new path when I don't even know the first step? How do I take a first step when I don't want to in the first place?*

I was interrupted by a flicker of movement in the distance. I expected to find Salinda returning to further counsel me. Instead, I found Maiya.

She walked toward me, wringing her hands before her. "Are you mad I told Salinda about the nightmares?"

I smiled. "Of course not, Maiya. You were only trying to help, and your mother did help me...I think."

Maiya sighed, and her face brightened. "Good. Do you want to talk about it more?"

"No, that's the last thing I want to do. I just want to be distracted." I unshouldered my bow and quiver and placed them behind the old log to retrieve later. I took Maiya by the hand. "Let's go do something fun."

"Did I hear you right?" asked another giggling voice with mock surprise. Ciela came walking arm-in-arm with another girl, Luna. "*You* want to do something *fun*? You mean, you aren't always such a serious stick-in-the-mud?"

"Very funny," I said as the two girls approached.

"If you're looking for fun, come with us," said Luna, a tall, buxom brunette with warm, golden skin and a mischievous smile.

"What do you mean?" Maiya asked.

Ciela bent in close to Maiya, pretending to whisper. "Luna has a date with a hunter tonight."

Maiya's eyes went wide as she blushed. "What does that have to do with us?"

"He's camping not too far from here, and his companions look wealthy," Luna said. "I'm sure we could get a decent night's earnings in exchange for an evening's worth of entertaining."

"Oh, I don't know." Maiya looked at the ground, kicking at dirt and leaves.

Ciela pouted, then turned her charms on me. "What

about you, stick-in-the-mud? You said you wanted to have fun. What do you say?"

I'd heard about Ciela and Luna's idea of fun, which consisted of flirting, drinking, and charming money from unsuspecting travelers. It never sounded appealing to me, but after the week I'd had, any distraction was welcome.

"Why not?" I said with a shrug.

Ciela and Luna cheered, then danced around Maiya, begging her to come along.

Maiya finally gave in. "Oh, all right. If Cora's going, I guess I'll go too."

"Get ready for a good time," Luna said with a shake of her hips. She fumbled around in the bag that hung from her shoulder, then handed Ciela a reed flute, Maiya a bottle of what I assumed was wine, and me a purse full of fate cards.

Maiya stared wide-eyed at the heavy bottle in her hands, then looked at me. For a moment I wondered if I was making the right choice. What was I getting the two of us into? I shook the worry from my head and smiled at Maiya. She smiled back and took a small sip from the bottle. The adventure had begun.

BY THE TIME WE NEARED THE HUNTERS' CAMP, NIGHT HAD fallen. "We're here," Luna whispered as we approached the sound of raucous voices. We brushed ourselves clean of forest debris and adjusted our skirts and bodices. Luna and Ciela were dressed in their most festive dresses, skirts, and scarves while Maiya and I still wore our everyday dresses. I looked down at my tattered, faded blue dress under my worn, brown leather bodice and wished I'd had a moment to change.

"Ready?" Luna shook her hair from her braid, letting it cascade in long, brown waves over her shoulders. The rest of us nodded, and she waved for us to follow her. She stepped confidently forward, entering the hunters' camp with sumptuously swaying hips. I gulped. The three of us followed in her wake. I tried my best to sway my hips, nearly tripping in the process.

In the middle of the camp were about a dozen thick-set, burly, middle-aged men, drinking, cursing, and smoking. I couldn't imagine why Luna had described these men as wealthy-looking. They very well may have been wealthy, but it wasn't how I'd choose to describe them in terms of appearance. There was only one younger man, probably a few years older than I, amongst the hunters. His face brightened when he saw Luna. "You came back," he said with a shy smile.

"Of course I did." Luna walked over to him and planted a kiss on his cheek.

The talking halted and all eyes locked on us.

"What are you doing bringing witches among us, James?" A large brute of a man stepped toward us, hands balled into fists.

The young man named James looked at his feet. "They aren't witches. Just girls from the nearby village. I met Luna by the river when I was watering our horses."

The hunters eyed us one by one. I held my breath.

Luna let out a giggle, putting her hand over her lips. "Oh, look at you! You are all so serious. We came here to enlighten and entertain you tired hunters. I just love the sight of big, strong, manly hunters. It simply takes my breath away!"

A quiet rumble of arrogant laughter spread around the camp.

Ciela took the bottle from Maiya's hand and stepped toward the men. "Besides, who else will we share our wine with? Our village is so strict, and sometimes girls just want to let loose. But if we are not welcome, we can go have fun on our own."

"Let them stay, Gringe. Please," James said.

"Yeah, they seem harmless," said another, who had his eyes on Ciela.

"Fine," Gringe said. "But no funny business. I've heard stories about these forest-whores who enchant travelers only to leave them drunk with half their goods missing the next morning. I'm not so easily fooled." He eyed each of us with a warning, holding my gaze too long for comfort.

I did my best to giggle coyly and avert my eyes. It was then I realized I was not good at playing coy.

The evening passed as we entertained the hunters by singing, dancing, flute playing, reading their cards, and sharing wine. I did most of my drinking in act. Luna and Ciela, on the other hand, were clearly drunk and looked like they were having the time of their lives from the laps of their equally drunk companions. I looked over at Maiya sitting between two loudly chorusing men. She met my gaze with a bored smile and rolled her eyes.

The hunter I had been entertaining with a palm reading looked to be on the verge of unconsciousness, so I figured he wouldn't notice if I took my leave. I went to Maiya and extended a hand. "Let's dance."

Maiya's face brightened as she stood. We took each other's hands and began circling in a traditional dance of the Forest People to the tune of Ciela's clumsy flute playing.

"I'm sorry I dragged you into this," I whispered. "I just..."

"I know," Maiya said. "You've had a hard week. Besides, this isn't so bad. I'm having fun."

We both laughed at her lie and continued to dance, our steps growing lighter and looser as we circled the campfire. Before long, we truly were having fun. I was starting to think this adventure had been brilliant after all.

A pair of cold eyes froze me in my steps. Gringe stared at us, brows drawn together, mouth turned down in a hard frown as he muttered to himself. He spat in our direction and stomped out of the camp into the dark trees beyond.

The skin prickled behind my neck as I stared into the forest. I sensed darkness or danger, but for some reason I wasn't called to run. I was called to follow.

The singing hunters stood up and started dancing with Maiya and me.

"Oh, how my feet ache," I said to my stumbling partner and stepped out of his reach. "Let me catch my breath and rest for a few moments."

Without a word of protest, the hunter turned away to continue his dance alone.

"Cora?" Maiya looked from me to her dance partner and back again.

I felt a hollow feeling in my gut. How could I leave her alone? Still, I could feel the pull of the woods and had to see where Gringe had gone. "I just need to sit down a moment. I'll be right back."

Once Maiya's back was turned, I slipped quietly away from camp and followed Gringe's fresh trail. My eyes were half-closed as I let my inner senses lead me along through the darkness. Somewhere up ahead, a subtle illumination shone through the trees. I crept toward it until I found myself at the entrance of a cave that held firelight in its depths. I stood just outside, keeping my body in shadow while I listened to the muffled voices coming from deep within.

I focused on the sound, extending my power through all my senses, and heard the sound grow louder and louder until the voices became fully audible to me.

"It's those forest whores," grumbled the angry voice of Gringe. "They've got all our men drunk off their asses."

"Our instructions were clear. We are to have as little contact with outsiders as possible." The second voice was unfamiliar to me.

"Well, I know that, but I don't think the others care."

"You were responsible. You were on watch and you let them into our camp. Get rid of them, now!"

"Kill them?" Gringe sounded excited.

"Do whatever you need to do. Just get rid of them and hope Morkai never finds out."

I froze, losing contact with the voices. I could not believe the name I'd heard. *Morkai. Morkai. Morkai.* It rang through my head like a bell that marked the hour.

I must not have heard him right. It's not possible. I shook the name from my mind; there were more important things to worry about. If I *had* heard everything correctly, then Gringe was coming for me and my friends. I took a step away from the cave to quietly creep away.

"You," growled Gringe from behind me.

I looked back at his towering silhouette, black against the faint light from within the cave. I tore into a run. It wasn't long before I felt his crushing grasp.

7

AN UNWANTED ALLY

Teryn

I stared at the words on the page in front of me, but none of them made sense considering how they swam before my tired eyes. I reread the same paragraph four times in a row, then gave up, realizing the words weren't going to hold my attention any better with repetition. Instead, I flipped through the thin, yellowed pages and admired the illustrations.

Here, a young unicorn is drawn to the virgin princess, read the caption beneath an ink drawing of a small unicorn laying its horned head in the lap of a smiling, young girl. I looked up from the drawing and my mind began drawing its own picture.

Perhaps I can disguise Lex as a girl. I'm sure he's a virgin...

"What?" snapped Lex from across the table. "Why are you looking at me like that? You look insane."

I sighed. "I am nearly there. This is mind-numbing, all this reading! It's well past eighth bell and we aren't any closer to figuring out how to find one of these damned horned horses."

I slammed the book shut and pushed it away. I leaned back in my chair and stared up at the endlessly high ceiling of Dermaine's library. We had been thumbing through page after page of historical and mythological textbooks, trying to find some clue as to how to find and catch a unicorn. Half of what we read was useless myth, and the other half was merely descriptions of brief encounters. It appeared my library lacked the useful information we needed.

"Don't get fussy with me," Lex said. "I'm only here to help you, remember? It's not my fault Helios has made this whole process so difficult."

"Yes, that man is a nuisance," I said through clenched teeth.

Lex thumped his finger on a page. "It says here that unicorns were once common in *Le'Lana* five-hundred years ago."

"Le'Lana?" I echoed. "Where is that?"

Lex scratched his head and flipped the book from cover to cover. I caught a glimpse of the title, *The Once and Former Magic of Ancient Le'Lana*. "I don't know. Was Lela once called Le'Lana? I don't think this looks right. Here's a map."

I glanced at the map he pointed to. The image showed a vast land mass divided into several large kingdoms marked by rivers, forests, mountains, lakes, and streams. It did not resemble my homeland in the slightest; Lela was a modest land divided by three small kingdoms, with only a handful of notable landmarks. "That isn't Lela at all, Lex! What kind of books are you reading?"

"The wrong kind, apparently." Lex pushed the book away.

"I don't think we're going to learn any accurate information from these books, anyway. Most of them were written too long ago to be judged as fact, and the current writings are nothing but reflections on the past."

"Then what do we do? We've been up here all day and all night. I missed lunch...and dinner too! And we've only got four more days until we leave."

I dropped my head into my hands and rubbed my temples. "All we can do is follow the information we *do* have. Lex, write this down."

Lex grumbled, but took out a quill and paper. "Fine. What do we know?"

"We know there have been unicorn sightings somewhere in Lela. That means they do exist in this land, perhaps even in my own kingdom. Obviously, we start with the more remote forests of Lela. We can begin our hunt in the eastern forests of Mena, then move our way north toward Kero. We'll question the nearby villagers as we travel and see if they have any helpful information. If we hunt all day, every day, we're bound to find what we're looking for."

Lex slammed the quill on the table. "That sounds crazy! What if Helios has already learned exactly where to find the unicorns?"

"What other choice do we have?"

We were interrupted by a heavy knock at the library door. The young doorguard entered, eyes wide and shoulders tense. "Ahem...I apologize for the interruption, Your Royal Highnesses, but you have a guest."

"No one is welcome here while I am at my private studies. You are to guard the door from all visitors while I have my *current* guest over. Was I not clear?"

The doorguard's eyes darted between Lex and me. "You see, this new guest is quite persuasive, and he knows about your, um, current guest as well."

My mouth hung open. Who could possibly have known about our secret meeting besides a handful of palace staff?

"Who is this mystery guest?" Despite my irritation, I was curious. The last time this happened, I was gifted with Lex, for better or for worse. Perhaps it was another person willing to help us.

"Prince Helios of Norun, Your Highness."

"No. Absolutely not."

Lex looked like he was about to fall out of his chair. "What does he want?"

"He won't leave until you see him, Your Highness," the doorguard said.

I let out an agitated moan. "Fine, send him in."

A moment later, Prince Helios was before us, striding into the library with quick, deliberate steps. He gave us a quick bow, which I was loath to return. Lex's bow was even slighter than my own.

"Prince Helios of Norun, what a pleasure to make your acquaintance again," I said without joy.

"In other words, what do you want?" Lex narrowed his eyes at Helios. I bit back my laughter.

Helios returned Lex's glare beneath thick, bushy eyebrows. Turning a neutral gaze to me, he said, "I'm here to join your alliance."

His deep, toneless voice grated on my ears as much as

his overconfidence grated on my nerves. I fought back the numerous retorts that threatened to spew from my lips. "What alliance do you speak of?"

"The two of you are working together to complete the Quest, that I know. Why you have chosen to ally yourselves together is beyond me, but I want in." As he spoke, his expression remained a stony mask with only his mouth fluctuating. I hated to imagine that mouth anywhere near Mareleau and had to question her taste in men. *Did she really choose this brute?*

I kept my composure. "Why should we work with you? Two against one clearly has an advantage."

I saw a flicker of something cross Helios' face. Was it annoyance? His jaw shifted as if he were grinding his teeth. "I need your help."

Lex and I laughed. "You need *our* help?" I asked. "Aren't *you* the one bribing information from my kingdom's scholars and paying them not to tell *us*?"

Helios gave a quick nod but revealed no shame. "This is true. I have much information that you do not, which is why it would be wise for you to join me."

"I thought you said you needed our help. Why do you need it, and why should we help you?"

Helios made a grumbling sound in his throat, although his face remained impassive. "After completing my initial investigation, I decided the best course of action would be hiring a hunting party."

"Wait," Lex said. "Isn't that against the rules of the Quest?"

Helios again glared at Lex. "She said no guards. She didn't say anything about a hunting party."

I tried to keep from blushing. How had I not thought of that?

Helios continued. "I then researched the most reputable hunting parties within reasonable distance, narrowed it down to the parties skilled and qualified for our specific task, and offered them generous compensation. Yet, for every messenger I dispatched, I received a refusal, if any answer at all. It appears they are all currently employed."

I couldn't believe my ears. "You've literally queried all the hunting parties for hire?"

"All the reputable, skilled, and qualified ones," Helios corrected. "Unicorn hunting is not common sport. It is a very specific interest. Not any hunter will do."

I raised an eyebrow. "Is unicorn hunting really so different from any other kind of hunt?"

Helios' mouth twitched with a hint of a smirk. "I take it the two of you don't know the first thing about catching, killing, or de-horning a unicorn?"

My eyes went wide, making my answer obvious.

"Without a trained hunting party, you two are hopeless, which is why you need me. I, at least, know the basics of unicorn hunting."

"You still haven't explained why *you* need *us*." Lex crossed his arms over his chest.

Helios made another grumble. "I don't know what sport these hunting parties are currently after, but let's suppose they are also hunting unicorns. That creates a lot of competition. Without a skilled leader, you two will die in the forests before you even catch wind of a unicorn. And I will be more successful with assistance, even if it comes from the two of you. Our only choice is to work together."

"How do you suppose we do that?" I asked.

"The three of us combine our strengths to find the three gifts. Once we have the three, we will each take one and deliver them to Mareleau together, showing our equal effort and worth."

I threw my hands in the air. "That's ridiculous! Isn't the whole point of the Quest to show which *one* of us is most worthy? If we return as equals, we are no better off than where we are today."

"Exactly. We can end this ridiculous Quest with a tie. Mareleau will then be forced to choose a suitor herself or give us a more reasonable mission."

"Or choose none of us and send us all home."

Helios shrugged. "The choice is yours. This is my offer."

I turned and paced a few steps, rubbing my chin with my thumb. Was the risk worth it? Were things as dire as he said? How would Mareleau respond to a tie? I looked over at Lex, wondering how he was felt about the idea. He met my eyes with a look of uncertainty, followed by the slightest shrug of his shoulders.

That's when it dawned on me; Helios had no idea Lex had already forfeited to me. We could complete the Quest together, but Lex and I could somehow conspire for me to come away with two gifts, while Helios would have only one. It wasn't a perfect plan and the deception made me uneasy, but it was probably the best plan we could have.

I looked back at Helios, wondering if he had a similar

plot secretly in mind. "How do we know we can trust you? How do we know you won't betray us?"

"You don't, but what choice do you have? I have the information you need. I know how and where to find the unicorns. I know how to catch one, kill one, and remove its horn. Without me, you have nothing."

It made my stomach churn to admit he was right.

Helios took a step toward me. "I have no desire to betray you. I just want this stupid Quest to be over. So, do we do this or not? Are we in alliance, or do I walk out that door with all the information you so desperately need?"

I swallowed back the sick feeling rising in my throat. "Fine. We accept your assistance and welcome you into alliance."

Helios stuck out his hand, meeting mine with a bone-crushing grasp. Lex shook his hand as well, although by the look on his face you would think he was handling a snake. I tried my best to smile, but I couldn't help feeling like I had just sold my soul to the devil himself.

8

THE CAVE

Cora

Don't panic. Just breathe.

It was easier said than done, considering I was bound by wrists and ankles, and gagged with cloth. I could see nothing beyond the dark nook near the mouth of the cave where Gringe had left me. Gringe had gone to find my friends, yet the nameless man remained inside. Aside from him, the cave seemed empty.

But was it?

I extended my power, almost certain I felt other minds nearby, yet I heard no voices to prove it. I sensed a hint of distress, but its source was unfamiliar. With my outer senses, I heard an occasional scratching sound, like metal grinding against stone.

"The other two are gone, Jarod," came the voice of Gringe as he stormed through the mouth of the cave. I craned my neck to watch him pass in front of my nook.

Just before he disappeared from sight, I caught glimpse of a dark-haired girl hanging limp over his shoulder. *Maiya.*

"I sent the men to hunt them down," I heard Gringe say from within the cave. "They've been ordered to kill the two other girls and whomever else they come across. I put my sword through that young fool, James, of course."

"Why aren't you with the men, tracking the girls?" asked the man named Jarod.

"Because I had to return *this*."

"Why is she still breathing?"

"I figured we can use these two girls as bait in case the other two can't be found. Perhaps their people will come looking for them. If not, we can do whatever we like with them...and *then* kill them." The laughter in Gringe's voice made my teeth grind.

"We didn't come here to play with witches or their rat following. If our men are as drunk as you say they are, then what good will they do tracking the girls? Go after them and clean up this mess you've made!"

I heard a growling curse and saw Gringe stomp past as fast as he'd come in.

Now think, think! I tried my best to ease my terror and steady my mind, allowing me to access my power. I had to do something. I had to at least try.

Let the dark feelings go, I imagined Salinda saying in her calming voice. There was no better time to use all the wisdom she'd instilled within me. She'd trained me to be stronger than this, to be stronger than fear.

I emptied my mind, breathed deep, and summoned my inner power. I filled my consciousness with nothing but the rope wrapped tightly around my wrists and ankles. I focused on the harsh feeling against my skin. I thought about every strand woven together, every fiber that made up each strand. I thought back through its very composition to the beginning, until it was indistinguishable from the skin it touched.

It was no different from me. Therefore, it was under my control.

I saw the fibers moving, transforming. I saw them change the formation of the strands. I saw the strands loosen from their tight coil within the rope.

The sound of slow footsteps from the inner cave threatened to shatter my concentration, but the rope was loosening.

The footsteps neared.

My heart quickened but my focus held steady. Finally, I felt the rope fall from my wrists. Suppressing my surprise that I had accomplished such a feat, I continued to free myself, removing my gag and untying the ropes at my ankles. I pushed myself deeper into the nook, pressing myself against the cold, hard stone. I felt nothing but stone all around me. I became the stone.

I held my breath as Jarod crept slowly in front of the nook. "Now, where is that other little beast?" He was half obscured by shadow, but I could see that he was tall and muscular with wiry, shoulder-length hair, and an angular, bearded face. The way he walked, slinking step by step, reminded me of a wolf stalking his prey. It was obvious why he was the authority amongst the pack of hunters.

He looked into the nook and saw my discarded ropes and gag. He strode forward to retrieve them, his fierce gaze scanning the walls within. At one point, he looked directly at me, and I feared the glamour I had conjured had failed, but I kept my focus on the stone around me until his gaze moved elsewhere.

He cursed under his breath and took his search to the mouth of the cave. "Where are you?" I heard him shuffle from one side to the other. I extended my power and opened myself to sense his distress; he wanted to go after me, but also wanted to guard the cave.

I moved my focus to one of the trees outside the cave. I thought about the bark, the branches, the leaves. I thought about the snap of a twig from one of its boughs.

A moment later, I heard the loud snap coming from outside, followed by a curse from Jarod and his pounding footsteps as he left the cave.

I slipped out from the nook and crept into the inner cave. It was a wide space, lit with a modest fire burning in the center. The high cave walls were lined with massive wooden cages. Next to the nearest cage laid Maiya.

I ran to her and put my hand on her cheek. It was still warm. I braced myself to lift her when movement from within one of the cages caught my eye. I paused and stared between the filthy bars, suppressing a shout when I saw what was behind them.

A unicorn. The cage held a unicorn.

Never had I seen such a creature, but the Forest People revered them in their tales. I loved hearing about the majestic unicorn and their gentle yet powerful magic. However, the unicorn before me was anything but majestic. It was a mud-splattered white, and wobbled back and forth on its thin, bony legs. It blinked slowly at me, as if every subtle move was strained.

I looked down the row of cages. Each one appeared to be occupied by the massive form of a unicorn. Yet, of the dozen cages, all but two held corpses. The only other living unicorn was in the next cage over from the white. It was a deep chestnut brown, even thinner than the white, and had thick clumps of dark-red blood surrounding the base of its long, ivory horn. One of its eyes locked on mine and I felt as if I had been struck in the chest—pain, hunger, distress, and insanity flooded my awareness. I felt like I would retch from the agony.

I took a deep breath and released the feelings. I could still sense them, but I kept them at a distance. *I can't help them if I'm a mess.*

I lifted my palm toward the brown unicorn, making a soft hushing sound. He turned away and stuck his horn through the slats of the cage, pressing it against the wall. A sharp grating sound rang through the cave as it tossed his head up and down. My stomach lurched as I realized what he was trying to do. "Stop!" I slammed my fist into the splintery wood of the cage. "You are hurting yourself!"

The brown unicorn turned his maniacal gaze back to me just long enough for me to see fresh blood oozing from the base of his horn. The horn itself was left undamaged, yet he returned to his fruitless efforts.

I spun around, searching the cave for what I needed, and saw an ax lying next to one of the cages further down. I ran to retrieve it, brought it to the unicorn's cage, and began to hack at the ropes binding the wooden frame. Once I had the door ajar, I did the same to the white unicorn's cage. I looked at the unicorn, who was no longer blinking sleepily. His ears twitched, and his muscles quivered. As he held my gaze, a shiver ran down my spine.

Danger.

"What?" It was almost as if the unicorn had spoken to me. I shook the idea out of my mind. "Don't just stand there. Get out! Both of you!"

I bent down to Maiya and slapped her lightly on the cheek. "Wake up. Please, wake up." I put her arm over my shoulders and pulled her up by the torso.

Her head lolled as she gasped and mumbled.

"Don't speak. I just need you to walk." I pulled her forward, forcing her to take one weak step at a time. Sweat beaded at my forehead.

I looked over my shoulder, shocked when I saw neither unicorn had left its cage. The brown still ground his horn against the wall, while the white stared at me, motionless.

"What's wrong with you? Get out of here while you can!"

Danger

Again, I felt the word so strongly I thought I'd heard it out loud. Before I could make sense of it, I heard the thundering sound of feet coming from outside the cave. I bit back a cry as I looked around for somewhere to glamour myself, wondering if I had the power to hide Maiya as well. I looked back at the white unicorn that now stood outside his cage.

Danger.

"I know, I get it!" I said through clenched teeth. I turned to run—or hobble—toward the cave wall, when the white unicorn came to a halt before me and lowered his head.

Mount. Safety.

My eyes grew wide, yet I made no move to obey the words that somehow spoke to my mind. I hadn't mounted a horse since I was a child. How was I supposed to mount a unicorn? And with Maiya too?

The footsteps resounded on the solid stone of the cave entrance, and I knew I had no other choice. I hefted Maiya with all my might onto the unicorn's back, and then flung myself up as well. The unicorn righted itself as Gringe, Jarod, and the other hunters found us.

They paused when they saw us, but quickly recovered with a roar and a flash of swords. The men came at us. The unicorn backed away, but they were too fast. Inches away, steel flashed near my foot. The unicorn continued to back away, darting this way and that with nowhere to go. We were surrounded. A wave of steel swelled before us.

A flash of brown flew in front of me. As if from nowhere, the brown unicorn was standing between us and the hunters, and the swords met his hide instead. But the brown fought back, thrashing his horned head at the hunters, giving us a chance to skirt around the fray to freedom.

As we raced from the cave, I looked behind, just in time to see the brown fall beneath the hunters in a bloody heap.

I wrapped my arms tightly around Maiya's waist as we sped through the dark forest on the galloping unicorn. My head was pounding, and I could feel myself growing weak. I had used more of my power in one evening than I'd ever used in my entire life; it wasn't surprising my strength was failing. My eyes slid out of focus, yet I held tight to the thought of home. It was my only comfort until even that slipped from my mind.

THE SKY WAS STILL DARK WHEN I OPENED MY EYES. MY LEGS were numb, yet I had somehow managed to stay righted on the unicorn's back. My arms were still wrapped around Maiya's waist. I looked around and saw that we had stopped in the middle of a large clearing.

I shook Maiya until her eyelids fluttered and she lifted her head from the unicorn's neck. "Where..."

I hushed her and helped her slide to her feet. I followed suit and looked around. What I'd first seen as an empty clearing, I now realized was once a camp. Debris littered the ground. Embers from freshly extinguished fires softly glowed. The smell of smoke and herbs and meat clung to the air.

I let out a cry. We were home, but the Forest People were gone.

"What is happening?" Maiya whimpered, trembling as she took in our abandoned camp. She wrapped her arms around me and sobbed into my shoulder.

I didn't have the strength to raise a hand to pat her back or stroke her hair. I couldn't offer a single consoling word. I couldn't even cry with her. There was nothing left in me.

The sound of nearby movement shook me from my brooding. Maiya lifted her head and put her hand over her mouth to stifle her cries.

"Cora. Maiya." The voice was quiet, yet vaguely familiar. It called out again.

Roije entered the clearing, arrow nocked and trained on us. His face softened when he saw us. He lowered his bow and ran to our side. "I cannot believe I've really found you. You won't believe how worried everyone has been."

Maiya and I let out sighs of relief. Maiya fell to her knees, and Roije bent down beside her to assess her injuries.

"What happened? Where did everyone go?" I asked.

"Salinda received a vision. She urged everyone to pack their belongings and prepare to move camp. Many heeded her, and those who didn't quickly responded when Luna and Ciela returned to camp. They were incoherent, trying to explain what had happened to the four of you. After that, we left camp with haste, as you can see. A few of us, including myself, remained behind to track you. How did you make it back?"

"We rode," I said.

"On what?"

"On a—" I looked to my side where the unicorn last stood, but he was gone. My shoulders slumped. I'd wanted to thank the heroic unicorn before we parted ways. I looked back at Roije. "On a horse. We stole one of the hunter's horses. It ran away when we got here."

My eyes flashed toward Maiya, who made no indication that she knew otherwise.

Roije seemed to accept my story as well. "Now that the two of you are safe, we can call off the search and rejoin our people."

As we walked through the moonlit trees, my eyes fell on the place I had stood just hours before, shooting arrows into a log. *My bow and quiver*! I remembered my stash and ran to retrieve them. Shouldering my bow felt like coming home to my own body. I sighed and took one last look at the old log. I could almost hear Salinda's words. *Your path is changing.*

No. I'm coming home.

I turned away from the log and ran to catch up with Roije and Maiya, yet my feet felt heavier with every step.

Coralaine.

This time, it was another voice I heard. One that made my skin crawl. That's when I remembered the conversation in the cave. No matter how hard I tried to convince myself otherwise, I knew I'd heard right—Jarod had spoken Morkai's name. In my gut, I knew the name could belong to none other than the man who'd destroyed my childhood. Somehow, he was involved with the killing of the unicorns in the cave. It was more than sport. There was evil involved.

I paused and looked over my shoulder. *Back there is danger. Forward is home.*

"Is something wrong? We need to keep moving," Roije called from ahead.

I felt like my feet were planted in the dirt below. My head felt heavy as I forced it forward. I lifted a foot, and again felt as if I were weighed to the ground. A tear slid down my cheek. "I'm not going with you."

Roije's eyes went wide. "What are you talking about? I promised Salinda I would bring you back if I found you. I can get us back to our people."

I took a deep breath. "Tell Salinda she was right. I have found my path. She will understand."

Maiya whimpered and ran to me. "What are you talking about? You have to come with us!"

I gathered her into my arms. "Maiya, I love you like

my dearest sister, but I have to go. There's something I must do."

"You're talking crazy. What could you possibly do?"

"I don't have the answers. But you were right about my dream. It means something."

Maiya lowered her head and sobbed.

"I'm so sorry I'm leaving you. But I'll find you again, I promise."

Roije came to us and put a hand on Maiya's shoulder. "We must keep moving," he said gently.

Maiya released me and nodded. "Stay safe, Cora. And come back soon."

"I will."

Roije removed his dark-brown hunting cloak and draped it over my shoulders. Even though it was large on me, its length and heavy weight provided comforting warmth. "I don't know what you are doing," Roije said, "but I trust your spirit is guiding you."

"Thank you." I brushed the tears from my cheeks and took one last look at their faces—the last faces of home I would see before I turned toward the unknown. It took all my strength to close my eyes, turn away, and walk in the opposite direction. I didn't look behind me until I was sure Roije and Maiya were out of sight. They were gone. I was alone.

But then I wasn't.

Feeling a quiet presence beside me, I lifted my head saw the white unicorn. My heart softened, my shoulders relaxed. The unicorn walked so close, I knew I could touch him. I reached out a tentative hand and placed it on his mud-splattered, white coat. A calm warmth flooded me. "I'm glad you came back. I wanted to thank you for helping us."

You helped me.

My eyes widened. So, it wasn't just in the cave. We really could understand each other. I opened my mind, my senses, and could feel the gentle spirit, the love, the gratitude, and the loyalty of the unicorn. I wondered where his home was, where he would go next.

Once again, my mind heard the feelings-turned-to-thoughts-turned-to-words, *I stay with you.*

My heart leapt, and I felt a smile stretch across my face as I walked alongside my new companion, knowing nothing would ever be the same again.

9

GOODBYES

Teryn

What have I gotten myself into? I asked myself, as I packed the one bag of belongings and survival necessities Helios was allowing me to take. *Do I really need to do this? Do I really need Helios? Do I really want Mareleau that bad?*

It was too late for second guessing. I breathed a heavy sigh and finished packing. With feet that dragged as if made from lead, I made my way to my chambermaster, handed him my over-stuffed bag, and ordered my horse to be ready before third bell. I took a wistful look around my room, and my eyes lingered on my already-made bed. According to Helios' plan, I wouldn't be sleeping in a bed again until after we completed the Quest.

Perhaps I should have slept in longer.

My thoughts were interrupted by a message that my father was expecting me in his study. I took one last look at my comforting, familiar chambers before turning my back on them, and heard the mournful sound of my doors closing behind me.

"My boy!" my father exclaimed as I entered his study. He pushed away the stack of papers he was signing as a young serving boy pulled out a seat for me at the king's desk. Father ordered a goblet of wine to be filled for me. "I know it's barely morning, but we must share one final goblet for luck."

"I'll need all the luck I can get." I forced a smile, then took a drink.

Father waved his hand dismissively. "Come, now, I know you'll do fine. You've always been an excellent hunter. If these unicorns truly exist, I know you'll find them. And if not, surely Mareleau will tire of such a silly flight of fancy and call you boys home."

"I'm sure you're right," I said without feeling.

"However, I'm astonished she has forbidden you to travel with guards." Father ran his fingers over his dark, short-cropped beard. "Are you sure I can't send some of my guards to tail you at a distance? Or any men of the Royal Force? The Red Force would be best, but the Black Force could remain unseen. Or how about your brother? He's trained with the Black. Besides, you could use a companion."

I shuddered at his advice. Take Larylis with me to win the heart of the woman he thinks he loves? Our last conversation came to mind, sending waves of dread through me. I shook my head. "Don't worry, Father, I have it all figured out. I won't be hunting alone. I'll be hiring a team of assistants in secret once I'm away. I just don't want word to get back to Mareleau that I'm employing help, in case she uses it as grounds to disqualify me."

My father nodded, accepting my tale. Helios had prepared me with numerous well-constructed lies in order to keep the alliance a secret, as well as pacify worried or suspicious minds.

"That does make me feel better," Father said. "Still, I must warn you to be careful. I know this seems to you like a lighthearted adventure—"

Oh, how wrong you are, Father.

"—But some places in Lela are...less safe than Mena. I pray you stay close to home, if you can help it."

"I'm only traveling to Kero, Father." That, at least, was true. From what little I'd been told about our plan, I knew we would be traveling to northern Kero where rumors of unicorn sightings circulated most frequently.

Father's eyes widened for a moment. "That's what I was afraid of."

His expression made my heart race. "What do you mean?"

"There are things you just don't understand, Teryn. Things I don't even understand. Kero has become a *reserved* kingdom, for lack of a better word. Ever since King Dimetreus took the throne, things have been different."

I didn't want to let the fear show on my face, but I had never heard him speak ill of our neighboring kingdom before. I remained quiet, hoping my father would elaborate.

"It's so sad what happened to King Jeru and Queen Tiliane," Father said quietly, eyes unfocused. "I knew them well. They were both younger than your mother and I, yet they died well before us. Every report coming from Kero since then has been nothing short of strange."

Although I knew about the tragic incidents that had befallen Kero and the royal family, I hadn't given them much thought. When forced to consider it, Kero did seem like a distant and reserved kingdom. In terms of location, Mena was just as close to Kero as Sele. However, Sele felt like our true neighbor. We were kept constantly informed about Sele's affairs as if they were our own and were always invited to the celebrations and festivals at Verlot Palace. Kero, on the other hand, had never felt nearly as welcoming.

"What exactly are you worried about?" I asked.

"What concerns me most is King Dimetreus has yet to sign the Tri-Kingdom Peace Pact of Lela." Father's brow furrowed as he took a deep drink of wine. "Perhaps the Pact seems insignificant to him after centuries of peace, but as long as the Pact has existed, each new king has renewed it upon taking the throne. He has yet to follow suit. Ten years have passed since his coronation, and not one attempt has been made by him to solidify the Pact."

"What does that mean for Lela? Does he not agree to peace?"

"Perhaps he does, but without his name on the Pact, we can't be certain. Every effort we've made to meet with him has been thwarted by one justification or another. It could simply be that he sees the Pact as an archaic ritual that he will participate in when he sees fit. Or it could be that he doesn't agree to peace."

I was speechless. How were there concerns for my

kingdom I didn't even know about? As crown prince, I shouldn't be so ignorant.

My father let out a sigh and forced a smile that didn't reach his eyes. "I know you will be safe. Just be careful."

"I will," I said, yet I couldn't shake the weight of his warning.

Father sat upright, regaining his composure. "Besides, when you and Mareleau are married, our kingdoms will be unshakably united. No one would dare oppose us."

So, I had yet another reason why I could not lose. I had to make Mareleau mine.

After exchanging our goodbyes, I left the study hoping my remaining farewells wouldn't be so burden-some. If the sinking in my gut got any heavier, I wouldn't be able to mount my horse.

As I walked toward the stables, I saw a small retinue waiting for me. My mother ran to me and threw her arms around my neck, sobbing her worries and goodbyes. I didn't think she would ever let me go until Larylis approached.

"May I have a word with my brother?" he asked.

My mother nodded, wiped her teary eyes, and reluc-tantly released me. I was left to face the unreadable Larylis. We walked a few paces away from listening ears and stood in awkward silence, neither of us meeting the eye of the other.

Larylis spoke first. "You know how you promised me you would forfeit the Quest if I asked you to?"

I nodded, my stomach tightening. When I gave that promise, I had expected him to answer me at once. Instead, he had stormed from my study and hadn't said a word to me since. Would he really ask me to keep my promise after I'd already made it this far? I imagined forfeiting the Quest, giving up on the alliance, on Mareleau, on my dreams, and turning my back on two weeks of preparations, secrets, and inner turmoil. For one incomprehensible moment, I felt relief.

Larylis met my eyes with a blank expression. "I'm not going to. You were right. Mareleau and I will never be together. At least with you, I know she will be loved and taken care of. You deserve her. Go get her."

I opened my mouth but could find no words. I hadn't imagined Larylis would forgive me any time soon, much less give me his blessing. I felt my shoulders relax, and for the first time in two weeks, I felt I could breathe. "Do you really mean it?"

Larylis attempted a feeble smile. "I can't say I'm happy for you, but I promise I will no longer get in your way or fight with you about Mareleau. I want her to be happy. And I want *you* to be happy."

"You know I want the same for you, right? I want you to be happy as well. I meant it when I said I would give her up for you. I hoped you wouldn't ask me to, but I would have kept my promise."

"That means a lot to me, but I'm ready to let her go. Also, she sent you this." He handed me a white rose tied to a scroll.

I took it from him, unrolled the scroll, and read: *My faith in you will outlast this white rose. I wish you the best of luck and anxiously await your triumphant return. With all the love in my heart, Mareleau.*

My heart pounded as I reread her words over and

over until they were branded on my memory. I embraced my brother and said my final goodbyes, feeling like my feet were floating as I mounted my horse. For that moment, I could forget the uncertainty of the future and charge forward with determination. The Quest had begun.

~

Larylis

I watched my brother until he faded from view. As I walked back to my chambers, I pulled out two other pieces of paper I had stuffed beneath the neck of my tunic. The first was a letter I had sent to Mareleau just days before. I could barely make out the words, crumpled and smudged as they were. It read: *Do you honestly think you could love my brother?*

The other paper held Mareleau's response, equally smudged and carelessly scrawled with: *All you need to know is that I can't love you.* The paper itself looked like it had been torn in half and stained with water; it likely came from the wastebasket. Meanwhile, Teryn's letter was written in an elaborate script on a beautiful scroll, not to mention the rose she had sent with it. I couldn't imagine a crueler way to get her message across.

I entered my study, slumped into the chair at my desk, and reread the scribbled words until my eyes began to blur. *Just let her go,* I told myself as I closed my eyes on the tears that threatened to fall. *She doesn't love me. She loves Teryn.* I grit my teeth and felt my hands turn to fists, crumpling the small pieces of paper in my palm. *Let her go.* I took a deep breath, then tossed the two letters into the fireplace. *Let her go.* I watched the paper disappear into the flames.

I hardened my heart and pushed all my memories of the golden-haired girl of my youth out of my mind. I pushed away her smile, her laugh, her sparkling, blue eyes. Never again would those eyes haunt my dreams. Never again would she taunt me with her cold, cruel demeanor. Because never again would I be so foolish to love a woman who did not love me back. For the first time, I saw her for the monster she really was.

I let out a deep breath, and with it went my commitment, my love, and my heartache for her. I stared into the flames, imagining all those things burning to ash along with her stupid note.

I let her go.

~

Mareleau

"They've all left," my mother said as she barged into my chambers.

I rubbed my eyes and sat up on my lounge.

Mother stared down at me with her hands on her hips. "Were you sleeping? Here you are, lazy as a cow, while your three champions depart on your Quest. Did it ever occur to you that you should see them off?"

"No." I cast her a scowl and reached for a bowl of chocolate on the table next to my lounge. I stuffed three pieces into my mouth at once. "Why would I do that, Mother?"

Mother looked at me with disgust. "Because it is respectful. You could have at least seen Teryn off."

"I don't care about Teryn!"

"Well, you should. He is the son of our closest allies, and we can't afford to disrespect them. Luckily, I sent him a gift on your behalf."

I jumped to my feet. "Why would you do that? And without my permission?"

"Because you are too selfish to do it yourself."

I opened my mouth to argue but didn't have it in me. Not today.

"Listen, young lady. I agree with your father that you *should* favor Teryn over the others. As much as I think you and Helios would make a beautiful match, there is no doubt that a union with Teryn would benefit our kingdom the most."

"Oh, so I'm a pawn now?"

Mother threw her hands in the air. "You really are a spoiled, little fool, Mareleau. You know nothing about leading a kingdom, which is why we aren't making *you* our heir!"

Again, I was too stunned to argue.

Mother looked equally as shocked as she stood, chest heaving. She closed her eyes, her face softened, and her shoulders relaxed. She moved slowly into the seat next to me. "I didn't mean it like that." She reached a willowy hand towards my face.

I turned away, letting her hand fall on my hair.

"What I meant to say is...you are important to us. You are not a pawn, but you do have a destiny to fulfill for the greater good of Sele. It is unlikely your father and I will produce another child, much less a son. If your father dies before adopting a legitimate heir, our kingdom could fall into chaos, even war. Your uncles would inherit the crown and fight over it. They are capable men, but too ambitious. Your father and I want the crown to remain under our direct lineage."

"Since I'm completely useless, what does this have to do with me?"

"That's just it, Mareleau. You are not useless. Once you marry your prince, you can start producing children. Your son can be *our* heir."

I spun around in my seat to face her. "Not only have you planned *whom* I can marry, but you've also planned the life of my future child? That's disgusting, Mother!"

"That's not disgusting, Mareleau, that's your duty. Besides, we have not planned whom you marry. You are responsible for that choice, and you are turning it into a farce!"

My arms began to shake. I clenched my fists around the folds of my skirt. "If I'm free to choose whom I marry, then why do you and Father insist I marry a crown prince? If you only care that I produce an heir for *you*, why does it matter whom I produce it with?"

"Don't you understand? A kingdom is only as strong as its rulers. Do you think our people will follow the son of some *nobody* prince? Do you think your uncles will be content to serve and follow him? Do you really think Sele will be safe from invading forces with such a weak claim to the throne?"

"Fine," I said through clenched teeth. "I get it. I need to marry a crown prince. But why Teryn? Why does father, and now you, keep pushing me toward him? Father knows Teryn is the last man I want to marry."

Mother sighed, a small smile playing on her lips. "Yes, I know, dear. The union between you and Teryn has always been your father's vision. But it is not without reason. If you were to marry Teryn, we *could* make you our heir. Then, when our rule passes to you and Arlous' crown passes to Teryn, the two of you could rule Sele and Mena as one. Our kingdoms would merge without war, without strife. We would become a strengthened force."

I leaned back in my seat and stared at the ceiling. I was even more of a pawn than I had originally thought.

Mother stroked the hair along my forehead. "I'm sorry this is so hard for you. I just want you to understand what's at stake. I want you to learn to care."

"That's too bad because I *don't* care."

Mother stood and glared down at me, her mouth opening as she prepared to argue.

I wouldn't give her the chance. "What are you going to do now, Mother? Yell at me? Insult me? Then are you going to apologize? Instead of wasting your time, why don't you just leave?"

My mother gaped like a fish out of water. "You would make a terrible queen," she finally managed to say, then left my chambers in a huff.

I paced around my room, trying to forget our irritating exchange. I stared out my window at the palace grounds, remembering the endless sea of men whose hearts I had crushed. I let out a sigh of relief, knowing I wouldn't have to deal with any more poems any time soon. Perhaps being practically engaged had its benefits. No more love letters. No more marriage proposals. No more serenades from below my balcony. No more lustful eyes, groping hands, and empty promises.

My three possible suitors were gone on what I hoped to be an endless, fruitless mission, and I promised myself I would enjoy every quiet moment they were away. I smiled for the first time in days and realized—for the time being, at least—I was free.

10

THE HUNT

Teryn

Every inch of my body was sore. I was filthy; dirt filled every gap between finger and nail, a fine layer of grit blanketed my skin, and my hair felt like one mass of collective straw. In the firelight, I watched a bug crawl over my arm as I hugged my knees toward my chest. My first instinct was to swat it away, but the thought of moving was effort enough. I let the bug make its way to my other arm before I rested my head on the trunk of the tree behind me.

"There are no unicorns here," Helios said from across the campfire.

Tell me something I don't know, I thought as I scowled at him. After three weeks of the grueling hunt, I wasn't sure I believed there were unicorns *anywhere.*

"What does that mean?" Lex asked weakly as he raised his head from his hands. Dark circles hung beneath his heavy-lidded eyes.

"It means the other hunters have been here already. There are no unicorns left in the area." Helios stoked the fire, showing no signs of fatigue.

"No kidding. Got any more obvious information?"

"Is my information beneath you, Prince Lexington? Would you prefer I left you in the dark?"

"I'd prefer to be sleeping in a comfortable bed!"

"Then you should go home."

"Come on, enough," I said, sitting upright. "Helios, what is the plan now?"

Helios grumbled and turned to face me. "We will continue further north, although I doubt we will come across many unicorns, if any. These other hunting parties appear to be more thorough than I had anticipated."

"How is that a plan?" Lex said, glaring at the back of Helios' head.

Helios closed his eyes for a moment, and I could see the muscles tighten in his jaw. "I'm not finished. While I realize we are in previously hunted territory, I can also see that we aren't far behind the hunting party that was here before us."

"And how do you know that?" Lex snapped.

"If you paid any attention to your surroundings you would know too," Helios said through clenched teeth, still looking only at me. "Last week we made camp in a clearing which appeared to have housed a group of hunters, perhaps two months ago. The hunting paths we've been traveling the past few days show even more recent use. And here, in this very camp, I can see it was vacated no more than three weeks ago."

I looked around me. "How can you tell?"

"Hoof marks from their horses, faded footprints,

packed earth where beds had been made. I even found a cave nearby with wood scraps, likely from cages, and dried blood smeared in the dirt and on the cave walls. They've got unicorns, I know it."

I was chilled by his thorough observations—I hadn't noticed a single thing out of the ordinary. "What do you propose?"

"From the look of their former camps, they settle into a main camp for weeks at time and hunt the surrounding areas. They've likely moved on and settled into a new camp just a few days' time from here. I say we track them and catch up to them."

"And after that? Do we surpass them somehow?"

"If we can. But first we will find them and see what they have to offer." Helios smirked, making my stomach uneasy.

"What exactly does that mean?" Lex's voice held a tentative edge.

"You'll see. Do you want to make a quick end of this Quest, or not? We could spend every day in this forest for the next month without even a glimpse of a unicorn, or we could do this my way."

Lex and I exchanged a quick glance. Did we really have a choice? Neither of us said a word.

"I take it we do it my way, then."

We sat in tense silence. Helios stared into the fire, his face a hard mask. Lex leaned to the side, arm propped on his knee, face resting in his palm. I looked around the camp, trying to find the signs and marks I had previously overlooked. If only I had the skills Helios had, Lex and I wouldn't be stuck with him. My upbringing felt suddenly inadequate. "Helios, how did you learn what you know?"

Helios raised an eyebrow but said nothing.

I tried a different approach. "You obviously have a lot more experience than Lex and I have. How did you become so proficient at hunting, tracking, and scheming?"

"You must know nothing of my homeland."

"Not so much," I admitted.

"I do," Lex said under his breath.

Helios grinned at Lex, then turned to me. "Didn't you know? Tomas and Norun are neighboring kingdoms."

This I knew, but I didn't understand why that was significant. Both kingdoms belonged to the land of Risa, and both lay just above the border between Lela and Risa, north of Kero. I shrugged.

"Do you know anything about the world outside Lela?" Helios looked down his nose at me. "I'll educate you. Norun is one of the wealthiest, most powerful kingdoms in Risa, and kingdoms in Risa are often larger than the entire land of Lela. Norun has conquered over nine of these kingdoms since the rule of my father, King Isvius. I've assisted in conquering five. There's a lot to learn in war. But you wouldn't know anything about that, being from Lela, the peaceful little land of nothing."

I scowled at him. "Are you saying peace is a bad thing?"

"You tell me. Here you are, nearly clueless when it comes to hunting or self-sustainability. If your kingdom was invaded, could you defend it?"

I felt my blood getting hot. "I've trained with my kingdom's Red Force and I know how to wield a sword. We're not as clueless as you think. Just because we don't conquer everything around us, doesn't mean we can't fight."

Helios shrugged. "Sure. And what about you, Prince Lexington? What do you know of war?"

"Quit calling me that," Lex said through clenched teeth. "And I *do* know how to fight. We are trained well, in case some monstrous kingdom like Norun tries to add us to its conquests!"

"Ha! You really think Norun would *want* Tomas under its rule? It's even smaller than Lela."

Lex turned scarlet as he pressed his lips tight together.

"I'd like to convince my father to invade Tomas just to see you fight. What a pathetic spectacle that would make. You can barely walk more than twenty paces without complaining."

"That's not true."

"And who trains you to fight in the first place? The farmers? Your father? Your unmarriageable, hideous sisters?"

"Just leave him alone." My voice came out stronger and louder than I had intended, ringing out in stark contrast to the quiet night.

Helios glared at me unblinkingly, laughing when I finally averted my gaze. "How sweet. The young princes of two pitiful, little kingdoms have become friends. My father would die of shock if he saw me cavorting with the likes of you."

I remained silent as unspoken insults spewed from my mind and hit the wall of my closed lips.

"Well, it's been nice chatting. I'm going to sleep now." Helios' face shone with pride as he laid out on his bedroll. "Must get a fresh start on tomorrow. Sleep well, I know you'll need it."

Lex and I sat silent in our humiliation. Only once Helios began snoring loudly and I could see the rhythmic rise and fall of his wide chest, did I feel my shoulders relax. I looked at Lex, who met my gaze with a roll of his eyes.

"I *do* know how to fight," he whispered, inching closer to me. "What an arrogant bastard."

"You know he's only acting that way to annoy us. He knows we need him, and he wants to keep it that way. Don't let him get to you."

Lex sighed. "I hate him. And I hate that he's right about how badly we need him. But at least this way we've got a chance. Or *you* do, at least. I just want to go home. I want to see my family again. And Lily."

"Lily? Is that your lady back home?" It was a relief to have a change of subject.

"Yes. Father doesn't approve of her. She's highborn, but not a princess. I was almost positive he was ready to agree to our marriage, until word of Mareleau's stupid contest got around. He wanted a better match for me, so he sent me to compete. I'm hoping after I return home a brave-yet-narrowly-defeated finalist, I'll earn his respect and he'll finally approve of my choice. If he doesn't...I don't know what I'll do. I'd do anything for Lily. I can't live without her."

I'd never heard so much passion from him that wasn't about food or comfort. "You must really love her. What's she like?"

Lex brightened as a smile took over his round face. "She's got the curviest body I have ever seen, auburn hair the color of fall leaves, skin like warm milk, and breasts like two overstuffed pillows. Nothing like that skinny Mareleau."

I laughed. "As unbelievable as it might sound, I happen to like *that skinny Mareleau.* She's a goddess in my eyes."

Lex shrugged, his expression full of bewilderment. We both laughed. "Do you love her?" Lex asked.

"Of course," I said in a rush. "I mean, it isn't quite the same as you feel about Lily, but I suppose I would do anything to make her my bride. I am on this Quest, aren't I?"

"Do you think she loves you?"

I reached into a pocket inside my hunting cloak and pulled out the withered rose Mareleau had sent me. "I think so. She believes in me, at least. It is now my duty to fulfill that faith and make it back to her."

"You will. We both will. We'll return home to the women we belong with."

I smiled. "That's the most positive thing I've heard you say in three weeks."

"Don't get used to it. In the morning, Helios will still be here."

It was a sobering truth. With a sigh, I tucked the rose back into my pocket and retired to my bedroll.

As I drifted to sleep, I summoned thoughts of my beloved—her golden hair, her blue eyes, her bold stance, her sultry voice. I remembered the moment she stepped onto her balcony, how my heart had stopped. I remembered her beautiful yet scowling face as she stood high above me, and how she had looked at me. Wait, *at* me? No, she had been looking *through* me. Her eyes were always somewhere else, somewhere in the distance. My pockets were full of an endless supply of jewels, but no matter how many I placed before her, I couldn't get her to look at me. I shouted her name to get her attention. I sang, I danced, I did magic I didn't even know I could do. Nothing could captivate her. Without a word, she turned and left her balcony, closed the door behind her, and took all the light from the world. I was left standing in darkness.

I woke in a cold sweat next to the dying embers of the campfire. *Just dreams,* I told myself, yet try as I might, I couldn't shake the darkness lingering behind my closed eyes.

11

THE OTHER HUNT

Cora

I t felt good to be clean again. The cool water of the sunlit river washed over my naked body, taking with it all the tension from my mind and muscles. I tilted my head back and let the sun warm my face. Holding my breath, I dunked my head under the gently rushing waters, letting my long, tangled hair flow in the current.

I stood back up and looked downriver where my unicorn companion, whom I'd named Valorre for his valorous rescue, bathed in the deeper waters. Now that he was clean, I could see the sun reflecting off tiny speckles of silver in his gleaming white coat. His strength and health had improved significantly since we'd begun our travels together. It was hard to believe I was looking at the same unicorn I'd fled the cave with. *Feels nice, doesn't it?* I directed the thought to him.

Very.

Valorre's health wasn't the only thing that had strengthened in our time together; our connection had become so deep that communicating with him seemed no different than conversing out loud with Maiya. Sometimes I even spoke to him aloud, just to remind myself I had a voice.

Once my skin became wrinkled, I reluctantly left the river and returned to the sapling where I'd left my freshly washed clothing hanging to dry. I put on my ivory chemise, still slightly damp, and sprawled out on the riverbank beneath the mild heat of the sun while I waited for the rest of my clothing—pants and bodice—to dry.

One of the first things I'd done after embarking on my new path was to raid the hunters' camp for necessities—extra arrows, a few knives, a small traveling bag, and a pair of leather pants. The pants took a good deal of washing, cutting, and stitching to forge a pair that would comfortably fit me, but the effort had paid off. I couldn't imagine stalking bloodthirsty hunters in a dress.

I closed my eyes, reveling in what would probably be the last calm moment of my day, until a shadow fell over me. I looked up and saw Valorre standing at my side. He'd been so quiet I hadn't even heard him approach.

The hunters. They move, he said.

Then let's go.

I rose and pulled on my pants, tightening the laces up the sides of the legs until they fit snugly. I tucked the bottom of my chemise into my pants and laced my brown leather bodice over the top. Next, I belted my bag around my waist, strapped on my boots, and draped Roije's cloak around my shoulders, followed by my bow and quiver of arrows.

I felt heavy after being so free and naked just moments before, but I was eager to start my day. There was much work to be done.

After I had parted ways with Roije and Maiya, Valorre and I had retraced our path back to the hunters' camp. It was, of course, abandoned by the time we arrived, but we were then able to follow their tracks. Keeping about a quarter-day's safe distance behind them, we continued to follow them for the next week until they settled into their new camp. Every day since then, I'd made it my mission to gather as much information as I could by stalking, watching, and listening. When the opportunity arose, I would sneak into camp, steal what I could use or eat, and search for anything significant that might provide answers. So far, I'd only gathered enough information to leave me with more questions.

It was late in the morning by the time we reached the hunters' camp. I crept quietly between the trees, crouching below the cover of leaves and branches as I peered into the clearing. Just like Valorre had said, the hunters had left for their daily hunt. As usual, only two men were left to guard—I'd come to learn they were named Nym and Arrin. They were new arrivals, replacements for young James and a hunter who'd been killed in the fight with the brown unicorn.

I looked at the cages; all but three were empty. In the time the hunters had been at their new camp, they'd captured three unicorns. They'd been kept alive so far yet didn't appear to be fed or cared for in any way. Just like Valorre and the brown.

I'd learned from Valorre that he'd witnessed the hunters in the cave harvesting the horns from the other unicorns only when they were at their weakest. Sensing the diminishing life-energy of the three unicorns, I knew they didn't have much longer. I wanted so badly to free them, yet I hadn't figured out a way to do so without putting my mission in danger. If I made any significant move, the hunters would know of my presence. It wouldn't be so easy for me to follow them if they expected me. I needed a plan and answers. Soon.

While I knew the hunters only harvested the horns when the unicorns were near death, I had yet to learn why. Why would they want a horn from a weak unicorn as opposed to a strong one? Was it just so it would be easier to remove? Was it so the unicorns didn't put up a fight? Why did they even want their horns in the first place? What were they doing with them? Most importantly, what were they doing for *Morkai?*

No matter how many times I asked myself these same questions, I couldn't figure it out. I'd tried probing the hunter's thoughts and intentions, but the results were unsatisfying. *I need to question them directly, but how?*

I watched Nym and Arrin idly pacing the perimeter of the camp and wondered how difficult they would be to overpower. They looked no older than James had been, and both were of lean build. *Perhaps I can kill one and wound the other for questioning.* I shuddered at the thought of ending human life. The Forest People had taught me to hunt and defend myself, but they'd also instilled within me a deep reverence for all life. I knew I could kill if it were necessary to defend my own or another's life. *But can I plot the end of a human life, even if the ends justify the means?*

Kill is never to be done lightly, Valorre said.

I know, but we're running out of time. I need answers and I need to free the unicorns before—

We were distracted by the rumbling of voices approaching from beyond the camp. Gringe and Jarod appeared. I'd expected them to be hunting with the others for many hours more.

Nym and Arrin looked just as surprised to see them as I was. The guards immediately began pacing the camp with more attention, their weapons held more firmly in hand. "What brings you back early?" Nym asked.

"Orders." Jarod looked flustered as he stormed across the camp and bent down next to one of the cages. After kicking some things to the side, he stood holding an ornate red chest with gold detail along the sides and corners.

Gringe followed clumsily in his wake, looking equally unnerved. "It has to be tonight?"

"Isn't that what I said?" Jarod barked.

"Not a lot of warning..."

Jarod turned to Gringe, fixing him with a fierce glare. "When I get my orders, I follow them. I suggest you do the same." He heaved the chest at Gringe who begrudgingly accepted the burden.

"Your orders for tonight remain the same," Jarod shouted at Nym and Arrin, then motioned for Gringe to follow him back into the dense forest.

I was torn between terror and curiosity as I debated what to do next. I could stay and formulate a plan to question one of the guards and free the unicorns, or I could follow Jarod and Gringe. As badly as I wanted to make sure the unicorns remained unharmed, I couldn't shake the feeling that Jarod was up to something dark. I had to know what it was.

Valorre and I quietly crept away from the camp and began to track Jarod and Gringe.

Dark had fallen by the time Valorre sensed the two hunters had stopped. When we caught up to them, we found them standing in a wide clearing with the box open at their feet. I could see something gleaming from within, reflecting the white light of the moon. *Unicorn horns.*

I extended my power to catch Jarod and Gringe's whispered conversation.

"Are you afraid of it?" Gringe asked.

"No," Jarod answered flatly.

"What will it do?"

"You'll see."

A few moments of silence passed, then Gringe said, "It wouldn't hurt us...would it?"

Jarod slowly turned his head to look at Gringe. "Will you shut up?"

Gringe growled his acquiescence.

The silence that followed grew hauntingly still. Not the rustle of a leaf nor the hoot of an owl could be heard. I was afraid to breathe in case the sound ruptured the stillness and revealed my hiding place.

After endless moments of the tortured silence, sound returned, but not in any familiar or comforting way. It was a sound that could be felt more than heard at first, a rumbling of the ground beneath my feet. Then a pounding reverberated through the trees as shadows moved and shifted in the distance. The rumbling grew heavier, faster, mimicking the beat of my frightened heart. Something was coming.

And then I saw it. A dark form stalked from between the rattling trees at the far end of the clearing. Bathed by the light of the moon was a huge, hideous creature resembling something between a boar and a wolf. Its head, which seemed too large for its shoulders, had a boar-like snout and tusks, but no visible ears. Its front legs had hooves while the back legs had enormous paws. The rear of its body was narrower than its shoulders and ended in a long, pointed tail. It was a hairless thing with raw-looking flesh. Tiny spikes protruded from its body, mostly surrounding its head and neck like a mane. It plodded toward the hunters, its immense hooves and paws leaving turned, loose ground in its wake.

The hunters scrambled back, quivering with fear.

The Beast towered over them, its beady, black eyes flickering from the hunters to the box of horns. A bellowing roar erupted from its open mouth. Moonlight glinted off rows of sharp, black teeth. With one swift move, the beast swung its head down and devoured the pile of horns. After another loud roar, it shook its body from head to tail like a wet animal. Perhaps it was just a play of the moonlight, but I could swear I saw a cluster of new spikes spring from the skin on its upper back.

My throat was dry as my heart hammered painfully in my chest. I could feel Valorre's panic as he stood trembling behind me. *We need to get out of here,* I told him.

Keeping my eyes fixed firmly on the beast, I took a tentative step back, then another. To my relief, the beast turned and began padding back in the direction from which it had come, making the ground rumble once again. I let out a breath I didn't know I was holding as Valorre and I quickened our pace, backing further and further away from the horrifying creature.

Just as the Beast was at the far edge of the clearing, it halted mid-step, and I froze as well. It lifted its snout as if sniffing the air, then swung its massive head back around —back toward us.

Valorre lowered his head, and I pulled my body over his back just as I heard the pounding of monstrous hooves behind us. We flitted between the trees as fast as Valorre could go. I took a wary glance behind me and saw nothing but quivering branches and a massive shadow gaining on us. It was only a matter of time before I felt hot, sticky breath on my back. I inhaled a shaking breath, stilled my mind, and reached for my bow. As quickly as I could, I nocked an arrow, swiveled my torso around and shot.

The Beast's snapping jaw loomed above me as the arrow struck its snout. The creature roared and faltered, but I was only allowed a moment's delay to nock another arrow into my bow as the Beast regained momentum. This time I shot it between the eyes. The Beast skidded to a halt, howling as it shook its head and rubbed it against a tree. I shot one more arrow into its thrashing hide and quickly nocked another one. I didn't lower my bow until I could no longer hear the Beast's thundering howls.

12

GLIMPSE

Teryn

"What do you think is worse?" Lex asked as he and I stood at the bank of the river, watering our horses. "Riding or hunting?"

"It's a tie. It's hard to believe I ever loved either. However, I do still love my horse, so hopefully I can find my love for riding again once this is all over." I gently stroked the neck of Quinne, my golden-brown mare.

"What do you think is better?" Lex said with a teasing smile. "A warm bed or a warm meal?"

"Why are you torturing me?" I laughed. "Both! Please!"

"You two are pathetic." Helios appeared behind us, sneering.

"I thought you were scouting," Lex snapped. "Back so soon?"

"Unlike you, I don't need all day to make myself useful. Follow me."

Lex and I exchanged a glance, and I shrugged my

shoulders. We left our horses and followed Helios down the riverbank. After a while, he veered toward the trees, then crouched down in the dirt. I stood behind him, looking over his shoulder as his finger hovered over the outline of what appeared to be a large hoof print.

"There. This print is larger than a normal horse, yet it leaves a lighter indent in the soil." Helios' voice was soft and full of awe, completely unlike his usual dour self.

"What does that mean? Big feet, skinny body?" Lex smirked as I hid my laughter behind a cough.

Helios turned to us, and I braced myself for a glare and a harsh word. However, Helios' eyes were wide, and a tight-lipped smile stretched across his face. "It means a unicorn has been here. Its trail continues deeper into the forest."

An excited chill ran down my spine. "Are we going to follow it?"

"*We* aren't going to do anything." Helios' face settled back into its usual scowl. "You two will stay here while I track further."

"We're supposed to be in this together," I argued. "We should all go."

Helios narrowed his dark eyes at me. "For one, I don't even know if there will be a unicorn at the end of these tracks. It could have been captured already. The hunters could even be nearby. For another, this is the most promising hint of a unicorn we've seen. I won't have either of you messing things up if I find one."

As Helios turned and stalked away, I tried to summon a clever retort. Instead, I threw my hands in the air and returned to our horses.

THE SUN HAD RISEN HIGH IN THE SKY, AND HELIOS STILL hadn't returned.

"What is taking him so long?" Lex frowned and threw a small rock into the river. "I don't trust that man. What if he's left us behind?"

"He wouldn't do that," I said, although I didn't quite believe my own words.

"Should we try to find him? Maybe he's been hurt!" Lex looked almost hopeful.

"I doubt that."

"That's a shame." Lex wrinkled his nose. "I'm so bored. I'd rather be riding or walking aimlessly than sitting here waiting like this. Besides, I'm starving."

"That I can agree with. I'll go check the traps." I shouldered my hunting pack and picked up my spear. "You wait here for Helios to return. I'll be back shortly."

"That's not fair! You get to go off and hunt while I wait around even longer?"

"Then here." I pushed the spear toward him with an innocent smile. "You can get lunch."

Lex eyed the weapon, leaning away from it. "Never mind. I'll wait here."

"Suit yourself." I walked down the riverbank toward where we'd seen the hoof print and entered the forest. Once I was under the blanket of trees, I felt a sense of calm settle over me. I felt free, free from Lex's complaining, free from Helios' judging eyes and condescending words, free from thinking about the weight of failure riding on my shoulders.

Luckily, two of our traps had been successful, and before long I had two large hares strung over my shoulder. I was on my way back to Lex and our horses when I got the uneasy feeling I'd lost my sense of direction. Relying on Helios so much had made me careless.

I just have to find the river. I checked the position of the sun and adjusted my direction. I followed what I thought looked like a familiar path, relieved when I heard rushing water. But as the sound grew nearer, I knew something was wrong. *Too gentle to be a river.* Moments later a small stream came into view. My shoulders slumped. *Perhaps the stream is running from the river.* I looked to my left. *Or perhaps it's running to it.* I looked to my right. And froze.

My eyes had to be deceiving me. I blinked once. Twice. But no matter how I tried to clear my vision, there was no denying what I saw downstream. There stood a large, white unicorn, staring at me with unblinking eyes the color of chestnuts. It was the most beautiful yet terrifying thing I had ever seen in my life. I could do nothing more than stare, too afraid to move, too afraid to startle it, too afraid I was dreaming.

My legs began to tremble. I slowly leaned forward, shifted my stance, and winced as a twig snapped under my foot. I held my breath as I waited for the unicorn to dart away. However, it continued to look at me, then lowered its head to drink in the stream. Sweat beaded at my neck, and my muscles quivered with excitement. This was the moment I'd been waiting for, the moment I was starting to doubt would ever happen. *I'd* found a unicorn. Not even Helios had managed to do that!

The spear felt suddenly heavy in my hand, and I

remembered what I was supposed to do next. *Lift. Throw. Kill.* The thought made my stomach churn as I imagined throwing the spear into the beautiful creature's hide.

But this is what I came here to do. I cannot let this opportunity pass. I must try.

I took three deep breaths, then once again shifted my feet. The unicorn didn't even flinch. Keeping my eyes fixed on the creature, I slipped the two hares from my shoulder and raised my spear. Still, the unicorn remained unperturbed. I pulled my arm back, preparing to throw. My muscles tensed. Sweat dripped down my forehead and into my eyes. I knew what needed to be done, but my body wouldn't respond. *I can't do this.*

Something stung my neck and I flinched, dropping my spear to the ground. I hissed, slapped my palm to the stinging pain, and felt something wet and warm dripping from my neck. I turned and saw an arrow protruding from the tree behind me. Before I could fully turn around, I felt the sharp tip of something press against the other side of my neck. Without moving my head, I looked out the corner of my eye and saw a blurry figure standing next to me.

"Who are you?" an angry voice demanded.

I slowly raised my hands, opening my palms in surrender as I carefully shifted to face my opponent. My eyes widened as I found myself confronted by a young woman. She was at least a head shorter than me with fierce, dark eyes and wild, brown tangles of hair escaping the hood of her cloak. She had a bow over her shoulder and a knife just inches from my neck.

"I said who are you?" She leaned forward until the tip

of the knife was once again against my skin. Girl or no, she was serious.

"T...Teryn." I tried to move my head as little as possible as I formed my words.

"Who do you work for?"

"No one!"

"You lie. Who sent you here to hunt the unicorns?"

My words were getting increasingly difficult to find. "Um...Mareleau."

She cocked her head. "So, why did this *Mareleau* send you to hunt them?"

"It's just...it's what she chose as the object of the Quest. She demanded one horn, one pelt, and one pet." I tried to keep my voice from shaking, but at that point, every part of me was quivering.

I felt the tip of her knife draw back slightly, giving me a chance to let out a deep breath as the girl's face twisted with confusion. "Who is Mareleau? Where does she come from? Why do you work for her?"

"Mareleau, Princess of Sele," I said in a rush. "I'm competing for her hand. To win I must complete her Quest."

"Who did you say you were?"

"Teryn. Prince Teryn. Of Mena."

The girl's eyes widened for a moment and I thought I saw the faintest hint of a smile twitch at the corners of her lips. She lowered her knife a few inches and eyed me from head to toe. I eyed her back, trying my best to steady my ragged breathing. Before I could consider relaxing, she thrust the tip of her knife right back under my chin. "You tried to kill my friend, you idiot!"

"I would never try to kill your friend, honestly. I wouldn't kill anyone..."

"Then what exactly were you attempting to do with that spear? Tickle him with it?" She nodded in the direction where the unicorn had stood.

"No. Well, at first I...but I couldn't, and...Wait. Your friend? The unicorn?"

She raised an eyebrow. "You really have no idea what you are doing, do you?"

"Not really." I attempted a shaky smile.

The girl sighed and rolled her eyes. "You're in way over your head. Go home, little boy."

Little boy? I'm certainly older than she is! However, the weapon in her hands made her impossible to argue with. Before I could say a word more, she lifted her leg and sent her foot to my gut, making me stumble back and fall against the tree behind me. My vision swam as I heaved forward, grasping my stomach.

"If you ever come near a unicorn again, I will kill you. I will not spare your life twice." She now stood a good twenty paces away.

My mouth hung open with the realization that I had been bested by a girl. "How will I finish the Quest?" I muttered to myself, realizing too late I had said the words out loud.

"I don't care," she said with a sneer. The girl turned to leave, then paused. Before I knew what was happening, she removed her bow from her shoulder, nocked an arrow, and sent it soaring straight at me. I shuddered as it struck the tree directly above my head. The tree was now riddled with two arrows that had nearly been the death of me. "And don't follow me."

My breath came out in ragged gasps. "Good aim."

"How do you know I didn't miss?" The girl eyed me with one final glare, then stormed away, leaving me to stew in my humiliation.

13

BLOODSHED

Cora

"**W**hy did you put yourself in danger like that? Why did you let him see you?" I asked Valorre as we left the boy at the tree.

He was harmless.

"You sure have a strange concept of harm then. He had a spear raised at you! He could have hurt you. I wouldn't have let him, of course."

He wasn't going to throw it.

"You're not the least bit bothered by the possibility? How do you know he wasn't going to throw it?"

Same way I know you would never hurt me. I know danger. I know darkness. The boy was neither. Just confused.

"Stupid is more like it," I mumbled. "What a fool. He's going to get himself killed, gallivanting around like a unicorn hunter. Gringe and Jarrod would have that boy for breakfast if he got in their way!"

And you? What would they do to you?

"I'm careful, Valorre. Besides, I've got a mission. A *good* mission." A failing mission, I did not add. I was still reeling from the shock of learning I'd missed my opportunity to save two of the unicorns. When I'd arrived at the hunters' camp earlier that morning, I'd found only one cage occupied. From what I'd learned, Nym and Arrin had killed and dehorned the two weakest unicorns while I'd been busy following Gringe and Jarod. I had to formulate a new plan, and quickly. The remaining unicorn was growing weaker.

You'll think of something, Valorre said.

I nodded and hoped he was right.

My mind wandered as we made our way through the sun-speckled forest, and again I thought about the boy and what he had said. "I can't believe that spoiled little princess has demanded unicorns in exchange for her hand. And even more unbelievable is the prince's pathetic willingness to please her! What is wrong with these people? Is that normal behavior for royalty these days? Yet, who am I to talk? I'm supposed to be dead, but here I am, traipsing through the woods like a wild woman, talking to a unicorn."

Valorre rippled with something like laughter. *The boy agitates you. Or interests you.*

I blushed, wondering if Valorre could sense my embarrassment. "It's just the first time I've met someone like me—like who I *used* to be—in a very long time. It was kind of exciting."

I thought back to nearly-forgotten moments from my childhood. I could vaguely recall the names Teryn and Mareleau, yet I'd known them long ago. I could almost remember their young faces from the royal festivals I'd seen them at. The face I'd confronted with an arrow revealed just how much time had passed since then. *We were all just kids last time I saw them! Now the snotty little blonde and the haughty little boy are grown and practically engaged.*

I felt a hollow sinking in my gut. That life was not for me to think about anymore. I shook the memories, the thoughts, and the prince's face from my mind, focusing instead on the task at hand.

Teryn

The sun was beginning to set by the time I made my way back to our horses. Lex ran to me, eyes wide as they fell upon the wound at my neck. I looked beyond him and saw Helios had already returned and was roasting something over a fire.

"He wouldn't go look for you," Lex whispered, nodding toward Helios. "I've been so worried. What happened?"

I shook my head, not wanting to talk until I was seated. I stumbled over to the fire and sank down, putting my head in my hands.

"Where have you been?" Helios sounded more entertained than concerned.

I lifted my eyes to meet his, my head pounding. "Checking traps. Hare." My voice came out raw and weak.

"Where is it then?" His eyes flickered to my neck,

smirking. "Did it do that to you? You know you're supposed to kill it first, right?"

My face flushed as I realized I'd forgotten to retrieve the hares I'd dropped during the unicorn fiasco. I opened my mouth but couldn't find the words to defend myself.

Lex sat next to me and offered me a skin of water, which I gratefully accepted.

"You better pull yourself together," Helios said. "We have a big day tomorrow."

"What's the plan?" I asked.

"I followed the unicorn's trail. Didn't find it. It's likely been captured, as I saw what seemed to be human footprints near it. However, it did lead me to the hunters we've been tracking."

I was about to mention my encounter with the unicorn and the angry girl but stopped myself. There was no way I was going to reveal the humiliating details of that event. Besides, it felt good to know something Helios didn't.

Helios continued, "I was able to watch their camp and gather some information. And the best part? They have a unicorn." Silence followed as I stared blankly back at him. "Did you idiots hear me? They have a *unicorn.*"

I let out a sound of mock awe. The truth was, after my encounter with the girl, I wasn't sure I wanted to see another unicorn ever again. In fact, the Quest was seeming more insane than ever.

"Tomorrow we claim our first prize for Mareleau." Helios wore his deepest grin. Even Lex was smiling. But all I could hear were the girl's words: *If you ever come near a unicorn again, I will kill you.*

THE NEXT MORNING WE ROSE EARLY AND FOLLOWED HELIOS to the hunters' camp. My muscles tensed with every step I took, yet I couldn't bring myself to turn back.

"You say you know how to fight," Helios said, interrupting my thoughts as Lex and I walked behind him along a narrow trail.

Lex and I exchanged a wary glance. "Yeah. So?" I said.

"Here's your chance to prove it. If my observations were correct, when we arrive at the camp, you will see two armed guards. The two of you will kill the guards while I get the unicorn. Got it?"

My heart began to race. "Wait, what? You never said we were going to kill anyone."

"How else do you expect to invade their camp?"

"I don't expect to! We're just following your plan without any say in the matter!"

Helios stopped walking and brought his face close to mine. "That's because my plan is the only one that will work, remember? You can do what I say, or you can go home. In fact, do me a favor and quit. Both of you. Leave Mareleau to me."

The look in his eyes when he said her name made my stomach churn. My imagination was quick to conjure up a flood of unwanted images. I ground my teeth. "I'll do it." I looked over at Lex, whose face had gone pale. "Just let Lex get the unicorn. Please."

Helios sneered at Lex. "Yeah. I figured he wouldn't have it in him, anyway."

When Helios turned his back to us, Lex released a deep breath and whispered his thanks.

Outside the hunters' camp, Helios silently communicated our instructions, pointing out a target for each of
us. I was to take on the guard at the left side of the camp,
Helios was to take on the right, and Lex was to free the
unicorn. Helios held up his hand and we prepared for
invasion. Helios and I unsheathed our swords. Lex balled
his fists and went a shade paler.

Helios gave the signal, and we were off, storming the
camp with a blur of swords, shouts, and curses. The
surprised young guard I confronted fumbled with his
spear as I approached him. My sword was at his neck
before he could thrust his weapon toward me. The guard
dropped his spear and raised his arms in surrender. Our
eyes met yet I remained still, unable to move my sword.

"What are you doing?" I heard Helios say behind me.
From the silence in the camp, I could tell he'd already
killed his target. "Kill him!"

I knew how to fight, but this wasn't fighting. This was
slaughter.

"I knew it. You can't do it. Pathetic. I won't do it for
you."

The guard at the end of my sword raised an eyebrow
and looked from me to Helios and back again. I could see
his breath begin to calm as his arms ceased their shaking.
His upraised hands slowly began to lower. I watched as
the fingers of his right hand twitched, and my eyes
flashed to the sword at his hip. His hand moved, firmly
closing around the hilt of his sword just as I plunged my
blade into his chest. As he sank to his knees, I kicked his
torso to free my sword and watched as he slid to the
ground in a heap of blood.

I dropped my sword at my feet and turned, glaring at

Helios' triumphant face. My blood boiled and my shoulders tensed as I opened and closed the shaking hand that had just ended an innocent life.

"I knew this would be fun." Helios grinned from ear to ear as he wiped the blood from his sword.

"I need help." Lex's voice distracted me from the hatred that burned my veins. I brushed past Helios and went to Lex, who fumbled with a set of keys at the unicorn's cage. His hands shook so badly, it was impossible for him to find the correct one.

"Step aside," Helios growled, nearly knocking me over as he pushed his way forward. He snatched the keys from Lex's hand and quickly found the correct key.

I looked at the creature lying within the cage, thin and miserable and nothing like the majestic white unicorn I'd seen the day before. Still, my feelings for it were the same; I did not want it to die.

"What are you going to do with it?" I asked as Helios wrenched open the door.

"You know what needs to be done. We need a horn, a pelt, and a pet."

"Then let's take this one as Mareleau's pet."

"This pathetic thing? It's half-dead already. She wouldn't want it as her pet. Besides, we can't capture the live unicorn until we are ready to return to Verlot. How would we be able to continue the Quest with a unicorn in tow?"

"Fine. Take its horn and let's go."

Helios' lips curled into a devious smile. "If you insist." He entered the cage and knelt next to the unicorn. He placed the unicorn's weak head in his lap, an almost tender gesture as he unsheathed his dagger. The unicorn remained limp, blinking slowly at Helios.

"This won't hurt, will it?" Lex asked.

"Oh, it most certainly will. You should probably turn around." Helios raised his dagger.

"I said to just take its horn!" I shouted.

"I am." And with that, Helios swung his dagger down into the unicorn's skull.

Bile rose into my throat as Helios tightened his arm around the unicorn's neck. The creature bared its teeth as it uttered a guttural sound. Blood poured from the base of his horn. "Helios, stop!" I shouted, yet he paid me no heed. I turned my head and closed my eyes.

"Don't you know how to dehorn a unicorn?" Helios' deranged voice was almost drowned by the tortured sound of the protesting creature. "You have to cut the horn from its head when it is still alive. Or else the horn's power fades and it eventually turns to dust."

"Why didn't you tell us?" I said over my shoulder. "That's not a minor detail. I would have forfeited if I knew!"

Helios laughed. Once the unicorn was silent, I gathered the nerve to turn around. I looked over at Lex, who stood trembling, a hand braced on one of the other cages, head hanging low. I brought my eyes to meet Helios as he stood in front of the now hornless unicorn, flourishing the bloody horn in his hand.

"I didn't tell you, because I knew you would find it distasteful."

"Why would you care? Why wouldn't you want to discourage me in whatever way possible?"

"I thought the two of you were going to be useful to

me. I thought I could use you to help me acquire the three gifts. Now that I see you are completely useless, I can kill you now instead of later." Keeping the horn in his left hand, he unsheathed his still-bloody sword with his right. "Who wants to die first?"

I was too shocked to move, too terrified to fight. "Please, Helios, just let us go. You've won. I forfeit."

"I can't risk letting you go." Helios took a step toward me.

I reached for my sword and found my scabbard empty. With a curse, I looked across the camp where I'd left it after killing the guard. I darted for it as fast as I could and gathered it into my shaking hands.

I turned to face Helios, who hadn't even moved. *He wants a fight,* I realized as he started toward me. My heart pounded; my whole body shuddered from the force of it. My knees trembled, and my feet rocked on the ground below me.

Then I realized it *was* the ground below me.

Helios froze mid step, and the three of us looked around. The entire camp was rumbling.

I threw myself to the ground just as a giant, blood-red abomination of a creature with a spiked mane of white horns pounded into the camp. I scrambled backward, but it paid me no heed. Its beady eyes were fixed on nothing but Helios. In the blink of an eye, it was upon him. The creature opened its giant, salivating maw and closed it over the upper half of Helios' body. I heard Helios scream as the creature pulled him further and further into its mouth. Blood poured over the creature's lips and dripped to the ground below. In a matter of moments, the screaming ceased—Helios was gone. The creature shook its body from mane to tail.

I remained frozen at the edge of the camp as the creature looked around, sniffing the air and nosing a few things to the side. Out of the corner of my eye, I saw Lex cowering by one of the cages. Then, just as quickly as it had come, the creature pounded away. I waited until the ground was steady before I scrambled over to Lex, pulling him to his feet.

"What was that?" I wondered aloud.

"The question is, who are you?" I spun around and saw two angry hunters enter the camp.

14

CONVERGENCE

Cora

We were nearing the hunters' camp when I heard the rumbling. The sound grew louder, and my heart quickened as I tried to discern which direction it was coming from.

We have to run, I told Valorre.

No time.

My throat tightened as I swung my head from right to left, looking for a place to hide. *Wait, maybe we don't have to hide.* I took a deep breath, emptied my mind, closed my eyes, and brought Valorre's muzzle close to my face. I placed my palm near the base of his horn as I thought about the trees around us, disappearing into them while cloaking Valorre's horn from view.

Fear and doubt flickered through my mind, and for one moment I could feel the energy falter. I pulled my power tighter and stronger around me as the rumbling grew closer. My breathing remained still. The rumbling stopped.

The Beast did not appear before us, but I could sense it close by. I held fast to the glamour as we waited. Sweat beaded above my brow. After agonizing moments, the rumbling commenced, then receded away.

The unicorn. Gone.

My heart sank, and I felt the glamour slide away. *Was it the Beast?*

Something strange, was all Valorre could say.

I blinked back the tears that stung my eyes. My hands balled into fists. *I'm done waiting. Let's go get our answers.*

We approached the camp, and I took in the scene before me—Nym and Arrin were both dead, the unicorn lay lifeless and hornless within his open cage, Gringe had his sword pointed at a chubby man who appeared to be surrendering, and Jarod was in active battle with another man.

Without a second thought, I drew my bow, nocked an arrow, and rushed into the clearing. I sent an arrow flying into the back of Gringe's neck, and another into Jarod's arm. Jarod spun around, and I sent a final arrow into his chest. I then turned my aim on Jarod's opponent and came face to face with the boy from the stream. He dropped his sword and raised his arms in surrender.

"You!" I said through clenched teeth. My eyes flashed to the dead unicorn. "Did you do that?"

"No, it was Helios! I tried to stop him, I swear—"

I pointed my arrow at the other man. "Him?" The chubby man cowered, covering his head in his hands.

"No!" Teryn shouted, darting toward me. "That's Lex. Helios...is gone."

"I don't believe you." I turned my arrow back to Teryn.

Not he, Valorre said, appearing at my side.

I scowled at Teryn, grinding my teeth. "Explain. Quickly."

Teryn hesitated as he stared wide-eyed at Valorre.

"Did you hear me?"

Teryn squeezed his eyes shut, rubbed his temples, and vigorously shook his head. When he opened his eyes, he was looking at me. "Yes. Remember when I told you about the Quest for Princess Mareleau's hand? Helios, Lex, and I were competing together. He brought us here to steal the unicorn from the hunters and take its horn. I didn't know how to stop him. I never knew...the horn..." Tears filled Teryn's eyes as his shoulders slumped. He looked back at the dead unicorn. "I know what this looks like, and I know you warned me. But please believe me when I say I'm done with the Quest."

I could feel the truth of his words. Still, I needed answers. "Where did Helios go? Where is the horn he took?"

Teryn opened and closed his mouth, shaking his head from side to side. "I don't even know how to explain. This creature. Huge and red and unlike anything I've ever seen. It...ate him. He was holding the horn."

I looked at the pool of blood in the middle of the camp. My stomach churned.

"Will you let us go?" Teryn asked. "I told you, I'm done with the Quest."

I lowered my bow. "Take your friend and get out. Now. Before I change my mind."

Teryn ran to his friend and pulled him from the camp, leaving me alone with corpses. I looked at the two hunters I had shot, hoping one of them might still be alive for questioning. Both Gringe and Jarod were dead.

I threw my head back as tears streamed down my cheeks. Now that Jarod was dead, I was sure the hunters would disband, especially after returning to such a gruesome scene. While that should have given me peace, it meant I no longer had a chance at getting the answers I needed.

And I had ended human life for the first time.

I shuddered, reflecting on how I'd loosed my arrows at Gringe and Jarod with as much ease as if they'd been logs and not men. I hadn't hesitated. I'd imagined it hundreds of times before, but it was one thing to imagine death, and another to look it in the face. I'd known what needed to be done and was grateful for how quickly I'd reacted, but that didn't stop me from feeling the pang of regret. "Mother Moon, may flesh return to your land." I whispered the traditional prayer of the Forest People under my breath.

Valorre nuzzled my shoulder, and I reached up to pat his cheek. I blinked the tears from my eyes and wiped my face dry. *Let's go.* As I stood and turned to leave the camp, something red and gold caught my eye; it was the chest I'd seen Gringe and Jarod bring the Beast. I ran to it and tried to pry it open. Locked. In a flurry, I turned over logs, bedrolls, and blankets, looking for a key. Finally, I spotted a set of keys dangling from the dead unicorn's cage. I retrieved them, ran back to the chest, and after a short struggle with key after key, it opened.

Within the chest lay two white horns. I swallowed back the bile that rose in my throat and reached into the chest. My hand hovered over the horns. *What am I even doing?* All I knew was I couldn't leave the horns to be used by the hunters or fed to the Beast. Trying to touch the horns as little as possible, I lifted them by my fingertips and stashed them in my quiver of arrows.

The boys need you, Valorre said as I stood.

"What do you mean? I don't want to help them."

Valorre was already leading the way. I let out a groan and followed him. Moments later, we found Teryn making his way through the trees with his pale-faced friend. I could sense Teryn's agitation as he strained to help his friend walk.

"Are you all right?" I asked, with more irritation than I'd intended.

Teryn turned to me, his face red and covered in a sheen of sweat. "I think Lex is in shock. He won't speak or even look at me. I can barely keep him upright to walk."

I sighed. "Where is your camp? Your horses?"

"We made camp by the river." Teryn looked at the trees around him. "But Helios was our tracker. He led us here. I'm not sure..."

We can help, Valorre told me, just as I was considering the best way to wish the boys luck and be on our own way.

I'm sure they will be fine, I said, but Valorre ignored me. He went to Lex and nudged him in the shoulder. Lex didn't respond.

Let him up. I will take him.

My mouth hung open. *You want to let him ride you?*

Valorre lowered his head in answer.

"Help your friend mount," I said to Teryn through clenched teeth.

Teryn looked back at me, eyes wide. "You want him to...mount? The unicorn?"

"Yes. We can help you find the river. And Valorre can carry him much faster than you can." Teryn still didn't make any move toward Valorre. "I don't have all day to watch you drag your half-conscious friend though the forest. I want to put as much distance between me and the rest of those hunters when they return, not to mention the Beast."

At that, Teryn began moving. Together, we hoisted Lex onto Valorre's back.

"Lex, can you hear me?" Teryn slapped Lex lightly on the cheek. "I need you to mount this...horse." Lex made no sound yet responded by assisting our efforts to seat him.

"You don't have a saddle, so hold onto his mane and his neck," I added. Lex's eyes remained unfocused, but he kept his seat as we made our way to the river. Once we found their camp, Teryn and I worked together to help Lex dismount. Teryn unrolled Lex's bed while I started a fire.

"Thank you," Teryn said in a weak voice as he helped Lex drink from a skin of water. "For everything. Sparing our lives. Bringing us back here."

I forced a smile. "Don't mention it." I was about to take my leave and find my own camp for the evening when I saw that Lex was still deathly pale and trembling. "He needs to relax." I bit back an irritated grumble. "I'll try to find something to help."

As I searched through the undergrowth of the forest surrounding the camp, I desperately wished I had the Forest People's stock of herbs and a healing pouch. Yet, despite my less-than-ideal circumstance, I found chamomile flowers and stinging nettles.

When I returned, Lex looked even worse. I got to work steeping my small harvest into a tea. When the brew was ready, I passed it to Teryn. "Get him to drink this. It will calm him."

Teryn convinced Lex to drink a few sips at a time. Before long, Lex's trembling began to subside. Once his eyes grew heavy, Teryn helped him lie down.

By then it was pointless for me to leave for my own camp. "I'll stay with you tonight and make sure he's well in the morning."

"I appreciate your help." Teryn looked at me, hesitated a moment, then added, "Are you some kind of healer?"

"Something like that. I was raised by healers, so I know a thing or two."

"I can't imagine what we would have done without you." Teryn's eyes slid out of focus as he gazed past the fire. "I can't imagine what would have happened if you hadn't killed the hunters, either. I can't imagine how I've endured anything since starting this stupid Quest."

"Why don't you tell me more about it? How and why did you find the hunters? Who are Lex and Helios?"

Teryn met my eyes with a small smile. "Still not convinced I'm not an evil unicorn murderer?"

"I'll believe you more if you explain." I matched his smile, and saw his shoulders relax.

He went on to explain the details of Mareleau's Quest, his alliance with Lex, and his surprise alliance with Helios. He mentioned how Helios had convinced them to join him and explained the overabundance of unicorn hunters in Kero.

I sat forward, my muscles tensing. "Wait, he said there were multiple parties of unicorn hunters? How many more were there? Where are they? Who do they work for?"

Teryn shrugged, his eyes wide at my outburst. "He didn't give us many details. This is the only other hunting party we've come across. My guess is that the others are further north."

The hair on the back of my neck stood on end as I was flooded with a mixture of horror and excitement. Teryn's information meant more unicorns were being tortured and killed every day, but it also meant I still had a chance to get my answers. *I must find the others.* "Tell me everything you know."

15

PROPOSITION

Teryn

The girl barely blinked, eyes wide and hungry as I finished my tale with as much detail as I could remember. Once I'd said all I could say, she stood and began pacing. "I have to find them," she mumbled, biting at a fingernail. "There are more of them. They're working for him, I just know it."

I raised an eyebrow. "What exactly is *your* quest about? Obviously, you are some kind of warrior of unicorns. But why?"

She stopped pacing and narrowed her eyes at me as if she'd just remembered my presence. Her shoulders tensed, and I felt one sharp movement from me would send her darting into the trees.

I smiled, trying to seem as innocent as possible. "You rescued me, and I don't even know your name. I just want to know more about you, that's all."

The girl's face softened. She sat back down by the fire

but refused to meet my eyes. "My name is Cor...Cordelia. But you can call me Cora."

"What's your story, Cora? I've told you mine."

Cora looked sideways at me but said nothing.

"As Prince of Mena, I could demand you talk to me."

"We're in Kero. What do I care about the Prince of Mena?"

I threw my head back and laughed. "See? It worked!"

Cora pressed her lips into a thin smile and turned her face toward mine. "Fine," she said with a roll of her eyes. "I stumbled upon this group of hunters by accident. I rescued Valorre from them...or he rescued me. Before that, I'd never seen a unicorn. When I saw what they were doing to the unicorns—what they were doing to Valorre —I vowed to find them again and stop them from harming more. But my goal wasn't to kill them. I needed to find out why they were hunting unicorns in the first place and who they work for. Now that I know there are more hunting parties out there, my work is of even greater importance."

"And you plan on doing this all by yourself? How? Are you just going to single-handedly take on one horde of brutal hunters after the next?"

"I take it you doubt my capabilities."

I shook my head. "From what I've seen, you're more than capable. But even though you're fierce and passion-ate, I have a hard time imagining you up against those brutes alone, not to mention that creature. What was that thing?"

"The Beast? I don't know, but it reeks of dark magic. I need to figure that out too."

"You've seen it, then?"

"Yes. It's working with the hunters somehow. They feed the horns to it." Cora looked down at her hands, her face slack. "I know it sounds impossible. I don't even know how far I will go, but I have to try."

"Isn't there anyone who can help you? Anyone at all?"

"Are *you* offering?" My mouth hung open until Cora laughed. "I'm kidding," she said.

I felt the blood return to my face and changed the subject. "Couldn't you go to your king? Surely he'd stop this."

Cora stared over my shoulder with a frown, eyes unfocused. "The king can't help. He could be giving the orders, for all I know."

Her words gave me a hollow feeling in the pit of my stomach. "Why would you say that?"

"Forget it." Cora stood and turned her back to me. "Like I said, I know nothing. That's why I need answers."

I stood and circled her until she was facing me. "If you know something about the king, please tell me. As Prince of Mena, I need to know about any threats in the land of Lela, even in other kingdoms. If it's serious, I can help you."

"I don't need help."

"Cora, please."

She sighed and met my eyes. "I heard a rumor that the king is growing his Royal Force, and I have a hunch that these unicorn hunters are working for someone from within Ridine Castle. Other than that, I know nothing. That's why I'm doing what I'm doing. There's really no more I can say."

My mouth felt dry, and my stomach churned at her

words. My father's warning echoed through my head. "The king is growing his army? This is no small matter!"

"I don't even know if it's true."

"But—" I was startled by the sound of whimpering. I looked at Lex, tossing and turning in his bedroll. It was then I realized I'd been yelling. I watched him, ready to race to his side, until he calmed back into quiet slumber.

"We should get some sleep," Cora whispered, not meeting my eyes.

I nodded, although I was far from satisfied with how our conversation had ended. I watched Cora curl up beneath her cloak by the fire, leaving the smallest portion of her face free from beneath the bundle. I searched my mind for something to say to release the sick, heavy feeling roiling in my gut, but no words would come, not even *goodnight*.

Instead I went to my bedroll and stared at the canopy of trees, the black sky speckled with stars, and at the curling tendrils of smoke from the campfire that unfurled across my vision. I thought about what she'd said about King Dimetreus. She'd said it was just a rumor. But was there really such a thing as *just* a rumor? Was the threat minor enough to ignore?

Something had to be done.

～

"You're what?" Lex asked, eyes wide and mouth gaping. "You're going with that crazy unicorn girl?"

I narrowed my eyes at him. "That *crazy unicorn girl* saved our lives, yours especially. You were in complete shock all evening. It was her care that calmed you enough to sleep."

"For all I know, that could have been poison she made me drink last night. She's probably a witch."

"Don't say that." I looked over my shoulder, hoping Cora hadn't returned from her errand. I had yet to even ask her if I *could* accompany her and didn't want Lex's careless slander ruining my chances. "She saved our lives, Lex. Why don't you trust her?"

"I'm finding it hard to trust *anyone* right now."

"I understand, but she's not some conniving, arrogant, deceiving fool like Helios."

"You don't know that." Lex stomped his foot, cheeks flushing pink. "Besides, why would you *want* to go with her? It's not like she needs help!"

"She *does* need help. She told me things last night that I can't ignore. My kingdom could be in danger. As Crown Prince of Mena, I have a responsibility to find out if there is truth in that threat. If there is, my father must know immediately. If I find there is nothing to concern myself with, I can return home with peace of mind."

"Isn't there a better way to find out other than risking your life?"

I opened my mouth but had no answer for him. Perhaps he was right. Perhaps I was being reckless. Maybe I should head straight home and tell my father to investigate the threat himself. Then again, what if it really *was* nothing and I caused a stir for no good reason? And what about Cora? "I've already decided. I'm going."

"What about Mareleau? She's still expecting her gifts, you know. As far as she's concerned, we are still competing to find them. What are we going to do about that?"

"I'll speak to her when I return home. Maybe Cora can help me find a unicorn that I can take back to Mareleau as her pet. Other than that, I'm done with the Quest. I will never attempt to harm a unicorn for as long as I live, and I will do whatever I can to stop others from hurting them as well. When I speak to Mareleau, I will explain the gruesomeness of the hunt and the cruelty of dehorning. If she remains unmoved by what I have to say, I'll be done with her as well."

"But what about *me*? We were supposed to work together. I can't go home without anything to show for it!"

"What else do you expect from me, Lex? I appreciate that you wanted to help me. I wanted to help you too, but we are running out of options."

Lex opened his mouth, yet all he could produce was a grumble and a moan.

I put my hands on his shoulders. "If I didn't go with Cora, I would go home. Either way, *you* would be going home empty-handed just the same. I can only think of one way to save your reputation, and that is for you to come with us. Help us stop the hunters. If we manage to do even one small act of good, people will forget about Mareleau's failed Quest. We will be heroes."

Lex's eyes went wide. "You're as crazy as the unicorn girl!"

"Fine, have it your way." I patted Lex on his back and went to wait by the fire, while he stomped over to the riverbank. I paced as I waited for Cora to return, steeling my resolve to confront her with my proposition. Why was I so terrified of her?

When Cora finally returned to camp, she was nearly unrecognizable. It was the first time I'd been able to see more than just her face beneath her hooded cloak. She strode toward me, spear in hand. At the end of the spear were three freshly caught fish. Her hair hung in a long braid over one shoulder and her sun-browned skin was exposed below her rolled-up sleeves and above her bodice. She was short and narrow, the complete opposite of Mareleau, yet I couldn't help but admit she was pretty.

"What are you looking at?" she snapped as she sat by the fire, making me realize I'd been staring. "Never seen a girl in pants before?"

I hadn't even noticed her pants, but now that she mentioned it, it most certainly was the first time I'd seen such a sight. "Honestly, no, but they look good, really."

She shook her head and unsheathed her dagger to gut the fish. "He seems to be well enough." She nodded toward Lex's sulking form. "Valorre and I will guide you to a road you can follow south. You should be able to find your way home from there or meet fellow travelers who can guide you."

"I was meaning to talk to you about that." I scrambled to her side, sat down, and took one of the fish to gut. My hands shook as I slit the fish's belly. "The things you told me last night have me concerned. I'd like to accompany you on your travels."

Cora's head snapped up. "What?"

I cleared my throat in attempt to steady my voice. "I'm worried about the safety of not only the unicorns, but also my kingdom. My father mentioned some things to me about King Dimetreus before I departed on the Quest. He warned me that Kero may not be safe." Cora's face softened as I mentioned this. "I need answers just like you. I need to know if there's a threat to my kingdom."

Cora opened her mouth to speak, and after a moment said, "I don't travel with strangers."

"You asked last night if I was offering my help."

"I was joking."

"But I'm not. I'm serious." My voice was stronger now. I held her gaze. "You spoke of dark magic. I saw the Beast. I can't go home and pretend yesterday didn't happen. Please, let me help you. You don't have to do this alone."

Cora closed her eyes, jaw moving back and forth. "Fine," she said through clenched teeth. "I guess I can handle one companion. Be prepared to do what I say."

"Don't get too comfortable." Lex sat down by the fire. "I'm coming too."

"You've got to be kidding me." Cora tossed the fish to the ground at her feet and stalked away.

16

ASSISTANCE

Cora

"They want to come with me. Both of them!" I told Valorre.

Why is that bad? Help is good.

"I don't want their help."

But you need it.

My shoulders slumped, but I didn't want to admit he might be right. "How do I even know they can help me? I had Teryn at my mercy twice. Jarod was about to kill him before I came to his rescue. And don't even get me started on Lex!"

Valorre didn't seem to think my complaints bore much weight. *There is bravery in both. Let them show you.*

When I returned to the boys, the fish had been cooked and their bags had been packed. I could sense their desperation to prove their competence. Teryn wordlessly offered me a fish, which I accepted. "You can't slow me down," I said between bites. "I move quickly, and I work quietly. Every day could pose danger."

Teryn nodded and Lex paled, freezing mid-bite.

"I want you to train with each other every day."

Teryn and Lex exchanged glances. "What do you mean?" Teryn asked. "With swords?"

"Swords, sticks, spears, I don't care. I need the two of you prepared and at your sharpest. I can't be distracted by saving your hides."

"I can fight," Lex said with a scowl.

"Terrific. Then you can show Teryn a thing or two."

Teryn and Lex sparred with two long sticks along the riverbank while I packed my few belongings. I cast a covert glance over my shoulder to discover the boys were in fact somewhat skilled in swordplay. *Now if only they can learn to implement their skills in dire circumstances, they might stand a chance.*

I finished packing and looked over at the horses, wondering if I should let one of the boys carry some of my burden. I then realized we had three horses in our company, one more than we needed. I approached the horse which had formerly belonged to the man named Helios. She was a lovely chestnut mare with a black saddle. I reached a hand toward her and stroked her soft neck. I could sense she was strong and had a good temperament. Despite the terrible things I'd heard about Helios, I could tell he'd at least taken care of his horse.

"Do either of you know the name of this horse?" I shouted over my shoulder.

"I honestly don't know," Teryn said through labored breaths as he blocked a blow from Lex.

"Harry, I think," Lex said, panting as he sidestepped Teryn's counterattack.

"Hara," I corrected.

"How do you know?" Teryn asked.

"It's engraved on her saddlebag," I said, but the name had come to mind a moment before I saw it. Looking at the ample storage provided by her saddlebags, it occurred to me that perhaps I should keep Hara for myself. Valorre and I had done much of our travels together on foot, but the boys and I would travel much faster if we were all riding. And even though Valorre seemed to enjoy letting me ride him, I would never consider saddling him.

As if sensing my thoughts, Valorre quietly came up beside me and Hara. I relayed my idea to him.

We shouldn't leave her behind, he agreed. I could sense the slightest hint of jealously, but I quickly assured him he wasn't being replaced.

I began to rummage through Helios' belongings to see what I should keep and what I should discard. Inside Hara's saddlebags were numerous survival necessities including maps, water skins, dried fruit and meat, rope, and an array of knives. I also came across a few personal items, as well as strange books regarding unicorn hunting. In one book, I found horrific illustrations about dehorning and designs for traps. Another book explained various items to be made from unicorn horns and corpses. I tossed them both on the ground to be burned.

The vile books brought to mind the horns I'd taken from the hunters' camp. I removed Helios' quiver from the side of the saddle and fetched my own, hesitating before I reached my hand into my quiver. I wrinkled my nose as I took the two horns from their hiding place, then set them aside before I combined Helios' stash of arrows with my own. Then, taking up the horns again, I began to wrap them in a spare piece of cloth.

"Where did you get those?" The words made me jump. Teryn was staring over my shoulder as he wiped the sheen of sweat from his forehead.

"I took them from the hunters' camp before I left. I found them locked in a chest. I couldn't leave them to be fed to the Beast." I finished wrapping the horns tightly in the cloth and put them at the bottom of one of Hara's saddlebags.

"Why do you think they feed the horns to the Beast? Do they somehow sustain it?"

I shrugged. "I'm not entirely sure, but I think so. Unicorns are magical creatures and have been said to hold great magic in their horns. I think the horns cut from starved, tortured unicorns contain a different magic that give the Beast its power."

"Who do you think is giving orders to these hunters? You seemed to have some inclination last night."

I turned my face away from his. "I told you everything I know."

Teryn took a small step forward and leaned his head toward me. "I know you know more," he said gently. "And I just spent the past few weeks being manipulated and deceived by Helios. He kept information from us and put us into danger we weren't prepared for. I can't do that again. I need to know what I'm getting into."

I met his eyes, glaring. "I'm not coercing you into

coming with me. I made it very clear that accompanying me would put you in grave danger. If you aren't prepared for that, you should go home."

"That's not what I meant. I know our mission will put us in danger, and I'm making the choice to take that risk. All I'm asking is that you respect me as a partner in this. Just give me honesty."

I ground my teeth and closed my eyes. It made my blood boil to share the things I was content to keep to myself. Then again, his frustration with me was understandable. He'd agreed to help me, and I'd accepted that help. For better or worse, I was now in alliance with him. I let out a deep sigh. "I will tell you as much as I can, but you will have to respect *me* if I keep certain things to myself. Some of the things I know are too dangerous to share. I will reveal vital information to you so long as you don't press me for anything more than what I give."

Teryn narrowed his eyes at me, head cocked to the side. "How am I to believe you really are telling me as much as you can?"

"You have to trust me, as I must trust you. I promise you, if I ever withhold something from you, it will not be done with malice. It will be done to protect myself and the two of you."

Teryn shrugged. "I can live with that."

I forced a smile, hoping we would live through this at all.

〜

Teryn

"What *can* you tell me?" I asked, as Cora resumed packing. "What is happening at Ridine?"

"I'm not completely sure, but it's something dark. I have reason to believe a sorcerer resides there and is the one commanding the hunters and the Beast. How involved King Dimetreus is, I can only speculate."

"Who is this sorcerer? How do you know about him?"

Cora pursed her lips and shook her head.

So that is all she would say. At least it was something.

"Now it's my turn," Cora said. "What else do *you* know? I know there's something you haven't told me."

I felt the blood leave my face. "What do you mean?"

Cora turned her head to the side, eyes unfocused. "Something about King Dimetreus. Some kind of warning..."

I thought about the warning my father had given me. I was almost positive I hadn't told Cora about that yet. "Are you reading my mind?"

Cora laughed. "Of course not! You mentioned your father telling you Kero wasn't safe. I have a feeling there's more to that than what you said."

I swallowed the dryness in my throat. "Well, my father warned me that King Dimetreus has yet to sign the Peace Pact of Lela. He's worried what that could say about King Dimetreus' intentions."

Cora nodded. "That is suspicious."

"I know. We've hardly heard from him in years. With this new rumor about him growing his force, as well as your hunch that he's working with a sorcerer, a threat seems likely."

"We won't know if any of it is true until I get answers. I need to find another group of hunters."

"Then let's go," I said. "Where will we begin?"

"Let's see if Helios left us any clues." Cora began digging through one of Hara's saddlebags. She pulled out a folded piece of parchment. As she unfolded and straightened it, I saw it was a map of Kero. Several circles had been drawn within the forested areas, with a word scribbled next to each. Cora ran her finger over the map until she came to a spot just below the southern half of the forest. A wide circle surrounded the area.

"Jarod," she said, reading the word next to the circle. "That was the name of the hunters' leader. The one I killed. Helios knew he was leading this party and he knew what area to find them in. It is where we are now." Her finger traced upward and to the right until it met another circle. "And here is the next closest group." She tapped her finger over the name. "Drass. That will be their leader."

My mouth hung open. Even dead, Helios continued to shock me with the information he had gathered. "Is that where we're going?" I asked, my heart pounding with a combination of dread and anticipation.

"Absolutely." By the look on Cora's face, she was feeling the same way.

I turned to ready Quinne's saddle for departure.

After a few moments of busy silence, Cora paused. "Do you know anything about the royal family of Kero?"

"Yes, don't you? I thought you would know everything about Kero, from how much you have shared with me."

"I was raised by the Forest People. We don't involve ourselves in royal matters. News comes to us sporadically, and I never know what is rumor. Hence my current need for answers."

I lifted an eyebrow. "The Forest People?"

Cora waved a hand in the air. "I'll tell you about them another time. It's...complicated. Is it true the royal family have all died?" Her voice shook slightly.

"Yes, aside from King Dimetreus, they are dead. My father was present for King Jeru and Queen Tiliane's burial. He had been close to them. Years later, word traveled regarding the death of Queen Linette followed by the execution of young Princess Coralaine."

"Execution?" Cora turned to me with wide eyes. "She was executed? For what crime?"

"Treason and murder. She was said to have been responsible for Queen Linette's death." My chest tightened. I hadn't thought about the grim details of Princess Coralaine's execution in many years. Now, after all that I'd begun to fear about Kero, this reminder only added weight to those fears.

Cora resumed packing, tightening the straps of Hara's saddle with a little more force than necessary. "How was she executed?"

I swallowed the lump in my throat, wondering how I hadn't been more disturbed by this event before. "She was publicly beheaded."

Cora remained silent and still for a few moments as she kept her back to me. Then, after a quick brush of her cheeks, she turned around, face blank. "That's a shame. She was just a child. Now, finish up. Time to move."

17

COMPANIONS

Cora

We followed the course of the river for a few days, allowing us to keep a wide breadth around the hunters' decimated camp, as well as staying oriented with the map that guided us. The river led us northeast, and once we appeared to be just south of where we expected to find the new hunters, we began traveling north.

The three of us rarely engaged in conversation during these travels, aside from discussing necessary details, and it suited me well. Most of the time I led the way on Hara, and the boys followed not far behind. They talked frequently with each other, practiced sparring morning and night, and stayed out of my way for the most part. They even assisted in setting traps and hunting small game for meals. I was starting to think having companions could benefit me after all.

On the sixth day of our journey together, as I rode

peacefully alone at the head of our retinue, I became aware of a silence behind me. Teryn and Lex's constant conversation had taken a suspiciously long lull, and I could feel an uncomfortable tension building in their energy. Before long, I heard hooves approaching as Teryn brought Quinne alongside Hara.

I bristled at the uninvited visit but took a deep breath and summoned my powers of cordiality. "Lover's quarrel?" I teased. Teryn looked at me, brows furrowed, clearly not getting my joke. "What's up with him?" I amended, tossing my head back at Lex who rode alone far behind us.

"I'm not sure," Teryn said with a low whisper. "He's much surlier than normal, which says a lot. I couldn't take much more of him today, so I lied and said I had to talk to you about something."

I forced a smile, not sure what to say. I wanted to find a kind way to dismiss him so I could return to my peace and quiet.

He wants to be friends, Valorre said, appearing in front of us. Since the start of our new journey, Valorre had been alternating between leading the way and meandering off to explore alone.

I never thought I'd be getting advice on social behavior from a unicorn, I told him. But Valorre was right. In the days I'd spent with Teryn and Lex, I'd hardly put any effort into bridging the gap between us as strangers. Teryn was simply making the first move. The least I could do was humor him.

I forced a small smile. "Since you're already up here having a fake conversation with me, how about we have a real conversation instead?"

Teryn's face brightened. "What can we talk about?"

"We really don't know much about each other," I said. "Why don't you tell me about your family? About your life in Mena?" Getting him to talk about himself would solve two needs—I could ride quietly and listen as he talked, and I could potentially learn some useful information about the royal affairs in another part of Lela.

Teryn shrugged, mouth turned up at one corner. "There's not much interesting to say about my life. I mean, aside from this current situation, which you obviously know about."

"What about Mareleau? You've told me about the Quest, but you haven't told me about your relationship. Do you love her?" I felt heat rise to my face as soon as the last words left my mouth.

Teryn's brow furrowed. "I think so."

"You *think* so?" I couldn't help but laugh. "That is why you've been risking your life for her hand? Because you *think* you love her?"

Teryn joined my laughter. "It's just...before the Quest, I thought I knew everything. I thought I knew everything a crown prince should know about his kingdom. I thought I knew how to hunt and fight. I thought I knew what I was willing to do for love. So much of what I'd known has turned out to be wrong. It feels safer to *think* for now, if that makes sense."

I nodded. "Then what about your family? Don't you have a brother?"

Teryn frowned. "How do you know I have a brother?"

My heart raced as I realized my mistake, but I kept my composure. "I may not know everything about royal matters in Lela, but I never said I knew nothing about your kingdom. I've heard some talk of the twin princes of Mena. Are you two close?"

Teryn's face went slack. "Yes, but it's...complicated. Speaking of complicated, didn't you promise to tell me about *your* family? About the Forest People?"

I was silent a moment, at war with my instincts to fight or flee from such a personal topic, but Valorre's words rang through my head. *This is a friendly conversation*, I told myself. *He wants to get to know me. I don't have to tell him everything.* "There's not much to say," I began. "We're a simple people. We care about nature and living in harmony."

"What are your homes like?"

"Tents, mostly. Especially in warmer seasons. In harsher seasons, we build stronger shelters."

"Do all Forest People dress like you?" Teryn examined me from head to toe.

"You mean the pants?" I let out a small laugh. "Yes, the men wear such pants, but the women mostly wear dresses, probably like what the common women wear in Mena. We make much of our own clothing, but we buy and trade many items too. Some of us prefer more modern fashions and luxuries, especially the younger generations."

"How do you buy things? What do you trade with?"

That question was much more difficult to answer without mentioning the Arts. I wasn't ready to share that side of my upbringing. I chose my words carefully as I continued, "The Forest People are practiced in ancient forms of healing. We make brews, teas, salves, and tinctures from herbs and flowers that hold great properties."

"Like a witch," Lex interrupted. I looked behind me, surprised to find Lex had caught up with us.

"Not like a witch." Teryn eyed Lex with a scowl. "Continue, Cora."

I turned my attention back to Teryn, trying to ignore the set of eyes burning into my skull. "We also weave and sew. We hunt. We craft beautiful bows and arrows and other fine weapons. We are skilled in many things. We offer our services and wares to nearby villagers or the travelers we meet on the road."

"Why do you live in such a way? It seems so antiquated."

"I guess you could say it is. We live based on the ways of the Ancient Ones, whom the Forest People are descendants of."

"Who are the Ancient Ones?" Lex asked.

I looked back at Lex and saw that his glare had been replaced with wide-eyed curiosity. *Maybe he wants to be friends too.*

"Yes, tell us about them," Teryn said.

I looked from one man to the other. "Well, if you both really want to know, I'll tell you. But don't hold it against me if the stories sound unbelievable. Most of my people's tales do sound more like myth than fact. I believe many of them, but that's how I was raised. I don't expect you to feel the same way."

Teryn shrugged. "We won't judge."

"Fine then. The Ancient Ones were a magical people who lived long ago. Of all the Ancient Ones, the two most powerful races were the Elvan and the Faeran."

"You mean elves and fairies?" Lex wrinkled his nose. "Are you seriously talking about magic people with pointed ears and the flying bug folk? I remember the stories from when I was small, but they aren't real."

I closed my eyes for a moment and tried my best to summon my patience. "Your childhood legends are not the same as my legends. But if you think you know them, by all means, continue the story for me."

Lex turned slightly red in the cheeks but made no argument.

I continued, "The Elvan and Faeran shared rule over their land while maintaining harmony with each other and with all other beings. While they shared the same vision of harmony, they had differences in tradition, talent, and appearance. The Elvan were a tall, slender, ivory-skinned, silver-haired, blue-eyed people. They were known for their elegance and grace and were skilled in music, art, and creating things of beauty. Their magic built the most majestic palaces, wove the finest fabrics, and created the most pleasing instruments. They wore elaborate dress, lived in shining cities, and held magnificent feasts.

"The Faeran, on the other hand, were small in height with thin, agile, youthful bodies. They had dark hair, skin colored in shades of soil, and dark eyes. They lived and worked outdoors, mostly in the forests. The Faeran were famous for their healing powers and for their connection with nature. They could speak to animals and plants. They could find a remedy by listening to the land.

"The legends of my people say that we, the Forest People, are descendants of the Faeran. That is why our traditions mirror their simple ways. Many of my people even resemble the Faeran in appearance. Especially Salinda, the woman who raised me."

"What do you mean she raised you?" Teryn asked. "Was she not your real mother?"

I was taken aback for a moment, realizing I'd mentioned something I had planned to keep to myself. "I was orphaned at birth," I improvised. "Salinda took me in."

"Wait, what happened to the Ancient Ones?" Lex frowned. "Where did they go?"

I was grateful for the change of subject. "Some say their harmony was eventually destroyed and war broke out between them, leaving their numbers nearly extinct. Other tales say they simply disappeared as magic faded from the land. It is a mystery, even amongst my people."

"Do you think the Ancient Ones ever lived in Lela?" Teryn asked.

"Some legends say Lela was once the very center of the Ancient kingdom, where all magic thrived. Perhaps it's true."

"I didn't even believe in magic before the Quest," Lex said. "Then I find out unicorns are real. Next, I watch a man cut a horn from a live unicorn's head. I then witness him being eaten alive by a monstrous demon. And I won't pretend I didn't hear the two of you talking about a sorcerer. I'm starting to think magic is nothing but trouble."

"It can be," I admitted. "Especially in the wrong hands."

Lex responded by going pale. That was clearly not the answer he wanted to hear.

"Are you really up for this?" I asked him. "Do you really want to put yourself in more danger? It's not going to get any easier."

Lex turned his head, scowling into the trees. "Yeah." He let out a long sigh that told me there was much he wasn't saying.

I turned to Teryn, who gave me a significant look. "See what I mean?" he mumbled.

My first instinct was to take my opportunity to end the conversation all together. Another instinct was a burning desire to discover what had Lex in such a mood. My final instinct was to honor my attempt at friendship. My last two instincts won, and I began to slow Hara's pace until Lex and I were side by side. Teryn took the hint and remained ahead.

"Hey, Lex." I forced my voice to sound warm and casual. "I know we haven't gotten to know each other very well over the past week, but I'm hoping that can change. I'm grateful you decided to come with us. Thank you."

Lex met my gaze, raising a suspicious eyebrow at first, then resigned to a half-smile that never touched his eyes. "Yeah. You're welcome."

Getting him to talk seemed equally as difficult as getting *me* to talk. "This is a dangerous mission. I know you know that. You're very brave to do this, even though I can tell you aren't quite sure you want to."

"Brave? Me? I doubt that."

"Why do you say that?"

"Because you're right." Lex's voice grew with force. "I *don't* want to do this. I don't want to be in danger. I never wanted to do the stupid Quest in the first place. The last thing I want to do is extend this pointless trek through the woods in search of new ways to get myself killed. I'm not brave. I'm stupid."

"Then why are you here?" I asked gently. "You don't

have to be here. I promise, I can help get you safely on your way home, if that's what you want."

Lex sighed. "I wish. I can't go home yet."

"Why? You can tell me about it, you know. I'll listen."

"I just...I have to prove myself. I have to show my father I'm capable of following in his footsteps. I have to show him I'm more capable than my younger brother, Ben."

"Why is that? You're the heir, aren't you?"

"I am, but Ben is *Savior of Tomas*. He led a charge to fortify our defenses between us and Norun. My father originally asked me to lead the fortifications. I refused. Seeing no current danger from Norun, I didn't think it was a valuable use of my time. My brother volunteered in my stead. It was the biggest mistake I could have made.

"To make matters worse, Ben then gets engaged to a daughter of one of our allies. A princess. She's ten years his junior, so he will have to wait to marry, but his prospects are higher than mine. The woman I want to marry is the daughter of a lord. Lady Lily. Highborn, but not a princess. You see the position I'm in? I'm seen as the lazy, fat, unambitious crown prince while my brother is the young, handsome, brave savior whom our people love.

"I have to prove that I'm worth the crown. That's why I agreed to compete in the Quest. I didn't expect to become a finalist, but once I became one, I knew I had to see it through as far as I could. That's why I formed a plot with Teryn to help him win. Now that plan has been destroyed. I'm lost now. I have no idea what to do. I have no idea what to say if I return home. I don't want to make the same mistake again. I don't want to turn down an opportunity to show I can be as brave or as useful as Ben."

"That makes perfect sense. You have nothing to be ashamed of."

"But it's all a sham. All I can ever do is fake it. I was going to fake the Quest. Now I'm faking this mission. Instead of being brave, I'm dragging myself along, miserable."

"Just because you don't want to do it, doesn't mean you aren't brave," I said. "You can be afraid and angry about something, yet still choose to do it anyway. You are being brave by making that choice. You are only miserable because you feel too guilty to forgive yourself for turning down the opportunity that Ben accepted. Once you forgive yourself, you'll realize you are brave after all." I wanted to laugh, realizing how much I sounded like Salinda.

"I don't know." Lex wore a frown, but his composure was beginning to relax. "Sometimes I think maybe I'm not worthy of the crown after all. If I was, I would have tried to win the Quest for real."

"You obviously didn't want to win. You want to marry Lady Lily. There's nothing wrong with finding a clever way to make the best of your circumstances. Being clever is just as important as being brave. And you're both."

Lex sighed, meeting my eyes for the first time. He smiled, then shyly looked away. "You really think that's it? That I'm being too hard on myself? That I need to forgive myself?"

"There's no harm in trying."

Lex nodded. "Maybe there's hope then. Maybe this won't be so bad. We'll go save a few unicorns, become heroes, and then Teryn can bring a unicorn back to Mareleau and I can go home with a smidge of pride."

I felt the color leave my face. "What did you say? Teryn...bring a unicorn to Mareleau?" My eyes snapped forward just as Teryn looked back at me, head lowered with a sheepish look on his face. "What's this all about, Teryn? Are you seriously planning on taking a rescued unicorn back to your empty-headed bride?"

Teryn's mouth hung open without a word as I brought Hara next to Quinne. "It...it was just an idea," he said in a rush.

"Is that the only reason you are traveling with me? Explain yourself!" I felt my shoulders tighten, my blood burning. Below my anger was a strange combination of disappointment, hurt, and shame. *I knew I shouldn't have trusted them! How could I be so stupid?*

"Cora, I promise you, I am here because I believe in your mission. I barely gave it any thought when I told Lex you might help me find a unicorn for Mareleau. I thought I might bring one to her as a pet."

"A pet? Are you out of your mind? A unicorn is not a *pet.*"

Teryn struggled to find his words. "I thought...because of you and Valorre..."

"Valorre is not my pet, he is my companion. We have a bond. He chooses to accompany me. I do not stable him, I do not saddle him. And I certainly don't braid his hair and adorn it with ribbons like some idiot princess would do to a pet!"

Teryn sighed. "I'm sorry. It was a stupid idea, but it was harmless. I didn't realize the difference, but I do now.

I didn't mean to offend you. I want to be here to rescue the unicorns. I want to—"

"Quiet," I interrupted. Teryn opened his mouth to argue as I brought Hara to a stop, but I held up a hand to hush him. I fixed my gaze on Teryn and Lex in turn. "I mean it. Stay calm and listen."

The three of us remained silent as the rumbling grew louder.

"The Beast," Teryn said with a gasp.

"Do not panic. Follow me." I led them off the path as I reached my mind out to Valorre. He had gone off on his own again, for what seemed like an unusually long time. *Valorre, please.* I continued to call to him as the three of us went deep within the undergrowth, stopping beneath the dense cover of branches and shrubbery.

Valorre appeared in front of us, eyes wild and legs quivering. *Come, Valorre, I'm here,* I soothed, making room for him to stand between me and Teryn. The horses became agitated as the rumbling grew even louder.

"Cora, I hate to say this, but I don't think hiding under a tree will keep us from the Beast's view," Teryn said.

"I know, but you need to trust me. Close your eyes, both of you. Stay calm. Don't focus on fear, don't even think." I looked from Teryn to Lex, trying my best to appear reassuring until they both closed their eyes.

Valorre, can you calm the horses?

Yes.

I then set to the task of calming myself, breathing deeply as I extended my consciousness to Valorre, Teryn and Lex. I focused on the trees around us, attempting to shield us within their boughs like I had with myself and Valorre the last time we'd encountered the Beast. But extending my power to two unknowing minds was proving more difficult than I had hoped. Their minds were too erratic, too panicked. I released them.

"Whatever happens, stay calm. Remember, the Beast is only interested in unicorns. He has no reason to hurt you." I resolved all my focus on shielding myself, Valorre, and Hara. I focused only on my own breathing, the scent of the forest, and the strength of the trees nearby. Instead of being jostled by the rumbling of the approaching Beast, I swayed with the overhanging boughs. I became soil, leaf, and bark. I became tree.

"Where did Cora go?" Teryn asked in a panic. His voice merely slid past my awareness as if it were coming from far away, while I held fast to the glamour. The rumbling grew until it brought with it the sound of pounding hooves. The sound raced past, sending a gust of air that felt like a storm wind tearing through my branches. I reeled with the wind yet refused to be torn from my power. I stayed within the trees until well after the rumbling had subsided.

I emerged from the glamour and found myself surrounded by chaos and confusion.

"Cora, where were you?" Teryn shouted. He and Lex were both on foot, searching for me. "Where did you come from? We thought...we thought..."

"I'm fine. I was...I was here..." The words felt funny in my mouth, and I found myself unable to remember what I was trying to say. The blood rushed from my head as my body grew heavy in my saddle. I put a hand to my forehead and started to tip to the left. A pair of hands caught me and pulled me gently to my feet.

"Cora, what's wrong? Are you all right? Are you hurt?"

Teryn's voice sounded unnaturally loud. I closed my eyes and braced myself against one of Hara's saddlebags. I took a few deep breaths to steady my mind and regain my strength. My short attempt to cloak our entire group at once had been too much. Even cloaking myself, Valorre and Hara had been a large enough feat to overexert me.

"I'm fine, just dizzy. Give me a few moments."

"Were you invisible?" I heard Lex say behind me.

"Lex, don't be preposterous," Teryn said.

"I'm serious. One moment she was there. The next she was gone. She reappeared right where she had been. I think she's a witch."

I squinted as I gingerly turned my head to look at Lex. "I'm not a witch, Lex, but I can protect myself when I need to." Every word sent a shooting pain through my skull. "I tried to shield all of us, but it was too much."

Teryn and Lex exchanged a wide-eyed look. I realized I was probably saying more than I would under clearer circumstances, but my lack of strength was clouding my judgment. "Don't look so terrified, we have much graver business to attend to."

"What do you mean?" Teryn asked, his face pale.

"The Beast is here, likely collecting horns. We've found our hunters."

18

ANSWERS

Cora

"**A**re you sure you don't want me to come with you?" Teryn asked for the hundredth time that morning. We'd made camp just within the new hunters' anticipated range.

"No, I'll be fine," I said, shouldering my bow and quiver. "I need to scout their camp and get perspective. We know nothing about them, except for the name *Drass*. For all we know, they could be heavily guarded."

"Which is why I should come too."

"No, Teryn. I'm small and quiet. I don't need an extra set of noisy feet lumbering beside me." His face fell, making my gut feel heavy for the insult. Even though I had resolved to foster a friendship with Teryn and Lex, it was still most natural to want to keep these strangers at a distance. *But he isn't a stranger, not anymore*, I reminded myself. *He's my friend.*

I put a hand on Teryn's shoulder. "I'm sorry. I didn't

mean that, but I do want to go alone. I think it's best for all of us that their camp is scouted before the three of us go there together. It's the smartest tactic. I will come back for you, and the three of us will formulate a plan together."

Teryn let out a grumbling sigh but nodded in agreement. Lex made no argument, likely preferring that he never see the hunters' camp at all.

I left my companions behind and followed a narrow path that appeared freshly traveled by our new targets. Valorre quietly followed—he was the only one I couldn't persuade to be left behind.

It was after midday when I began to sense we were nearing the hunters. I urged Valorre to wait for me while I searched out their camp. *I don't want you getting too close, just in case.*

Be careful. Not hasty. Safe, Valorre warned.

I quietly crept through the trees, following an inner pull toward what I could only explain as a feeling of density in the peaceful, flowing energy of the forest. It was a sense of rigid darkness. A place of death. I'd felt it before, at the previous hunters' camp. Now I understood what it meant.

Before long, I came to the outskirts of a clearing, and the camp unfolded before me with every step. Remaining in the shadows of the undergrowth, I took in every detail. The scene was like that of the previous hunters—messy, strewn-about belongings, wooden cages. My eyes lingered on the cages as I counted them. There were eight, and only one of them was occupied. The unicorn within was small and brown, not yet completely emaciated. Aside from the unicorn, the camp was empty.

Wait. Not empty. A young man, no older than four-teen, strolled slowly out of the woods at the far end of the camp and into the middle. There he began to pace aimlessly—bored—around the fire. He appeared to be armed with nothing but a belted dagger. My mouth dropped open at the sight. This young man was the great defense the hunters had left to guard their precious goods? This boy, whom I could have tied to a tree within moments? Whom I could easily force to answer every one of my questions?

I nearly raced forward, led by my burning exhilaration, until I reminded myself of the promises I'd made to both Valorre and Teryn. I clenched my teeth and surrendered to the fact that I would have to wait. *At least when we return we can free the unicorn, get the boy to talk, and there will be no bloodshed. Lex will like that too.*

My limbs twitched with resistance as I turned my back on the perfect opportunity for answers and returned to Valorre.

"ONE GUARD. ONE UNICORN. THAT'S ALL," I BLURTED OUT upon returning to our camp, breathless from my anxious, hurried pace.

Teryn and Lex raced over to me. "Does he look...dangerous?" Lex asked with a gulp.

"Not at all. He's pretty much a boy!"

"When do we leave?" Teryn looked at the late afternoon sky above us. "It's too late for us to go today. We wouldn't make it there and back before dark."

My shoulders fell, but I knew he was right. "We will have to go first thing in the morning."

"Hopefully the conditions of the camp will still be the same." Creases formed between Teryn's brows. "It seems unusual that they only have one guard."

I nodded. "We will prepare for the worst but hope for the best. If there really is only one guard, there will be no need for violence. Even so, I want the two of you to practice your sparring. Practice like your life depends on it. Tomorrow, it just might."

Teryn

It was exactly as Cora had said; one guard, one unicorn. I let out a sigh of relief. The three of us exchanged glances and Cora nodded once, signaling the execution of our plan.

We each went our separate ways, moving quietly to surround the camp. I placed myself directly behind the young guard, who was idly picking at his nails with a dagger. I waited until I saw the boy stiffen at a rustling in the trees at the other end of the camp. That was my sign to move forward.

I hooked my arm around the guard's neck before he even knew I was there. I knocked the dagger from his hand and pressed my palm firmly over his mouth. The boy struggled to pull free, but Cora was at my side a moment later. We quickly bound his hands and feet with rope, followed by a gag for his mouth and a cloth for his eyes. Cora kicked him in the back of the knees, and the boy fell on his side. I felt a twinge of guilt at how easily he was defeated.

We left the boy wriggling futilely while we went to assist Lex in freeing the unicorn. He'd nearly cut through the ropes that secured the frame to the cage door—Cora's suggestion, and a much easier method for freeing the unicorn than struggling with keys and a lock. Once the ropes fell away, we coaxed the small unicorn from the cage and hurried him from the camp.

"Go. Take the unicorn to Valorre," Cora said when we were back beneath the trees. "Once he feels safe, he will leave you and be free."

Valorre had remained behind, not far from us. Still, going to him without Cora had not been mentioned in the plan. "What do you mean? Why aren't you coming with us?"

"Teryn, we came here for two things. The unicorn and answers."

"Then we'll get the unicorn safely away and come back together to question the boy."

"No. The other hunters could be back any moment, there's no telling when. We need to do all that we can *now*. You take the unicorn, I'll get the answers."

I opened my mouth to convince her otherwise but knew it would do no good. Besides, maybe she was right. Perhaps this was the perfect opportunity to get what we wanted without bloodshed. "Fine," I said through clenched teeth, "but be quick about it. And stay safe."

"I will." Cora put a hand on my arm. "Valorre will know if anything is amiss. Watch him. He grows very still when he senses danger and fidgets when it comes near. But I'll be back before you even need to worry about that." Without another word, she turned and raced back into the camp.

I watched her go, wishing I had something else to say to change her mind. Despite our ideal situation, I couldn't help but feel wrong about leaving her. What if the hunters *did* return? What if that boy proved to be more difficult to manage than he looked? And if Valorre *did* sense danger, would we have time to respond?

"Teryn," Lex said, shaking me out of my stupor. "This little guy is trembling with fright. Let's get him to Valorre already."

I looked at the unicorn; Lex was right. Lex, however, was shaking nearly as much. I threw one last look over my shoulder toward the hunters' camp, then led the way back to Valorre.

The unicorn needed help as he was both weak and frightened, but we eventually made it back to our meeting place. Lex and I sat down and drank from our water skins as Valorre received the hesitant unicorn with a gentle nuzzle on the neck. We sat in silence for a few moments, catching our breath, until Lex shattered the somber atmosphere with his laughter. I stared wide-eyed at his apparent madness. "What's so funny?"

"Nothing," Lex managed through bursts of chortling. "I just can't believe it. We saved a unicorn! We really did it!" He was grinning like a madman as tears pooled in his eyes. It was the first time I had ever seen him in such a mood, and it wasn't long before his joy became infectious.

I joined him, laughing at the absurdity, the danger, the victory, the incredulity of our entire situation. "If someone had told me a year ago I would be rescuing unicorns, I never would have believed them."

Lex nodded, blotting his eyes on his sleeve as he attempted to sober himself. "What do we do with this little guy?" he asked, turning his attention to the rescued unicorn that seemed fixed to Valorre's side.

I shrugged. "Nothing, I guess. Cora said he will leave when he feels safe."

"You know, I wish he wouldn't leave. He's beautiful. I'm glad we could save him. Maybe this *being heroes* thing isn't the worst after all."

I opened my mouth to agree but was distracted as a flash of brown streamed past my eyes. It took me a moment to realize the rescued unicorn had fled our company.

"Was it supposed to leave like *that*?" Lex raised an eyebrow.

"I don't know." I went to Valorre, a chill creeping down my spine as I watched the unicorn grow rigid. "What is it?" I whispered. Valorre didn't flinch or meet my eyes. He stared off into the trees, listening, watching.

Lex joined my side. "Something's wrong, isn't it?"

I shuddered. "Cora."

~

Cora

I stood over my captive lying limp and helpless on the ground. The boy had short, rust-colored hair, a thin, angular face, and a lanky, youthful build. He had given up his struggle and had grown so still I wondered if he'd fainted. I kicked his foot and he flinched, turning his blindfolded face toward me. He made no attempt to struggle away as I unsheathed my dagger, pressed the tip to his throat, and roughly pulled the gag from his mouth.

"What do you want from me?" he asked flatly. I was taken aback by the lack of fear in his voice.

"I want you to answer my questions," I growled.

"Are you the one, then? The one who has been massacring the other hunters? Ha! But you sound like a girl! And to think we were told you were dangerous."

I felt the blood drain from my face. He knew. *They* knew about the deaths of the other hunting party. Somehow, they had been warned. It made completing my current task even more urgent than before.

I grabbed the boy by the hair and slammed his head hard on the ground. I then pressed my blade closer to his neck until it just barely broke the skin. "I'm doing the questioning here. Who do you work for?"

"Drass and his hunting party." The boy's voice was calm, his composure completely unaffected by my abuse.

"Why are you hunting unicorns?"

"Because those are our orders."

"Who gives these orders?"

"Drass."

"Who does Drass take orders from?"

The boy remained silent.

"Who do you *really* take your orders from?" I shouted in his face.

"Our master," he finally whispered.

"Who is your master?" Another stretch of silence followed, causing my blood to boil as sweat beaded behind my neck.

"Do you really need me to tell you?" The boy had laughter in his voice. "Or do you already know?"

My gut churned. Something wasn't right here, and I had been too ambitious to realize it before. This boy was not the pathetic, easy target I had figured him to be. This was not my perfect opportunity to get answers. This was a trap. I released the boy and stepped away from him, taking a deep breath to calm my sudden fear.

"You're dying to hear his name, aren't you?" the boy taunted softly. "You know who he is. You wouldn't be asking all these questions if you didn't already know the answers."

"What does he want?" My voice was shaking despite my attempt to steady it. "Why has he sent you here?"

"Ask him yourself." A wide, toothy grin spread across his face.

I felt a shadow fall behind me. I whirled around, stifling a scream as I found myself face to face with Morkai. With trembling legs, I stumbled backward until my ankle snagged one of the logs surrounding the extinguished fire. I caught myself as I fell and scrambled back to my feet. This shook some sense of awareness into me, and I remembered the dagger still in my right hand. Fury replaced my fear.

"What do you want?" I planted my feet and thrust the dagger toward Morkai as he took a step toward me. Just as quickly, I took a step away.

"It's a pleasure to see you again too. You look...dreadful." Morkai stared down his nose at me. "Just look at you, a wretched mess. And to think you used to be a princess."

I pressed my lips tightly together, lifted my chin, and looked at him through narrowed eyes. In the six years that had passed since I last saw him, he hadn't aged a day. His disturbingly familiar face was long, thin, and shockingly pale, his skin nearly translucent. His eyes were dark beads of black under an arch of thick, black, bushy eyebrows. His head was bald, yet he wore a long, braided beard that grew to his waist.

His clothing was familiar to me as well—a long, midnight-blue, velvet robe patterned with intricate designs in black and gold, belted with a sash of dark-brown leather. A dagger with a jeweled hilt adorned his waist. He wore a long, charred, wooden staff at his hip as if it were a sword. My eyes lingered on the staff, noticing the row of blood-red rubies running along its length. Atop the staff was a large, deep-purple crystal. His hand idly rubbed the top of the crystal, where I saw endless clusters of heavily jeweled rings on his fingers. *My family rings.*

"*You* look as disgusting as ever," I sneered.

"Thank you, my dear. Now, if you will be so kind as to come with me."

I opened my mouth to retort when a sudden pain struck my right arm, causing me to drop my dagger. Before I could react, I felt arms tightly encircle my torso and neck. The guard boy snickered behind me.

"Not so tough now," the boy teased.

I struggled to free myself, but he squeezed harder. Even though he was years younger than I, and had appeared puny in strength, I had greatly underestimated his height. The length of his long, lanky arms gave him advantage over me.

"Come, Coralaine." Morkai stepped toward me until he was uncomfortably close. "You can't interfere with my plans and expect me to let you get away. You will be coming with me now."

"You'll have to force me!" I roared, then spit in his face. I tossed from side to side, trying to free myself from the boy who still held me in an iron grip.

Morkai calmly wiped a hand over his cheek, eyes locked on mine. "I'm going to have to hurt you now, you see?" He stepped back, took his staff from his hip, and lifted it in the air.

The arms surrounding me finally relented, and I threw myself sideways, dashing for the trees surrounding the camp. Before I could run more than a few steps, I was brought to my knees by a searing pain in the back of my skull. My vision swam as I tried to fight my inability to stand. The ground sped toward me, then faded to nothing.

19

MORKAI

Cora

A dream. I was only dreaming. Or am I dreaming now? Or dying. Am I dead? I opened my eyes, startled as I found myself in the great hall of Ridine Castle. Confusion flooded through me but was quickly replaced with awe and a sense of ease as I took in my surroundings. My body relaxed. All worry and concern melted away as I stared at the familiar walls. I studied each picture, each tapestry, each crevice, each stone. Everything was exactly as it had always been during my youth.

Music floated upon my attention, but as I looked around, I could not find the musicians. All the tables around me appeared empty. I looked down the hall to the opposite end of the room at the head table. At first glance, I took it to be empty as well. Then, after a blink of my eyes, two occupants appeared. I nearly jumped out of my skin as I recognized the familiar figures. "Mother!

Father!" I shouted, vaguely noticing how small my voice sounded as I ran to greet them.

"Coralaine!" My smiling father threw his arms open wide to embrace me. "Come to me, my love. Why are you so upset?"

I opened my mouth to answer but couldn't remember any reason to be upset in the first place. "I don't know." Something pulled at my mind, feeling like a thorn in my happy thoughts. I pushed it away. "I'm just so happy to see you."

My father smiled down at me with only a hint of concern in his kind, olive-green eyes. I drank in his presence as if he were the most beautiful vision in the world, which in that moment, he was. There was beauty in every strand of his long, straight, brown hair and wiry beard, in every crease on his wise, smiling face.

"My, my, strange child," my mother whispered in her feathery voice as she touched my shoulder. "You *do* seem out of sorts. You act like you haven't seen us in ages!"

I turned around and looked into my mother's beautiful face surrounded by her long, velvety, black curls. I choked back tears as I stared into her dark-brown, almond-shaped eyes and relished the comfort and relief her presence gave me. *But why?* A dark thought or memory tugged at my heart. Again, I forced it away. *My parents are here. They have always been here.*

"Coralaine! Mother, Father!" I turned toward the voice, looking down the great hall as Dimetreus and Linette strolled in, hand in hand. Their faces glowed with love, as if they had just returned from their wedding bed. My happiness at seeing them was overwhelming, and I nearly tripped down the stairs beneath the dais as I raced to embrace them.

"Lovely Coralaine, how I adore you," Dimetreus said as he bent to kiss my cheek. His face was warm, youthful, and enchanting as always. His eyes were green like Father's, but a brighter shade, like that of a spring leaf. His hair was also straight and brown like Father's, cropped just above his shoulders. But unlike Father, Dimetreus' face was smooth shaven.

"Little sister!" Linette took my hands and spun me around.

"Yes, let's have dancing!" Father clapped his hands and the music increased tempo.

Linette and I continued to twirl and dance, laughing until tears fell from our eyes. My head began to spin, but I continued to dance anyway, my smile growing so wide that my cheeks ached. I was enchanted as I watched Linette, her beautiful face flushed with a rosy hue, her auburn hair flowing wildly, and her golden skirts swirling round like a windblown flower. *My family! My family is here! They are all here!*

When the song was over, we turned, out of breath and giggling, to curtsy for my parents. My mother and father held up their hands in applause, and I wished with all my heart that I could stay forever in that moment, beneath my parents' smiling eyes. But to my dismay, the nagging darkness crept forward again, reminding me something was wrong. *Nothing is wrong. My family is here. They have always been here. I have always been here.*

Without warning, the bright light from the candlelit chandeliers faded to a glow, dimming the hall until there was only a dull, gray light illuminating the room. "What happened? Where did the light go?" I asked my parents. Their smiles had faded with the light, and dark circles appeared under their cold, black eyes. The gray light threw them under a ghostly pallor. They reached their hands toward me as if in plea for help, but before I could take a step forward, they toppled limp and lifeless to the ground.

I gasped and turned to Linette for help. A cry escaped my lips as she too had been swallowed by the gray light. Terror fell over her face as she stepped away from me, one hand covering her mouth, the other covering her suddenly bloated belly. I reached out my hand to comfort her, but she cowered from my touch. With every step she took away from me, her body began to decay. Blood poured from her eyes instead of tears.

I covered my face in trembling hands and screamed. "Dimetreus! Dimetreus, where are you? Help me!"

"What have you done?" growled a voice behind me. I whirled around and met the angry face of my brother. He was no longer youthful, beautiful, and joyous; he was a man aged by sorrow and rage. "Get out." He took a step toward me, hand raised.

"Please, I didn't do anything," I whispered, retreating away from him.

He caught up with me in two great steps and sent his hand across my face. My entire body ached from the blow as I fell to the floor, sobbing, pressing my cold fingers to my burning cheek. A wave of memories and unanswered questions surged through me. "This isn't real, this already happened," I mumbled as I pressed my eyes closed.

"Look at me," demanded my brother in a fierce whisper.

Slowly, shuddering head to toe, I did as I was told. I opened my eyes and looked into the dark, beady eyes of Morkai.

"I'm your family now."

I sat up, screaming as I opened my eyes to darkness. I swung my head side to side, trying to fight the blindness. A muffled growl of laughter came from somewhere to my right, and I held my breath to halt my screaming. I heard a creaking noise, followed by a blinding, blue light. I blinked a few times and tried to regain focus. In the doorway stood a shadowed figure, an orb of blue light hovering over the silhouette of a palm.

"I figured it was time to wake you up," Morkai said.

"Where am I?"

"You're home. At Ridine Castle."

My breath came out in ragged gasps as I forced myself to calm. My heart continued pounding in memory of the nightmare, but I knew I must have my wits about me in Morkai's presence. I took one last deep breath and forced my mind to steady.

Morkai and the room slowly came into focus as my eyes adjusted to the strange blue light emanating from his hand. I looked around me, finding myself on a bed beneath a brown wool blanket. I looked back at the sorcerer. "How long?" I asked flatly.

"Three days. You've been out cold for three days." He lifted his palm, and the blue light faded, quickly replaced by a warm, yellow light glowing from oil lamps around the room.

The light brought a piercing throb to the back of my

head. I reached my hand to soothe it, only to find my arms wouldn't reach. I looked to my wrists and found them bound with a thin, gold brace connected to a shimmering gold chain. I eyed the chains, following the path from wrist to bedpost, where they'd been secured. I raised my eyebrows in question.

"What did you expect?" Morkai gave a dismissive shrug of his shoulders. "I couldn't have you wandering free in the middle of the night."

"Trust me, I'd do worse than wander."

Morkai threw his head back in laughter. "Ah, I have to admit, I do like your spirit." He walked to the side of the bed. My body trembled as he stood inches away, yet I held my glare unwaveringly.

"Oh, don't look at me like that." His voice was disturbingly gentle. He reached a hand toward my face, as if to caress my cheek. I flinched and pulled as far away from him as I could within the limits of my bindings. Morkai's eyes widened, shock passing over his face before he quickly snatched his hand back. His scowl returned. "Get up and get dressed." He snapped his fingers, and my bindings disappeared.

I massaged my wrists, surprised at how quickly he had let me free. *He must not find me a threat,* I thought with disappointment.

"Wear what is in the chest at the foot of the bed. Then come to me." His mouth twitched in the faintest hint of a smirk before he turned and left, slamming the door behind him.

Once Morkai was gone, I let out a breath I hadn't realized I'd been holding. The beating of my frantic heart began to slow, and my breathing returned to a regular pattern. I stepped out of the bed and looked around the room. It was spacious, yet sparsely decorated; the only furnishings were the bed and the wooden chest. The air was cold and damp, saturated with a stale, moldy smell. I slowly stepped across the chilly, stone floor to the window and looked out at the black sky speckled with clusters of bright stars. I wasn't sure whether it was early morning or late night. Shadowy silhouettes of the Ridine Mountains stood in the distance above a faint shimmer of light where the stars were reflected in Lake Ridine. The familiar view tugged at my heart. I sighed but could not let myself fall into sentimentality.

With a shiver, I crossed my arms over my chest and looked down at myself, surprised to find I was clothed in nothing but a chemise. It wasn't my own. My stomach churned at the thought of someone stripping and changing me in my unconscious state. The thought brought my attention to my hands, which looked completely clean. I ran them through my hair, which felt as if it had been thoroughly washed and combed. *I've been bathed.* I swallowed a lump in my throat, shaking unwanted thoughts from my head.

With no better options, I went to the chest to dress with the clothes Morkai had provided. Within the chest, I found a beautiful, midnight-blue gown patterned with silver threaded butterflies. Ivory lace ran along the bodice, hem, and sleeves.

As I pulled the gown over my shoulders, I realized I would not be able to lace myself into it—it was not the simple style of dress I was used to wearing. I ground my jaw and nearly tore the dress in two, when I was interrupted by a faint knock at the door.

"Stay out!" I barked, covering my chest and backing into the shadows against a wall. Without a word of reply, the door opened, and in walked an old woman dressed in filthy rags. She came to me without looking at me and reached for the dress. I flinched and nearly pushed her away, but then understood what she had been sent to me for. I took a hesitant step forward and turned around so she could tighten the laces at the back of the dress. My heart quickened at the unfamiliar routine. I hadn't been dressed by a maid since I was a child.

"Thank you," I whispered gently to her. "What is your name?" There was no answer, and I figured it best not to inquire further.

Once the job was done, the woman left as silently as she had come, and I was left again to the dark, empty room. The silence lasted only long enough for me to step into a pair of dark blue, delicately beaded slippers when another knock sounded on the door, this one fiercer than the last. I didn't have the chance to inquire who was calling before the door swung open, and in walked guard-boy.

"What are you doing here?" I crossed my arms and scowled. He replied with nothing but a sly smile. I took the moment to penetrate his mind. I searched...and searched. Nothing. He was blocking me. He must have expected my powers. In fact, he must have known about them long before I came into the hunters' camp, which would explain why I hadn't been able to sense the danger he presented. Morkai had him thoroughly prepared.

"It was a trap, wasn't it?"

Again, he gave me nothing but a smirk. "Come." He

reached toward my arm. "Morkai demands your presence."

I jerked away and stepped around him, exiting the room with my head held high. "I can walk myself."

The boy caught me by the wrist. "I am to lead you to him. Unless you'd rather struggle first." His voice was cold, and his eyes sparkled dangerously. It was hard to imagine I ever saw him as a pathetic, young boy.

I gave in and let him lead me forward. He was not rough, which I could have been grateful for if I were not so full of rage. The rage, however, kept the fear at bay, which was something I treasured so much more.

As we walked through the hallways, I watched my surroundings, finding them familiar yet vastly darker and less well-kept than I could remember. The tapestries were dusty and faded, with burn marks marring the once-beautiful designs. Cobwebs hung in low clouds from the ceiling. Only a few lamps and candles were lit, throwing shadows where there used to be light. I shuddered, remembering the vibrancy of my nightmare compared to the true vision before me, unable to decide which was worse.

After a long walk through the lengthy hallways, the boy led me up an even longer flight of stairs. Considering the heights we were ascending, we could only be heading to one of the towers. At the top of the stairs was a large, wooden door engraved with spirals and strange patterns. Below the door, I could see a faint red light. Despite my best efforts to control my emotions, my hands began to shake. I balled them into fists and held my composure as the boy opened the door and led me inside.

We were in a large, circular room, illuminated by

bright red lamplight that threw an eerie glow upon the room's contents. The first thing that stood out was the overabundance of books—shelves upon shelves of books covered the expanse of every wall. In the center of the room was a large table strewn with more stacks of books and unfamiliar tools and gadgets. Next to the table were two ornate, throne-like chairs.

But where is Morkai? I regretted the question as soon as I heard the creak of a previously unseen door hidden between two bookshelves. Morkai entered the room, and the door swung shut behind him, leaving no evidence of its existence. His face stretched into a disgusting smile as he assessed me from head to toe. "Now you look more appropriate, little sorceress. I knew Linette's clothes would fit you."

I deepened my glare and tried my best to appear unaffected by the knowledge that I was wearing my dead sister's dress.

"How did you like your old room? Did you find it cozy and to your liking, like when you were a child?" Morkai's voice was sharp and mocking.

My shock at this, I could not hide. My mouth fell open as I realized the dark, cold, empty room I had departed from had once belonged to me, had once held my own bed, my own chests and cabinets, my own dresses, mirrors, and tables. I could tell Morkai enjoyed my shock.

"You may go, Orin," he said to the boy. Orin released my wrist, then left me alone in the room with Morkai. I steadied my breathing and kept my gaze firm, ready to defend myself against whatever he would deliver next.

"Don't look so tense." Morkai went to his desk and

began flipping through his books as if my presence was nothing to be concerned with. "I'm not going to hurt you."

"Then why am I here?" I hoped he couldn't hear the quiver in my voice.

"You know why you're here. You attempted to sabotage my plans. I want to know why."

I put my hands on my hips and turned my chin up, forcing confidence. "Well, if you must know, my friends and I were nearly killed by one of your hunting parties. Then I found out what they were hunting. *Then* I found out whom they were hunting for. And, knowing your true nature, I assumed your intentions were nothing short of evil. I wanted to find out exactly what you were planning and why."

Morkai turned around to face me, folding his hands at his waist. "What exactly do you want to know?"

His reaction caught me off guard. "You will answer my questions?"

Morkai nodded. "Isn't that what you've been risking your life for?"

"Yes, but..." After all the time I had spent looking for answers, I found myself unable to form a single question. Could I even trust him to answer me honestly? Of course not! But the offer was too good to pass up. I closed my eyes, took a deep breath, and readied my first question. "How did you know where to find me?"

"I wasn't exactly trying to find *you*...at first. I had been given report that a group of my hunters was being stalked and sabotaged by someone. Then I found several of them had been murdered. While penetrating the mind of my Roizan—you have met him, have you not?"

"The Beast," I said under my breath.

Morkai let out a sharp laugh. "No, my dear Coralaine, he has a name. So, while I was penetrating the mind of my *Roizan,* attempting to come across some clue to the identity of my new foe, he showed me your face—so vaguely familiar and just as much of a nuisance as I remembered you to be. After a deeper look, I knew it had to be you. I assumed you were on some heroic mission and therefore would be easy to catch at the height of your stupidity."

I clenched my teeth and moved on to the next question. "Why are you hiring hunters to slaughter unicorns?"

"I desire their horns."

"Why?"

Morkai sighed, as if I were boring him. "Because they are useful to me. They contain power, magic."

"What do you use them for?"

At this Morkai grinned. "Where do you think my Roizan gets his strength?"

I nodded. This was no surprise. "But why unicorns? Why use their magic and not your own?"

"Why use up *my* magic when I can harness one of the greatest sources in this land? Those creatures have grown abundant in Kero, and I detest them. They are a sign of foreboding. So why not have them destroyed *and* use their power for my own needs?"

I swallowed my disgust. "What is the Roizan for?"

"Don't you know what a Roizan is? It is an ancient term. The Roizan is my weapon, my servant, and my channel to the magic within him."

"I don't understand."

"And I don't have time to explain ancient magic to you."

I clenched my teeth. "Fine, then. Why are the hunters starving and torturing the unicorns before dehorning them?"

"I don't want their horn for any pure, miraculous uses," Morkai said with a flourish of his hands and a roll of his eyes. "I want the dark horn of suffering. The horn of death. The horn of true power."

This corresponded with what Valorre and I had already concluded. "Why are the hunters working for you? How are you gaining so many allies?"

"They don't work for free, Coralaine."

"What do you give them in return?"

"They keep the unicorn pelts. I have no need for their stinking corpses, so I let the hunters have them to do with as they please. Since unicorn skin is a rare and highly desired luxury, my hunters fetch a high price for it."

Everything made sense, yet so much was still missing. I paused, searching my mind for the next question. "What are you planning?"

Morkai burned me with an intense gaze as his face stretched into a malicious grin. His lips pressed firmly together.

"You said you'd answer my questions."

"I will tell you later. First, there's someone I want you to see."

My heart began to pound. "Dimetreus?"

Morkai cackled as he strode forward to grasp my arm. I didn't fight as he led me out of the room, down the stairs, and down the endless hallways. I was in a daze as I thought about my brother. Was he in good health? Was he a prisoner? Would he be happy to see me? Would I be happy to see him?

After what seemed like an endless journey, we came to a dark stairwell. Morkai raised his hand, opened his palm, and ignited a glowing orb of red light. We descended the stairwell, ending at a large hallway lined with barred chambers. The dungeon. My heart sank. So, he was a prisoner. I tried to remain strong, but as we walked past the stinking, rusty cells, I began to tremble. I wiped a falling tear from my cheek.

We finally stopped at a cell. Morkai touched the lock with his hand, and the door sprang open. He stepped inside, flooding the cell with his red light. I ran in after him, halting with startled surprise as I found the occupant was not my brother after all. "Teryn?"

20

PLANS

Teryn

My breath caught in my throat as a beautiful woman rushed into my cell. It wasn't until she said my name that I realized it was Cora. "You're alive!" I nearly ran forward to embrace her, but then remembered the dark figure that had entered before her. I stole a quick glance at the sorcerer, whose pale, smirking face glowed under the strange, red light. He watched me out of the corners of his eyes. I kept my distance and remained silent; I didn't want anything I said to put myself or Cora in danger.

With nothing else to say, my eyes strayed over Cora, making sure she was completely safe and unharmed. Finding her whole and uninjured, I was suddenly aware of her drastic change in appearance. Her skin was clean and smooth, and her hair was free of tangles, flowing in long, dark waves over her shoulders. Her small waist was cinched above a light curve of hips in an elegant gown that displayed a modest bosom that rose and fell with her heavy breathing.

My eyes quickly snapped back to her face, which was full of anguish. She opened and closed her mouth a few times as if she couldn't figure out what to say, before she finally decided upon, "I'm glad to see you are well."

I could tell she was trying to appear collected and indifferent, but her eyes glistened with tears. She looked like she wanted to say more, to ask me something, but she kept her mouth pressed tight. To answer one question that I knew was on her mind, I glanced toward the corner where Lex sat, his arms folded over his knees as he quietly peered from the shadows. Cora followed my gaze and let out a sigh of relief.

"Well, this is a pathetic reunion, is it not?" Morkai waved the red light away from his hand. After a moment of darkness, the lamps along the walls in the dungeon hall began to glow, illuminating the dark cell. "I know the three of you are acquainted, although the boys refuse to confirm my suspicions."

"They had nothing to do with killing your hunters. Let them go." Cora's trembling voice betrayed her forced confidence.

Morkai barked a laugh. "This won't do. I answered your questions. Now I expect the same respect in answering mine. Who are these men?"

Cora looked from me to Morkai, eyes wide and brows furrowed. "Please, let them go."

Before I knew it, Cora was in Morkai's grasp with the blade of a dagger at her throat. "Now, will you speak?"

I watched as a tiny trickle of blood ran down Cora's neck below the dagger. My body flooded with a fury I'd never felt before. "Let her go. I'll tell you everything," I shouted.

"No," mouthed Cora, but no sound came out.

"Get on with it." Morkai tightened his grip around Cora's waist, eyes locked with mine as he brought his face next to Cora's. "I'm waiting," he whispered, his mouth brushing Cora's cheek as his lips turned up at the corners in a sly smile.

I had the sudden urge to take the dagger from him and plunge it into his heart. My shoulders tensed, and my muscles shook from head to toe. I swallowed hard and forced my voice to remain steady. "My name is Teryn. I am Crown Prince of Mena. Anything you do to her, Lex, or me, will bring forth the wrath of King Arlous and all our allies."

"The wrath of King Arlous? What a pleasure. What are you doing in Kero? And what are you doing with *her?*"

I replied with a hurried summary of my travels, sharing only the barest details of my journey with Lex and Helios, explaining Helios's death, and then lightly touching on my meeting with Cora. Finally, I confessed to my involvement with his hunters. I was sure my words were sealing my fate, but I was willing to do anything to make him take his hands off Cora.

"Now, was that so hard?" Morkai released Cora from his hold and pushed her forward.

Cora put her hand to her neck as she stumbled into me. I put a protective arm around her, and we faced Morkai, glaring as we awaited his next move.

The sorcerer steepled his fingertips, considering us silently. The quiet was shattered by his hissing laughter. "The things a man will do for a woman. First, he begins a ridiculous quest to impress one woman. Then he joins the pathetic quest of another, nearly getting himself killed in the process." Morkai smirked at Cora. "Men are quite fickle, my dear. You'd do well not to let your heart fall on this one."

I bit back my retort, and Cora remained silent as well.

Morkai turned his gaze on me. "You don't agree with me, Prince Teryn? You aren't chasing skirts, blowing from one fancy to the other like the wind? Oh, I see. You consider yourself to be a hero." Morkai shook a finger at me. "Silly boy. But if that's the case, I have a way for you to be a real hero. How would you like to save your kingdom?"

"What do you mean?"

"Come. All of you." He grabbed Cora by the wrist, tearing her away from me, and led her out of the cell. Two guard-like figures entered and wordlessly forced me and Lex to follow.

My heart raced as we were led through the castle. Cora stole anxious glances at me as Morkai dragged her on ahead. There was nothing more to see but shadowed halls as we were forced onward. Finally, we came to a door and stepped through to the outside. The men released me and Lex, but I could feel their presence close behind. I blinked as my eyes adjusted to the glowing starlight within a black sky as Morkai brought us to the edge of a dark field. I heard a strangled cry escape from Cora's lips as she stared at the empty expanse.

"The gardens," she gasped, a shaking hand held to her lips.

I followed her gaze and could see nothing resembling a garden. All I could see was a charred field with no sign of life, save for a few gnarled, black stumps that were probably once trees.

"What have you done?" Cora whispered.

"This isn't exactly what I brought you here to see, but I'm glad you are impressed."

"Then why are we here?" Cora asked, eyes filled with tears.

"Don't be so impatient, my dear." Morkai ran his hand down the back of Cora's hair with his bony, white hand. I clenched my hands into fists to keep myself from attacking him.

Cora stepped away from his caress and glared up at him. "Just show us what we came here for and get it over with."

Morkai smiled down at her as he again reached his hand toward her hair.

"Don't touch her!"

Morkai shot me an icy glare, grumbling as he turned back toward the field. He took up his charred, black staff from its place at his hip and raised it in the air. The rubies along the staff began to glow blood-red under the starlight, getting brighter and brighter until I had to look away. I could feel Lex trembling next to me.

Once the glow had died down, I looked back toward the field. I froze as I saw leagues of men dressed in indigo tunics standing in rows before us, filling nearly the entire field. Each set of dark, empty eyes was on the sorcerer, each set of rigid arms was held straight at their sides, and each waist was armed with a sword.

"What is this?" Cora asked.

"My Royal Force." Morkai spread his arms wide with a grin.

I shuddered.

"What are they for?" Cora took a step away from the field.

"War, of course."

I felt the blood leave my face. "What war?"

"The inevitable war that will result from anyone who fails to surrender to my rule. I am claiming rule over all of Lela."

"No." Cora stomped her foot.

"You can't!" I shouted.

Morkai walked over to me and brought his face close to mine. "Yes, Prince Teryn, I can."

"You'll never win," Cora said, and Morkai rounded on her.

"Of course, I will!"

Cora stood straight, chin lifted. "What, with this pathetic, ensorcelled army you've accumulated? Mena and Sele will fight you. Your men won't stand a chance against the real passion of Mena and Sele's Royal Force, not to mention anyone from Kero brave enough to stand up against you."

Morkai doubled over with laughter. "You think this is *all*? I still have time to recruit more men. In fact, Teryn has given me some valuable information that I can use to form more allies. But I've got more than men, silly girl."

Cora's shoulders sank. "What now?"

Morkai clapped his hands, and the men marched to the far end of the field, hidden within the shadows of the trees. Once again, Morkai raised his staff in the air, and again it shone the red light, this time sending a red fog rolling over the field. "Come," he whispered, his voice a chilling hiss.

At first, there was nothing to see but the red fog as I held my breath in anticipation. Then, distant shadows began moving toward the field. I thought perhaps Morkai's army was returning, but as the shadows came nearer, I knew something was amiss. I could make out the forms of bodies moving slowly and erratically forward, but I could see no faces. I watched as they neared, waiting for the figures to become clear, but the nearer they came, the less sure I was that they were human. They seemed both dead and alive at once. They were as transparent as the fog, barely discernible as they wandered through the field. Each figure carried an equally transparent weapon, and each looked equally lost and mindless. Soon the field was filled with these figures—hundreds of them.

"Wraiths?" Cora said with a gasp.

Morkai nodded. "Lost souls of the dead, trapped in the world of the living. These, as you may have guessed, are the souls of great fighters. These men have lost their lives in an ancient war you've never heard of. They are here to continue their legacy as warriors."

"Wraiths cannot fight," Cora said. "They are lost. They cannot grasp the physical world again. They only live as memories, memories that are not meant to be woken."

"You underestimate me too much. Of course I know what a wraith is capable of. I also know what *I'm* capable of."

Cora narrowed her eyes at Morkai, her face red and nostrils flaring.

"Now you're impressed. I knew it. Watch and I will demonstrate." Morkai faced the field of wraiths. "Fight!"

At that moment, the shadowed spirits seemed to gain

consciousness as each immediately sprang into action and began to fight. Arrows soared, swords were swung, and deathly voices cried out in agony as the mass of wraiths slaughtered each other. From the intensity of the fight, I thought the battle would last no more than a few moments, but it continued without end. Bodies fell to the ground only to get back up again, over and over. Many of the deaths repeated in sequence; one wraith was decapitated in the same manner over a dozen times, while another repeatedly raced forward with a fierce battle cry just before getting stabbed in the back.

It was a terrifying sight, but something about it was flawed.

Morkai clapped his hands, and the wraiths halted, then slowly dispersed. "You see, my wraiths *can* fight. They will fight mortal men just the same. And they never die, for they are already dead."

"You are horrible!" Cora shouted.

"Indeed." Morkai smirked. "But this can all be avoided. War does not have to be the answer. In fact, I have no desire to resort to war in the first place. I only wanted to show you my protection, show you what I am capable of. There is another way. A way free of bloodshed. A way of peace." Morkai turned toward me now.

"What do you mean?" I asked.

"This is where your heroics come in. How you can save your kingdom."

"How do you expect me to do that?"

Morkai's face stretched into a wide grin, the points of his crooked teeth showing between his thin, pale lips. "You will make Mena and Sele surrender to me."

"They never will."

"Even if it means your life?"

Before I could form an intelligent retort, I found my arms being bound behind my back by the guards.

"No!" Cora shouted as she ran forward, but Morkai grabbed her by the arm and forced her to his side. "What are you going to do to him?"

Morkai put his face disgustingly close to hers. "Nothing, if Prince Teryn's life is valuable to the leaders of Mena and Sele."

"What do you want from me?" I asked, forcing Morkai's attention away from Cora and back to myself.

"Look to the black, starlit sky. The moon is new. The power of my plans is being set forth in perfect timing." Morkai's face was full of elation as he stared at the sky. Seeing him full of such bliss sent a chill down my spine.

Once he lowered his head and returned his gaze to me, his face was once again cold and scowling. "I will send a message to Mena and Sele, explaining that I am holding you hostage. As the sun rises from the darkness of the next new moon, I will take you and my forces to Centerpointe Rock where the leaders of Sele and Mena will meet me. If they surrender to my rule, I will let you return to your family alive. If not, I will kill you."

"If you kill me..." I fell silent, as the full weight of his plan dawned on me.

Morkai smiled, nodding. "Yes. If I kill you, they will wage war on me. I never said this was going to be *my* war. I only said there would *be* a war if my rule was refused. And if there is a war, I will win. War or no war, Lela will be mine in one month's time. The only thing left to do is send a messenger. Come, Lex, you will make yourself useful."

"Leave him out of this!" I shouted, struggling against the firm hold of the guards.

Lex looked from me to Morkai, eyes wide as he trembled from head to toe.

"Lex, do you understand what I am saying?" Morkai spoke as if Lex were a child. Lex quickly nodded. "Good. You will ride to Mena, go to Dermaine Castle, and send King Arlous my message. In one moon cycle, he will either surrender to me, or lose the life of his heir. Understand?"

Tears streamed down Lex's red face as he gave a single nod. Morkai mumbled some unfamiliar words, and moments later, a horse appeared. "Now go," Morkai demanded.

Lex stumbled toward the horse, shaking as he climbed into the saddle. He turned his face toward mine. "Teryn," he whispered.

"Be brave," I said. "Remember everything you saw tonight. Everything you heard. Remember every detail. And tell my parents..." I couldn't finish my sentence, realizing I didn't know *what* I wanted him to tell them. Save me and surrender to Morkai? Sacrifice me and then go to war with Morkai's army of possessed men and fierce wraiths? "Tell my parents I love them."

Lex nodded.

Morkai placed a hand on the horse, mumbling a quiet incantation. The horse took off with unnatural speed, carrying Lex out of view into the forests beyond the field. "Now, take the prince back to the dungeons."

"Teryn!" Cora lunged forward, reaching for me. Morkai grabbed her by the wrist as the guards forced me back into the castle. My head spun, and my legs gave way beneath me. The guards dragged me on without a care. Once back in my cold cell, I was left with darkness and the pounding of my heart. My mind reeled with what I had learned. War. Death. My parents. Lela. Lex. Cora. Larylis. Slipping out of consciousness came as my only relief.

21

STRANGER

Cora

I bit my lip to keep the tears at bay and swallowed the painful lump in my throat as I watched Teryn being carried away. I forced myself to look away from the empty doorway through which he had been taken, and glowered down at my feet as I steadied my labored breathing. I could sense Morkai's beady eyes watching me. I felt his cold finger touch my chin, and I flinched out of his reach. He reacted by grabbing my jaw and forcing me to look up at him. His face swam behind a pool of tears.

"Don't look so upset, child." Morkai's voice sounded deceitfully gentle.

"What are you going to do to me?"

"Your fate is the same as Teryn's. I will do nothing to you if you comply with my wishes. It's up to you."

My stomach knotted. What could he possibly want from me?

"You don't have to be my enemy," Morkai continued. "You don't have to suffer. You could be on the winning side of this war. I know your powers are strong. I could use an ally."

"You are crazy if you think I will join you."

"No, Coralaine, you are crazy if you *don't* join me. Who are you fighting for? No one cares about you. Hardly a soul knows you exist. Not even your own people know or care who you are. You are dead to them, but I could bring you back. You could return to your place as royalty of Kero. You could join me and be queen of all Lela."

"Queen? *Your* queen? You really are crazy." I slammed my hands into Morkai's chest, forcing him to release me. "I would rather die than be your queen!"

His eyes narrowed, his jaw moved back and forth, and his hands clenched into fists. "Willing or not, you will comply. I have plans for you that you can't even begin to imagine. You will serve me. This is your last chance to do so willingly, Coralaine. Agree to be my queen or I will send you to rot in the dungeons."

"If those are my choices, I'll walk there myself." I turned on my heel toward the castle.

"I see. It's that boy. You think he actually cares about you."

I spun back around, my mouth opening, then snapping shut.

Morkai grinned. "You want to be *his* queen, don't you?"

"It's not like that." I turned my chin up as I glared into his mocking eyes.

"Of course, it is. But I should tell you right now, he

does not love you. It's the other woman he truly loves. The Princess of Sele."

"He can love whomever he wants. It doesn't matter to me. We are friends, and friends care about each other."

Morkai came toward me with slow, creeping steps. "You don't know anything about being a woman. You can't even tell when you're in love."

"I'm not in love!"

Morkai cackled, a rasping, grating sound from his throat. "I sure hope not, because you could never please him in any way. You are a wild thing, a creature. I can tell by looking at you that you have never known a man's touch. You are like a child in a woman's body."

His words sent ripples of nausea through me. It only made matters worse that he was right.

"You wouldn't know what to do with a man like Prince Teryn. He wouldn't have the patience for your childlike emotions to mature. I, on the other hand, would be gentle."

"Enough!" Fire flooded my veins. "You know nothing about me. I know what you are doing. You are trying to weave a web of insecurity around me, trying to break me. Trying to trick me into joining you."

"Oh, Coralaine, I do know much about you. More than even *you* may know. I only say these things because I want what's best for you. You don't need to fill your head with fantasies that can never be. You could never be Teryn's queen. The only thing more shameful than you cowering like a frightened dog at his intimate touch would be your unraveling when he sets you aside."

I raised my eyebrow and put my hands on my hips.

"You really think you're going to scare me with senseless threats like that?"

"It's not a threat, my dear. It is inevitable. You must be able to provide an heir to be his queen. Once he found out you were barren, he would have to set you aside, out of duty as king to his kingdom."

"What are you talking about?" My words came out with more of a tremor than I'd intended.

Morkai's face fell under a mask of sympathy. "Don't you know? Oh, you poor thing. My dear, you cannot bear children. You are infertile. I made you so since you were a child. You were so focused on what I was doing to your family, you never stopped to consider what I was doing to you."

My knees began to shake as the blood left my face. "What?"

"I don't mind your barrenness, Coralaine. In fact, I prefer my queen to be as such. I don't need any greedy little heirs being born, waiting in line for my throne. And I would be gentle with you. I would..."

"How could you do this to me?" My voice came out with a ragged sob. "You've destroyed my body! My womanhood!"

Morkai shook his head. "Now, now, don't act so ungrateful. I could have killed you, like your parents. Instead, I gave you a slow poison of a different nature."

"Why?"

"I had to end your family's bloodline." Morkai spread his hands out, a look of innocence on his face. "I knew I would someday rule Kero and then Lela, and your child would have been a plague to my rule. I've only killed those who would hinder me and my rightful legacy—

your parents, Linette, and her unborn children—but I was kind enough to let you and your brother live."

"Dimetreus is still alive?" A flutter of hope glowed faintly through the darkness of my pain, making me forget everything else he'd said.

Morkai smirked. "You expect me to kill the man who has been aiding my quest to his throne?"

"Where is he? Take me to him! I want to see him now!"

Morkai shook his head. "It is pointless, my dear. He will not know you. He will see nothing but a stranger. Don't you know? You are dead."

"He'll know it's me when he sees me."

"He saw you poison his wife. He sentenced you to death. He saw your head fall from the executioner's block."

"That's not true. None of that happened, and you know it."

"What may or may not be true is irrelevant. It is what he remembers that matters, and he remembers you are long dead."

"And why is that, Morkai?" I stomped toward the sorcerer, fueled by fury. "My brother banished me from my home. I was exiled. I wasn't a threat, I was a child with nowhere to go. Why would you turn my brother further against me? Poisoning his mind, twisting his memories? What was the benefit of making him think I'm dead? In making the people of Kero think I'm dead?"

"You are an ungrateful girl, Coralaine," Morkai hissed through his teeth. "I could have *really* killed you just as easily, but I let you live. You were a nuisance and I needed you gone. I needed to sever your claim to the throne. So, instead of killing you—as I probably *should* have done—I went through all the extra trouble to give you a new life. I even took the life of a kitchen maid to save yours."

"So, it was she you had beheaded in my stead."

"Yes. A simple spell over the crowd and they saw her as your spitting image. I sacrificed her life so you could live. I could easily have let it be you."

"You say this like I should be thanking you," I said with a shaky laugh, "but I'm sure your motives were far from selfless. You need me for something. Otherwise, you *would* have killed me."

"Oh, don't flatter yourself. I let you live out of the pure kindness in my heart."

"You have no heart. You love nothing but yourself. I can sense your hidden motives. You are keeping me and my brother alive for your own selfish reasons. Why?"

Morkai sighed, rolling his eyes. "I let you live because I respected the magic growing within you. You were strong, and I could sense your potential. A sorcerer respects a sorceress. I thought, perhaps one day, you'd even become my pretty plaything. But it seems you are more of a hassle than anything, and if you fail to satisfy me, I *will* kill you. As for your brother, he has been more than accommodating, and I still find him useful in many ways, including good company. So, I do not need to kill him just yet."

"Why didn't you kill him the way you killed my parents and claim rule of Lela at once?"

"There are things you don't understand about Lela." Morkai pressed the tips of his fingers together. "There is magic in the land. He who rules over the entire land rules the magic, but it can't be ruled by force. It must be inherited."

"If demanding the rulers of Lela surrender to your rule isn't considered force, then what do you call it?"

"I am not forcing my rule, I am claiming it as my right. If they refuse to follow, then it is by their own foolishness that they fall. There is a subtle difference, but the magic recognizes it."

"How do you intend to *inherit* the rule of Kero in the first place? It's impossible!"

Morkai's lips twisted into a thin smile. "It's not impossible. Dimetreus has made me his heir."

A chill ran down my spine. "How?"

"He adopted me. He was growing sickly and realized he had no heir to take his place should he die. A king with no heir is a vulnerable king, and he knew it. As his most trusted councilman, he saw no one better to succeed him to the throne. And he has already abdicated to me. I am King of Kero."

My knees nearly caved beneath me. I closed my eyes, gritted my teeth, and forced my head to stop spinning. "That can't be valid. For such an absurd appointment to be made, you would need the approval of—"

"All of the council? They were more than eager to agree. I can be very convincing."

My heart sank. If he was already king, there was no hope. "Please," I whispered. "Can I just see my brother?"

"It will do neither of you any good, but if you wish." Morkai clapped his hands twice. "Dimetreus. Come."

A shadowed figure strode forward from the castle wall. I recognized him as one of the hooded guards. I could barely make out the face beneath the hood, but I was certain it was not my brother. "I said I wanted to see my brother. Where is he?"

Morkai ignored me. "Dimetreus, remove your hood." The guard did as told, revealing a head of thin, gray-brown hair and a weathered, sullen face. His eyes were black and lifeless, lined with heavy shadows.

I gasped. It *was* my brother. "What have you done to him?" He looked so old. Far too old to be my brother, even after the six years that had passed since I'd last seen him. But I could see the shadow of resemblance, could sense the flicker of life that was barely left in him.

"I've done nothing. I told you, he grew ill. But he is happy to have me as his new king, aren't you, Dimetreus?"

Dimetreus gave a sharp nod, his black eyes staring blankly ahead.

I couldn't believe what I was seeing. "Dimetreus," I whispered. "It's me, Coralaine. Please look at me! Please remember me!"

Dimetreus let out a slow grumble as his eyes slowly slid down to meet mine. His eyebrows lowered, and his lips pressed into an angry frown. I could see no evidence that he recognized me.

"Don't listen to anything this girl says, Dimetreus," Morkai whispered into his ear. "She is a dangerous traitor. She refuses to accept my rule."

Before I could comprehend what had happened, I found myself sprawled on the ground with a pounding ache in my chest.

"You dare stand against King Morkai?" Dimetreus shouted.

I was frozen in shock as I looked at the man towering over me. No, this was not my brother. I shouldn't have been surprised. I already knew my brother was lost to me the day I was exiled.

"Take her to the dungeons," Morkai ordered.

"Yes, Master." Dimetreus roughly hefted me to my feet. Sobs tore through me as he dragged me through the castle. Once back in the dungeons, Dimetreus pushed me into a cell.

I turned around and looked into his dead eyes that revealed not even a hint of emotion. My whole body quivered from the rage that coursed through me. I took a step toward him. "How could you do this, Dimetreus? How could you let yourself become controlled by him? You have betrayed us all!"

Dimetreus grumbled as he raised his hand up and swung it toward my face. I raised my arm, blocking his blow. "No, Dimetreus, I will not let you hit me again!"

He took a hesitant step back, eyes wide as he frowned at his hand.

"That's right. You may not remember, but you have hit me before. You are dead to me now, but you were once my brother. You were once a good man. You were a son, a brother, and a husband. Now you are nothing but Morkai's slave."

"Morkai is a good master and strong ruler," Dimetreus said.

"Ha! Is that why he killed our parents? Is that why he killed Linette and your unborn children?"

"You lie."

"Oh, this conversation sounds awfully familiar, does it not? And, no, Dimetreus, it is not a lie. It is the truth, my brother."

"I am not your brother," Dimetreus said flatly, backing out of my cell. "My sister is dead."

"I *am* your sister, and somewhere deep down, you remember the truth."

"Enough!" Dimetreus slammed the cell door closed and locked it. "I don't know you."

I clung to the bars of my cell door, watching Dimetreus as he walked away. An intense mix of emotions coursed through me. I wanted to break from my cell and kill that man who wore my brother's face. At the same time, I wanted to run into his arms, feel his familiar embrace. I wanted him to remember me. I wanted my brother back. I wanted him dead. I hated him. I loved him.

"Dimi." The word slipped from my lips in a small, birdlike cry. I hadn't spoken that name since I was very small. The name filled my heart with a sorrowful tenderness as I remembered the youth who'd once loved me. "Dimi, please come back to me," I whispered. I almost thought I saw Dimetreus pause before he was out of sight.

22

HARBINGER

Larylis

"Prince Larylis, there is an urgent matter you must attend to."

I closed the book at my desk and looked up to find a red-faced guard panting in the doorway of my study. "What's the matter? What's going on?"

"We aren't exactly sure, Your Highness. Some man claiming to be Prince Lexington of Tomas came stumbling up to the front gates a few moments ago. As soon as he reached us, he fell flat on his face. We had someone fetch him water, but he just keeps mumbling that he must see the king."

"Is he truly Prince Lexington? What does he want with the king?"

"We don't know, Your Highness. He won't talk to us. He looks near death, and a horse was found dead just beyond the palace gates. It looked as if it had run itself into exhaustion. We have the man in the kitchens, trying to get him to eat something but he refuses food until he sees the king. Until your parents return from Verlot, you're as close as he's going to get."

He was right. My mother and father had taken a visit to Verlot—likely planning a hideous wedding in anticipation of my brother's return—and weren't expected back for another week. "You really think he's serious?"

"He could very well be a madman, Your Highness, but we must be certain before we dismiss him. He mentioned Prince Teryn and danger, but no one could understand what he was saying."

"Take me to him." I followed the guard down to the kitchens. Once there, the commotion was obvious. Near one of the cook fires, gathered a congregation of guards and kitchen staff, all huddled around a man in a chair. I pushed my way through and found a pale, chubby man with disheveled hair and filthy clothes.

I looked him over, raising an eyebrow. Was this man truly Prince Lexington? Considering I'd been banished from the spring festival, I had no frame of reference for what he was supposed to look like. He certainly didn't have the composure or cleanliness of a prince. However, if he was Prince Lexington...what could have brought him to this wretched state seeking the king?

"Prince Lexington?" I shook him by the shoulder. His eyes slowly fluttered open, and he mumbled something inaudible. "Speak up. I can't understand a word you say."

"Call. Me. Lex," he finally gasped.

"Fine. Lex," I said, trying not to sound irritated. "What are you doing here? Why do you need to see the king?"

"Message. For the king."

"The king is visiting Verlot. You will have to speak to me."

Lex bolted upright in his seat, eyes opening wide as some color began to rise in his cheeks. "Yes, let's go there. I can tell him. King Verdian too..." Just as quickly as he'd risen, he sank back down, eyes rolling and eyelids fluttering.

"Please, Lex. I am Prince Larylis, you can trust me. Tell me what you are here to say. If it is as important as you claim, I will take the news to Verlot myself."

Lex seemed to relax a bit. "Teryn. He's in trouble."

I swallowed the sudden dryness in my throat and forced my voice to remain calm. "What happened to my brother?"

"He's...been captured. By a...sorcerer. By the next new moon...war."

"War? What do you mean *by the next new moon, war*?" My stomach churned as I repeated the words, my mind reeling to comprehend what he could possibly mean. And what did he mean about a sorcerer? Perhaps he truly was a madman. "Are you playing some game here? How do I know you truly are Prince Lexington? And if you are, how am I supposed to believe the words of a man competing against my brother in the Quest?"

Again, Lex's eyes shot open, and he stood with more force than I thought he had in him. He fixed me with a glower. "You must listen to me! Teryn is going to die if you don't help him. Morkai has taken rule over Kero. He's going to kill Teryn unless King Arlous surrenders to him. We must do something! He's my friend."

The ferocity in his eyes frightened me, but his words

made no sense. "Since when are you friends with my brother? How can I believe you even *know* him?"

Lex sat back down, his energy draining again. He slumped to his side, rubbing his brow as he struggled to maintain consciousness. "We made a secret alliance." His voice was again quiet and strained. "With Helios. Things got out of hand. Helios is dead. I know it sounds crazy, but you must believe me. We need to tell the king. Teryn is in danger. Lela is in danger."

I nodded. I wasn't sure how much I believed, but I couldn't risk dismissing him if he was telling the truth. "Eat up and regain your strength. As soon as you are rested, we are going to Verlot, and you will tell my father everything you know."

Lex relaxed, and his eyes darted toward the nearest plate of food. It was barely in his hands before he began devouring its contents at a rate I never thought possible.

I shuddered, his warning echoing in my mind. I hoped beyond hope that what he said was not true. But why else come all this way? Why else nearly starve himself? *Lela, help us all if he isn't simply a madman.*

23

DARK WORDS

Larylis

I felt like I was going to retch. I shivered with an inner chill, yet my body was sweating buckets. I gripped the arms of my chair to keep myself still. *Air. I need air. I need to get out of here.*

I could no longer hear Lex's words as he stood at the center of the Verlot's great hall, a small audience of shocked faces surrounding him while he relayed the grim details of his encounter with the sorcerer, Morkai. Lex had already told me everything on our way to Verlot. There were many times during his story that I was close to turning back to Dermaine and dismissing him as a treacherous liar, but each time he assured me with a cold certainty that he was telling the truth.

I thought I could handle hearing Lex's message one more time with grace and calm, but I was wrong. This time I listened without apprehension, without the comfort of second-guessing his words as false. He repeated the same message he had said to me, word for word, then went on to describe Morkai, his control over Ridine Castle and all of Kero, his dark magic, his terrible Beast, his Royal Force, and his ferocious wraiths.

Morkai's ultimatum echoed over and over in my head, *Surrender or Teryn dies.* There was no way to win. There was no way out. We were going to have to surrender Mena to the rule of a crazed and powerful sorcerer. Or I was going to lose my brother. Could we really make that choice? Would my father make that choice?

My eyes flashed to my father, who sat still as stone with the most fearsome expression I had ever seen, matched only by the look King Verdian wore. The two kings urged Lex on, probing him for every detail that he could remember. I admired my father more than ever for his strength in the face of danger and wished I could be half the man that he was.

My mother squeezed my hand from her seat between me and my father. She was usually so composed; it was hard to see her in such a disheveled state. Her graying, sandy brown curls fell in stray tendrils around her anguished face, and her brown eyes were rimmed with red. I tried to force a comforting smile, but she wouldn't even meet my eyes as she sat quivering, sobbing silently into her handkerchief and flinching at every dark detail she heard. I wished she didn't have to hear any of this, but it was her choice. She demanded to be present.

When Lex and I had arrived at Verlot the morning before, Lex immediately sought my father and quickly delivered his message. My father was as apprehensive to believe such an outrageous claim as I had been, but after convincing him that I thought there was at least some truth to Lex's words, Arlous decided to give Lex a formal council meeting the next day to explain the details. My father's councilmen had been summoned for their hasty attendance by way of the fastest messenger horses, and by the looks on their faces, they hadn't had a moment to spare for sleep or rest.

In fact, the only person who appeared to be unaffected by the news was Queen Helena. She maintained a perfect calm as she sat tall and proud, her face blank and emotionless. It was clear whom Mareleau had gotten her constant air of indifference from. *Queen Helena must be even more callous than her wicked daughter*. But, upon a further look, I saw a subtle light catch her cheeks where tears slowly streamed. I blinked my own eyes dry and rested them on an empty seat next to the queen, which I assumed had been reserved for Mareleau. *Spoiled girl couldn't even trouble herself with the affairs of her kingdom*.

I looked to the middle of the floor, realizing Lex had stopped speaking and was now seated. His message had been delivered, and the kings had run out of questions. A long and painful silence followed.

"What are we going to do?" my father asked, his voice deep and strong.

"We have to get my boy back," my mother cried. "We cannot let him die!"

"And we are not going to surrender!" King Verdian pounded his fist on the arm of his chair.

"Then we bargain." Father released a heavy sigh and rubbed his temples. He rose and stood at the center of the floor. "We will take our forces to Centerpointe Rock. I will face Morkai and offer him whatever I can. He's a sorcerer, he can't possibly want only land. We'll offer him money, title, whatever we can bargain with. And when we have him where we want him, we will kill him."

A rumble of agreement came from the councilmen.

"And if he doesn't want to bargain?" King Verdian said.

Arlous' chest rose and fell as he took a slow, deep breath. "Then I will demand he take me in place of Teryn."

My mother cried out in anguish while I stood, my hands shaking. "No, father, you cannot give your life to that sorcerer! Trade my life instead!"

"No, my son."

"You are king, and Teryn is crown prince. Mena needs you both," I said.

"I said no."

"But I am expendable."

"No!" My father's shout and fierce glare silenced me and put me back in my chair. He walked up to me, his features softening as tears glazed his eyes. "You are not expendable," he said quietly. "You are my son, and you are important to me and your mother. You are important to our kingdom. You may not be crown prince, but you are next in line. Our legacy will live through the lives of your children."

I swallowed a lump in my throat and lowered my head under his caring gaze.

Father walked back to the middle of the room. "Teryn is crown prince and we need him alive. If Morkai will not bargain, I will convince him to take me in Teryn's stead, but I will not give him my life without a fight. He must be convinced to keep me prisoner, and we will agree to war. In the chaos of battle, I will escape. We will have men assigned to the task of freeing me. There is a chance that I will be killed, but it is a chance I am willing to take. We will not surrender to this madman. We will fight him to the death."

My head was spinning. I wanted to argue, but I could think of no other plan. What else could we do? I looked to Father's wide-eyed councilmen, waiting for them to speak up and talk him out of such a foolish plan, but they were clearly as dumbfounded as I was. I put my head in my shaking hands, realizing we were all doomed. In less than one month, I was going to lose my brother or my father. Maybe both. Maybe I would lose my own life.

"You know you have Sele's support," King Verdian said. "This is an attack on us as well. We will organize our forces immediately."

A rumbling of voices followed as plans were further discussed and messengers dispatched. Through the din, an unexpected voice stood out, saying, "I'll go to my father."

The rumbling subsided as all eyes turned to Lex. "You need more support than you have. I'll convince my father to join Tomas' army with yours."

"And what about Norun?" King Verdian said. "Their son was killed by this sorcerer's Beast. We should ally with them as well."

King Arlous nodded. "We will send a message to Norun. Lex will go to Tomas by messenger horse. Let us hope they believe us."

"I'll go with Lex in support." I heard the words spill from my mouth, surprised it was I who said them. All I knew was that I couldn't sit idle in preparation for my father to sacrifice himself. I needed to get out. "I'll represent Mena and confirm Lex's story. The messenger sent to Norun can report to me in Tomas. If Norun is open to our alliance, I can meet with them as well."

"Don't expect much from Norun," Lex said. "But your presence might help convince my father."

I looked to my father to gauge his response. He considered me for a moment, head cocked slightly to the side. I held my breath as I waited for his expression to turn to disapproval. However, his eyes twinkled, and his lips twitched with the smallest of smiles. "I'll allow it, Larylis. You may accompany Lex to Tomas."

With that, the kings returned to discussions with the council, the two queens linked arms and dismissed themselves from the room, and Lex sat pondering silently. With no eyes on me, I took the opportunity to slip behind a tapestry and out one of the hidden doors into a dark hallway. I closed my eyes and pressed my back to the cold, stone wall behind me. *War. We are going to war.* I wished so badly that I would wake and find I was only dreaming.

A soft sound startled me. My eyes shot open, and I looked across the hall where a female silhouette stood in the shadows of the opposite wall. She stepped forward into the dim light of the singular lamp lighting the hall. My heart stopped. It was Mareleau.

My tongue felt heavy as I sorted out what to say to her. Compliments I had always yearned to give her came to mind, and I nearly succeeded at delivering one before I reminded myself that I did not love her anymore. This was not my beloved, carefree childhood sweetheart—this was the selfish, cold, spoiled ice princess.

"You're a little late. The meeting's over," I finally said, trying to appear aloof.

"I know. I heard everything." Her voice was barely above a whisper. Her hands were behind her back as she took another step toward me, her face unreadable as she eyed me with piercing intensity.

I had to avert my gaze to keep my eyes from taking her in. Instead, I looked down the dark, damp, windowless hallway. "What are you doing here? Aren't these the servants' halls?"

"I could ask the same of you." She took another few steps forward.

My eyes locked on hers and my mouth opened to respond but I remained speechless. *Damn this woman. How does she still manage to make me feel so foolish?*

"You obviously remember these halls from when we were little. Do you remember how we used to hide in them?"

"Yes, I remember. I'm surprised *you* do." I hoped my words sounded as sharp to her as I'd honed them to be.

Mareleau ignored my comment. "You were brave in there." Her voice lacked all emotion as she leaned against the wall next to me. "To offer yourself in your brother's stead. You must fear for him greatly. And for your father."

"Don't you fear for him? For my brother, I mean?"

Mareleau was silent a moment. "We are to be married," she said flatly.

"Oh?" I shrugged as if I were indifferent to the news. But who was I fooling? My heart sank into my gut.

"As soon as you and Prince Lexington arrived here with a rumor that Teryn was in trouble, my father blamed me and my Quest. And that was before he learned all the details of the coming war. He is done letting me choose my husband. I will be forced to marry Teryn, like it or not. If he survives the battle, I should say." Her voice held not even a hint of concern for my brother, and her tone implied she found *herself* to be the victim.

"I imagine you are happy, then?"

She turned her head and slowly met my eyes. "Not really, no."

Heat rose to my face as I felt my shoulders grow tense. "You have finally found the man who would go out of his way to win your heart, and you are not happy? My brother may not have completed the Quest, but I'm sure he would have if he hadn't been captured by a sorcerer! Can you not see his devotion? Do you not care that he is risking his life for you? He might be killed because of you!"

Her eyes widened slightly at my sudden outburst, but the rest of her face remained passive. "I know."

My hands turned to fists at my side. "Prince Lex nearly exhausted himself to death delivering the message to us. And Prince Helios is dead! And you don't even care?"

Mareleau shrugged. "I feel bad for them, I guess. I'm afraid for the war. But I never knew these men, save for your brother. I never asked them to put themselves in danger. It was their choice to be so stupid—"

"Are you serious? You sent them on the Quest!"

"I didn't ask them to...I didn't want..." Her mouth hung open, but no more sound would come forth. It was the first time I'd ever seen Mareleau at a loss for words.

I clenched my teeth. "How many people have to die

before you realize how selfish you are? When will you quit torturing others with your carelessness?"

"Larylis—"

"Oh, so now you know my name? All these years I've been in love with you, and you've pretended not to remember me. Then you chose my brother. And now not even he's good enough for you? Will no man ever be good enough for you?"

"It's not that..."

"Then what? Why do you treat men in such a way? Why are you such a heartless bitch?"

"How dare you speak to me like that!" Mareleau's eyes went wide, her anger matching my own. "You don't know anything about what I've been through!"

"What *you've* been through? What could you possibly have experienced that is worse than what Teryn is going through now? He's going through all of this because of you, and all you can think of is yourself."

"I don't love him, Larylis."

"That much is obvious. I don't think that's an emotion you're capable of."

"I love *you*, you fool!" The words erupted in such haste, I could barely understand them, much less believe them. She took a step back, bringing her hand to her lips as if she too couldn't believe the words she had just spoken.

I couldn't breathe. My heart pounded so hard that my chest hurt. My legs shook. A rush of conflicting emotions seared through me. I had to close my eyes to steady my spinning head.

She said she loved me. I had waited so long to hear those words. My heart threatened to melt as I pictured myself sweeping her up in my arms and covering her with kisses, the way I'd always imagined. Then I remembered my brother. She was now betrothed to him. More importantly, I remembered how she had treated me all those years. How she tortured and ignored me. I remembered the letter she sent me. *All you need to know is that I can't love you.*

No. If she loved me, she could have had me long ago. She chose Teryn.

I steadied my resolve, opened my eyes and met hers. "Am I to hear you right? That you love me? And I am a fool for it? Even in your expressions of love, you manage to be insulting."

"Insulting? It is you who insulted me first!"

"I insulted *you* first? Shall we go back, then? To all the times you've ignored me? All the times you acted like you didn't know me? How about to the time so very recently when you demanded I be taken away from your pathetic poetry competition?"

"Please," Mareleau said, her eyes filling with tears. "You must let me explain."

I so badly wanted to hear an explanation, to hear the words that would justify all the pains of my past and give me what I had always wanted. But what good would that do, given the smallest chance it could be true?

"You don't love me." My voice sounded rough, distant, as if it wasn't my own.

Mareleau lowered her head and let out a heavy sob.

"This is another one of your games, isn't it?"

"No!" She lifted her face, twisted with distress as she looked at me through tear-filled eyes. She was doing an excellent job at pretending. "I swear it's true. I do love you!" She reached a hand toward my shoulder

I stepped away from her. "Your games would have worked on me before, but I know who you are now. You are wicked. You will do whatever it takes to make every man go crazy over you. But you are too late for me. You belong to my brother now."

"Just let me explain!"

"What is there to explain? You have treated me like the lowest of beings. There is nothing you could say to make me believe you somehow loved me. You had your chance with me long ago, and you tortured me instead and played with my heart like it was nothing more than filth under your shoe. You might as well have ripped it right out with your bare hands!"

"Larylis, please." Again, she tried reaching for me, but paused with her hand midway between us. Her tear-filled eyes turned hard as she put her hands on her hips. "I command you to stay and listen to me!"

"You don't command me, Mareleau. You have no command over me or my heart. Not anymore." I paused for only a moment, knowing that turning away from her would feel like ripping the flesh from my bones. I took one last look at her, then ran until I could no longer hear her pleading cries.

24

POWER

Cora

I awoke with a gasp as ice-cold water covered my face. I came to my feet, heart pounding as I backed against the wall of my cell, blinking into the dim light as two figures entered.

One leaned against the cell doorway, arms crossed and snickering—Orin, Morkai's little servant-boy. I wanted nothing more than to claw the smirk off his face. "That water was sent for you to bathe." He tossed an empty wash basin at my feet. "Enjoy your bath?"

I scowled as the second figure came to me and began brushing straw debris from my gown. My face softened when I recognized her as the woman who had helped me dress in my room days before. She handed me a cloth, which I took to my face.

This was the first time I'd been offered anything close to a bath, so I eagerly took advantage of the small plea-sure of wiping down my skin. In the five days since I'd been put in the cell, I'd had contact only with the few guards who brought my meager meals, and Teryn. Teryn and I had managed to have a few hushed conversations, which always ended with a guard stomping by and demanding our silence. This sudden offer of cleanliness, while welcome, made me suspicious.

"What's this all about?" I tossed the now-filthy rag at Orin.

"Morkai demands your presence, and he demanded you be clean first. Although, I can't see why he'd bother. Dress you in a gown. Clean you up. You're still ugly."

I ignored him, swallowing my self-consciousness as the woman re-tightened the laces of my gown. Then she brushed my hair, smoothing it down my back.

"Come." Orin grabbed my wrist. "If you struggle, I'll kill you." With his other hand, he tapped the hilt of his dagger. I obeyed and let him lead me out of the cell.

"Cora?" Teryn ran to the door of his cell as we passed him. "Where is he taking you?"

"That's none of your business," Orin said.

"I'm fine, Teryn." I forced my mouth into a weak smile.

"Don't hurt her!" Teryn shouted as Orin dragged me further down the hall.

Orin led me down a familiar path through the castle and out onto the charred, black field of the former gardens once again. Morkai stood in the same place I'd last seen him, his back facing me. The stars shone above. I'd lost my sense of time, but I guessed it was late in the evening.

"Coralaine!" Morkai turned and greeted me with a sickening smile. "Leave us," he said to Orin, who quickly obeyed, receding into the shadows outlining the field.

"What do you want, Morkai?" I kept my breathing steady, my face passive. Only my racing heart could have betrayed my calm exterior.

"I wanted to show you some things so you could have the opportunity to see my power before you truly decide to stand against me."

"There's nothing you could show me to convince me to join you. You're a fool for even considering it."

Morkai's eyes narrowed but his smile remained. "No, Coralaine. You're a fool to doubt me. You're a fool to even question me."

"And you're a fool for keeping me alive. Why is that again? Because you respect my magic?" I let out a small laugh. "I still don't believe that's the only reason."

Morkai considered me as he rubbed the purple crystal at the top of his staff hanging at his waist. "All in good time," he said quietly, almost as if he was saying it to himself. "You'll see. I have a purpose for you. I'm willing to be patient this time."

I balled my hands into fists, wishing so badly I could access the Arts and find some power within me to use against him. But in the time I'd been at Ridine, I'd felt a blockage between me and my power. I couldn't disappear into the walls of my cell. I couldn't slip through the bars. I couldn't tap into the minds of the guards. I was helpless.

Morkai seemed to forget me as he turned back toward the field and raised his staff. I felt a chill as the rubies on the staff began to glow, and before long, the ground began to rumble. I didn't have to guess what was coming. It was the Roizan.

The Roizan plodded through the field, halting in front of Morkai. Its open mouth panted as its enormous, red chest heaved. It pawed at the ground, seeming agitated. Morkai held out a hand, and the Roizan seemed to calm. It brought its gigantic snout to Morkai's hand until they were touching. Both were still a few moments.

My breathing became shallow, and I wished I could be invisible. I knew the Roizan had a bloodthirsty attraction to unicorns alone, but I didn't know what to expect with it under Morkai's direct command.

Morkai stepped away from the Roizan and turned toward me. The Roizan plodded over to a spot of charred land and lay down, curling up in a crude imitation of a sleeping pet. "You remember my Roizan. Now, let me show you what we can do. What would you like to see? What is your favorite room in Ridine Castle? The dungeon?"

Morkai turned toward the castle and reached a hand toward the base. I felt a rumbling beneath my feet that seemed to be coming from the castle itself. The sound of stone grinding stone shattered the air as the foundation began to shake.

"No!" My first thought was of Teryn. I couldn't help but imagine his terror as stone crumbled around him. "Stop, Morkai!"

Morkai lowered his hand, smirking as he met my eyes. "You're right, I need the dungeon. And I suppose I need the prince alive as well. How about that tower? Do you like it? Or could it use a bit of remodeling?"

I raised my head to look at the lowest tower, unable to remember where within Ridine it was. Before I could contemplate it further, the castle again began to shake. Morkai raised his hand and stones began to crumble from the tower, falling against the castle walls and crashing to the ground below. I stepped back from the sharp debris that rained down to the ground before us. Morkai let out a jubilant laugh as, piece by piece, the tower crumbled until it was nothing but a pile of crushed stone.

"What was the point of that?" I rounded on Morkai. "So, you can destroy the castle you call home. What good is that doing you?"

"Power, Cora. You fail to see the power."

"I see the power. It is a power you don't deserve. A power you have no right to. You have no right to destroy *my* home. To enslave *my* people. To hurt *my* friends. You have no right to rule Lela!"

"I do have a right." Morkai's eyes bulged as he brought his face close to mine. "My blood is the blood of the Ancient Ones. My blood is the blood of the rightful King of Magic. The rule is mine by right, and I will reclaim it."

I refused to falter under his glare. "If you really believed that, you wouldn't have gone through all the trouble of inheriting the crown from my brother and trying to convince me to be your queen. If you were the rightful heir of the land, the magic would know, wouldn't it?"

Morkai stood tall, backing a few slow steps away from me. "There's nothing wrong with being too careful. I am now the rightful heir by rule of magic, blood, and succession." His face looked confident, but I could sense a flicker of doubt. "Moving on."

Morkai turned back toward the field and again raised his staff. This time, the wraiths returned, filling the field with their slow, transparent bodies. With a mumbled incantation from Morkai, the wraiths stood at attention.

"Attack!" Morkai shouted, planting his staggered feet as he faced the horde of wraiths racing toward him.

I watched with confusion as the wraiths neared Morkai, hoping that somehow his plan had gone wrong and he'd accidentally brought their wrath upon himself.

However, it was no accident. Morkai raised his palms toward the oncoming horde. As he thrust his arms toward the wraiths, an invisible force sent the entire mass reeling back.

The wraiths fell, still and defeated. Dead.

It was moments before they got back up and returned to their original positions. Again, Morkai demanded their attack, and again they were defeated in one swift motion. Again. Then again.

My mouth felt dry as I imagined his power being used on mortal beings. Beings who would die once and never get back up again. Beings who had no defense against such a power.

Once Morkai seemed to grow bored of the demonstration, he sent the wraiths away and returned his attention to me. "You see? There is no fighting me."

"No matter how much power you have, we will still fight. The kingdoms of Lela will fight you. I will fight you. You may be able to kill an entire army of wraiths at once, but you are no match for Lela's fighters." I wasn't sure how much I believed my own words, but I couldn't give in to the fear that threatened to unhinge me.

Morkai's sickening grin spread over his entire face. "Orin," he called, without taking his eyes from mine.

Orin stepped out of the shadows and came to Morkai's side. "Yes, master."

Morkai faced him, placing his hands on his shoulders. "You have been very obedient. Do you wish to serve me to the end?"

"Yes. You will teach me your power."

"Of course." Morkai looked down at Orin indulgently.

The two stood still, eyes locked for a few quiet moments. Orin began to tremble, subtly at first, as if he was simply nervous or excited. Then his eyes began to roll, and his entire body became racked with convulsions. Just when I thought he would fall from the force of his body's jagged motion, he went rigid, eyes wide as blood trickled from his nose. Morkai lifted his hands away from Orin's shoulders, and the boy crumpled to the ground in a lifeless heap.

I stared at the body at Morkai's feet. "Why?"

Morkai laughed. "Don't tell me you feel bad for the boy!"

"I don't. It was just...senseless."

"No, Coralaine. It was to give you a sense of my power. I can destroy an entire group of fighters in one motion. I can kill a living being within moments by my touch alone."

"Are you trying to intimidate me? This doesn't change a thing. I will never follow you."

Morkai stepped toward me and reached his hands toward my shoulders. I sprang back, and his hands grasped only air. He came toward me again, and I felt a fire ignite within me. Every fiber of my being burned with it, flowed with it. It coursed through my blood and my veins. My mind felt suddenly clear, as if the fire had burnt all fear and hesitation from it.

"No!" The fire erupted in the form of a shout. My palms struck Morkai's chest, sending him reeling backward as if I'd struck him with the force of a galloping horse.

Morkai quickly recovered his footing and looked at me with the closest thing to fear that I'd ever seen in his eyes. His face twisted with rage as he reached his hand toward me. He wasn't near enough to touch me, yet I felt his grasp. I felt it in my throat as I struggled to breathe. The air escaped my lungs. My gut wrenched as if I had been punched. My eyes closed as I struggled to find consciousness through the agony of my mind.

I felt the ground shake below me and heard Morkai shout as his hold on me released. Gasping for breath, I took in the scene before me—the Roizan was pounding off toward the line of trees as Morkai stared after him with his mouth open.

"It's your damn unicorn, isn't it?"

Valorre! The thought brought me both terror and elation. I hadn't any clue what had happened to him or the horses after I'd been captured by Morkai. Teryn couldn't tell me anything of use, as all he remembered was that Valorre disappeared before he and Lex were captured. I was happy to think of Valorre alive and well, but terrified to think of him drawing attention from the Roizan.

"Get her to the dungeons!" Morkai shouted.

Teryn

I heard the dungeon door creak open and ran to the bars of my cell door, hoping it was Cora returning unharmed.

The sound of feet approached, followed by shouting. "Get back here," I heard a male voice call.

Cora appeared outside my cell, wrapping her hands around the bars as she pressed herself against my door. "You're safe." She was nearly breathless. "I was worried. Did you feel the shaking?"

The brief shaking of the dungeon walls was the last thing on my mind as I saw the frantic look in Cora's eye and what appeared to be bruising around her neck. "What did he do to you?"

"I told you not to run," the guard said, catching Cora by the elbow. I recognized him as the man I'd heard Cora refer to as her brother. Since that first day Cora had been brought past my cell and into her own, Dimetreus had returned only to alternate keeping watch with the other guards. He seemed to have no tender feelings for his sister at all.

"Dimetreus!" I shouted, as he roughly pulled her away from my door.

Dimetreus cocked his head as his eyes met mine, as if he wasn't sure the name I'd called was his.

"Do you see those marks on her neck? Did you do that or did he?"

Dimetreus looked at Cora as if he were seeing her for the first time. He shrugged. "Morkai. He can do what he wants with her. She's bad. He told me not to trust her."

"But he didn't tell you not to trust me. She's your sister. You should be protecting her."

Dimetreus stared blankly at me in response.

"It's no use, Teryn." Cora glowered at her brother. "He's not in there. Dimi is gone."

Dimetreus pulled Cora away from view. I heard the door to her cell open.

"She is your sister!" I yelled, even though I knew it was useless. "You have to believe me. She needs your help and your protection! Do you want him to kill her?"

I heard Cora's door slam shut. A moment later, Dimetreus struck the bars of my cell, and I jumped back from his angry glare. "I don't have to believe anyone." He left with a sneer and stomped off out of sight.

25

CONFESSION

Mareleau

I sat in the dark room, lit only by the flames of a dying fire. My eyes darted toward the door again and again as I sat huddled for warmth amongst the cushions of the couch. Anxious moments passed, hours perhaps. But I would not budge. I would wait. I would rather freeze than be ignored.

Footsteps approached the door, followed by fumbling of the handle. I took a deep breath and straightened myself, chest, shoulders, and head held high.

Larylis entered the room, his footing unsteady.

I stood. "Hello, Larylis."

Larylis jumped. I could see him blinking into the light, searching for my face. I stepped closer to the fire. Larylis remained where he was.

"What are you doing here?" he asked after a pause.

"Waiting for you."

"Why? How did you get in here?"

I looked behind me at a tapestry at the far end of the wall. "Back door. Servants' hall. This is *my* castle, you know."

Larylis walked toward me with uneven steps. I held my breath as he stood before me on the other side of the hearth. His eyes met mine for a moment before he turned toward the hearth, grabbed the fire iron, and began stoking the meager flames with more force than necessary. "You didn't answer *why*."

"I need you to let me explain." I hoped he hadn't heard the slight tremble that accompanied my words. "I don't want things to end the way they did. For you to go to war and never know..." I swallowed a lump in my throat. I could have done it for dramatic effect, like I'd done many other times to get my way, but this time it was real. This time, I fought back tears that stung my eyes like a thousand angry bees.

He let out a sigh that ended in a grumble, dropped the fire iron with a clatter, and went to the desk to pour a goblet of wine. I wondered how much he'd already drank that night. He looked at me and raised a second goblet inquiringly.

"No, thank you. This conversation is important to me. *I'd* prefer to remember it in the morning."

Larylis narrowed his eyes at me, then slammed the goblet on the desk. "Fine. Let's have a conversation to remember." He filled the new goblet from a pitcher of water and drank from it deeply. Leaving the wine behind, he walked back toward the hearth and took a seat across from me.

I watched him, waiting for him to meet my eyes. He looked everywhere but at me.

"Go on. Tell me all about your love for me." Larylis rolled his eyes, then settled his gaze on the fire.

"I do love you, Larylis. Even when you make it difficult to do so."

Larylis shook his head and took another drink of water.

"I've always loved you." I felt my cheeks get warm. I wasn't used to this sort of conversation. It was a wonder I'd managed to say as much as I already had. "First, it was the love of a friend, a playmate. I loved you as my favorite companion with the innocence only a child can have. Over time it developed into more. I hardly realized it until the day you were taken from me.

"I was twelve. My father called me into a council meeting to discuss my future marriage prospects, which was a great honor for me, being not only a woman, but also a child. It meant my father respected me and deemed me mature enough to discuss political matters amongst his councilmen. But things went far from expected.

"It wasn't a meeting to discuss prospects with me. My husband had already been chosen. The meeting was a charade to make me feel important, and even at twelve that was obvious to me. It was still an honor to be blessed with such a charade, but I didn't see it that way at the time.

"A contract was placed before me with the name of your brother written next to mine. I erupted with the fury of my adolescence, my innocence, my feelings of being betrayed by my father, and my need to protect myself all culminating in my declaration that I would never marry.

"Father's fury matched my own. My two uncles, the most respected men of the council, looked at me with disgust. Little did I understand at the time, I had shown weakness in front of the very men who could take my throne, should I prove to be unworthy.

"My father quickly yelled me into submission and assured me I would marry. My rage turned to fear and pain. I cried, begging him to let me marry you instead. Before I realized what I was saying, I blurted out that I loved you. It was the truth.

"Again, I met my father's rage and the disdain of my uncles. 'The runt? She wants to marry the runt prince?' they taunted. They didn't see you the way I saw you, as who you really were. They only remembered you as the second, sickly son. It didn't matter that they were wrong. What mattered was that, again, I had shown weakness in their eyes.

"I was banished from the council with every admonition that I, a spoiled child, would not get her way. I would marry Teryn, like it or not."

I paused, watching Larylis as he considered the fire in silence for countless moments, eyes slightly out of focus. Finally, he spoke. "Teryn never told me you were promised as children."

"I doubt he ever knew. I didn't let it get very far."

Larylis set down his goblet and leaned forward with his hands on his knees, now fully looking at me. His face was full of question.

I continued my confession. "I may have been youthful, brash, and angry, but I knew enough to calm my emotions and redirect my motive. I knew I had to use my strengths and appeal to my father's love of power if I were to turn the situation around in my favor.

"After days had passed and we'd both cleared our heads, I approached my father, apologizing for my behavior with all the grace and maturity I could muster. I asked for a second chance to discuss my marriage prospects, telling him I'd thought it over and was ready to let go of my childish ways.

"He agreed, although I wasn't allowed back on the council. We spoke alone. I told him I would marry, but not Teryn. Wealth, power, and influence were now my aims. I convinced him Sele wouldn't benefit from a marriage with a kingdom we were already allied with. A wealthy prince from a powerful kingdom would surely solidify Sele's position.

"My father was intrigued and agreed to open my prospects. While I was saddened that I would never be with the one I truly loved, there was a naive part of me that thought I might be content if I married a man who could provide me wealth and freedom.

"But wealthy men have greedy hearts and greedy hands. I was engaged to one man after the other and was repulsed by each one. They spouted their undying love for me. Me! A child, a stranger. Some made promises. Others made advances." I crossed my arms, hugging them tightly over my chest at the memories. "I saw through their loving exteriors to the lustful beasts within. Again, I decided no marriage would suit me. I grew disenchanted with love all together. Love had lost me the respect of my father and his council. Love had brought me heartache. Love had gotten me pawed over by strangers.

"Years went by as I destroyed every engagement I had, yet men still pursued me. My parents were confounded. I finally held the power. When I could see my parents were growing desperate, I changed my motive yet again. I insisted I must marry for love, for only love could bring my engagements to fruition. Neither knew the meaning of the word, so my idea for the poetry contest and Quest seemed a likely solution.

"All the while, I have continued to love you. Since I couldn't be with you, I would be alone for as long as possible. Yes, I'm selfish. Yes, I've been cruel. To you, to your brother, to every man. I've made a mess of things, I know. But it was the best I could do for myself."

Larylis put his head in his hands, running his fingers through his hair. "Why didn't you tell me long ago?"

"What would have been the point? There was nothing to do about it. Besides, I knew if I told you, you'd try to do something heroic. And that would have failed. You'd pine for me always, knowing I loved you. You'd never move on."

"I pined for you anyway! Tell me, what's the point now?"

"I don't know, Lare." I let out a sigh. "I don't always think things through. I just knew I couldn't bear it if you died in battle thinking ill of me, never knowing—"

"So, that is what it all comes down to?" Larylis sprang to his feet, throwing his hands in the air. "This is all about you. How *you* would feel if I took ill thoughts of you to my grave. Not because you can't stand to be without me. Not because your love is so strong you can no longer hide it."

"You expect too much of me!" I stood, placing my

hands on my hips. We were nearly eye-to-eye. "*You're* the one with the dramatic declarations of love, not me. I'm not controlled by my emotions, I survive them and create the best situation for myself in any given moment. You let your passions eat you alive and then blame your circumstances on your unfair lot in life."

Larylis opened his mouth to argue but no sound came out.

"I love you, Lare." My voice softened. I look a step toward him, fighting the urge to place a hand on his chest. "I love you and your passionate fire. I love your stubbornness. I love you in all your melancholy. You've hardly changed a day since you were young. But I have. I'm not the same little girl I was. And I'm not even close to the girl of your imagination whom you *think* you love."

"What do you mean *think*? I *know* I love you." Larylis' voice was quiet, strained.

"You hardly even know the real me. What's my favorite color?"

"Pink. It's always been pink."

"No, it isn't. It's a deep crimson red. You see? You still think of me as my child self."

"Are you saying my love for you isn't true? Where does that leave us? What are we to do about any of this?"

"I don't know. I told you, I don't always think things through. With our kingdoms going to war, we don't know what the future holds. I want to love you in whatever time I have. And if you'd like to take the time to know the *real* me, I'd like you to love me back."

"You're promised to my brother."

Our eyes were locked. We were so close I could see his chest heaving and feel his breath on my face. I slowly reached my hand to his cheek. "I know you love him, Lare. But think about it. If you decide you'd finally like to claim something you want, you know where to find me."

I turned to leave. Fingertips encircled my wrist, catching me mid step. Larylis gently pulled me toward him until we were again face to face. He placed a finger beneath my chin and brought our lips to meet.

26

APOLOGY

Cora

"Teryn," I whispered. "Are you awake?"

I heard rustling down the hall, followed by Teryn's hushed voice. "Yes."

I pressed my face to the bars of my door, making sure the guard was still nowhere to be seen. The guard had stopped his pacing some time ago, and although I couldn't see him, it was safe to assume he had fallen asleep.

"We have to get out of here," I said. "Valorre is out there. I think he's waiting for me."

"How do you know?"

"I saw the Beast—the Roizan—tonight. Or...last night. He ran off, chasing something. Morkai said it must be Valorre, and I know he's right. I can feel Valorre's presence."

"The two of you really have a special bond, don't you?" Teryn said.

"Yes."

Teryn was silent a moment. "Can I ask you something, Cora?"

I felt a little uneasy at the hesitance in his voice. "Of course."

"Remember that time you disappeared when we saw the—what did you call it?"

"The Roizan. That's what Morkai calls it."

"Roizan," Teryn echoed. "Lex called you a witch, and you told us you can protect yourself. Was he right? Can you really do magic?"

I couldn't help but laugh, despite the pit in my stomach. "I wouldn't call myself a witch or say I *do* magic, but I am practiced in the Arts. Most of the Forest People are. I'm sorry I never told you. It took me some time to trust you. I didn't know how you would react."

"But now that I've seen what I have..."

"Yes, now I think you can handle it."

"You also never told me you were Princess of Kero. That you're Princess Coralaine."

I felt my stomach sink even further than it already had. Through the chaos of the past few days, I hadn't realized I'd left Teryn to discover the truth on his own, never explaining myself or what had happened. "I'm so sorry Teryn. I didn't realize..."

"I'm not upset, Cora. I was surprised and confused, but it didn't take long for me to put the pieces together. With everything this sorcerer has done here, it's easy to see why you've been hiding your identity. If you still don't feel comfortable talking about it, I'll respect that. I just wanted you to know I understand."

"I'll tell you everything," I said in a rush. As soon as

the words left my mouth, I felt relief. I was filled with an urgency to free myself of the truths I'd held inside for so long. And I did. I told him everything, from the deaths of my family, to my exile, and to meeting the Forest People. I told him about my power, about the Arts.

Teryn listened quietly, asking a few questions here and there, but never judging, never admonishing. "So, you're basically saying you *can* do magic." The laughter in his voice made me smile. "Is this the part where you use your powers to break us out of here?"

"I wish I could. Morkai has been blocking my power somehow, but—" I paused, remembering the internal fire that had surged through me when I unknowingly attacked Morkai. Perhaps I was somehow regaining access to the Arts. "It wouldn't hurt to try again."

I took a deep breath and cleared my mind. Closing my eyes, I focused on the feeling of the cold bars beneath my palms. I thought of the energy flowing through them, until their composition unraveled in my mind's eye into something malleable. I gently pulled the bars toward me.

The door swung open.

I stared at the open gap, mouth hanging wide. "It...opened."

"What? You used your power?"

"I...I don't even know if it was me. It was almost too easy." My heart pounded in my chest as I faced the unbelievable prospect of freedom.

"What are you waiting for, Cora? If the door is open, get out!"

His voice propelled me forward, and I ran to his cell, looking left and right for any sign of the guard. "I have to get you out of here too."

"No."

"I'm not leaving you." My hands shook as I fumbled with the lock, trying to calm my mind. I was overcome with the prickling fear that—at any moment—the guard would wake and come strolling down the hall.

"You need to go. Now." Teryn reached through the bars and put his hand on mine, halting my fruitless efforts. "I'm the only reason Morkai is waiting to wage war. He needs me alive. If I go missing, what's to stop his wrath from exploding in some unpredictable way?"

"I can't leave you here." My voice cracked, panic flooding my body.

"You have to." Teryn's voice was firm. "This is your chance. This is *our* chance. Go gather allies. Find the Forest People. You can make a difference if you take your chance to escape. Go."

I inhaled deeply and exhaled slowly through my mouth. The anxiety drained from me until my mind became clear. "You're right. I must go."

"Don't worry about me," Teryn said.

My eyes fell on his hand, still clasped over mine. The heat of his skin was an unexpected comfort, although I couldn't explain why it made my cheeks feel so warm. I pressed closer to his cell. "I will worry about you whether you like it or not."

He nodded, forcing a weak smile. "And I will do the same for you. Now go. Stay safe."

My throat felt tight as I pulled my hand from his. It took everything in me to turn away from him, and my heart sank with every step that took me further away. Despite my reluctance, I forced myself onward. At the end of the row of cells, I pressed myself against the wall, looking for signs of movement. Still, no guard could be seen. I crept quietly forward, up the stairs, and came to the dungeon door. It was slightly ajar.

With bated breath, I pressed it open.

The hall was dark and empty. I followed the only route from the dungeon I was familiar with—the one that would take me to the charred field.

I felt an anxious chill, as every door along the way was left slightly open. No guard was in sight. I could no longer attribute my luck to my own powers; I was not responsible for the open doors and lack of guards. All I could do was press on without fear, hoping I wasn't running into a trap.

A rush of cool air met my skin as I came outside and stood at the edge of the field. Under the light of the breaking dawn, I ran toward the line of trees in the distance. A silhouette appeared at the end of my vision, galloping toward me. *Valorre!*

I felt a rumbling in the ground. With a quick turn of my head, I saw the unmistakable form of the Roizan rounding the corner of the castle. I doubled my speed as the rumbling surged behind me.

As the distance closed between me and the racing silhouette, I realized it was not Valorre, but Hara, still adorned with saddle and bags. My heart sank for a moment, wondering if Valorre was alive after all, but shook the question from my mind as I ran to meet Hara and hefted myself upon her back.

The Roizan continued its gain on us as Hara dug her hooves into the ground and abruptly turned us around, speeding toward the tree line. I held tight to the reins with one hand while searching for my bow with the other.

It felt like I was returning to my own skin as I gripped the familiar weapon in my hands, the smooth wood like an extension of my arm. Releasing the reins, I reached into my quiver, withdrew an arrow, and nocked it into place. I swiveled and aimed at the Roizan racing behind us.

Before I could release it, a flash of white sped between me and the Roizan. The Roizan skidded to a halt and stared after Valorre. Valorre raced away from us, and the Roizan followed. Again, I raised my bow, training my arrow on the Roizan's fleshy face.

I released the arrow, puncturing the Roizan's snout. My next arrow found the corner of its eye. The creature bellowed and rolled to the ground, rubbing its face into the dirt below. Hara continued racing forward into the forest, and soon Valorre was at our side.

Thank you, I said to him. *Now take me home.*

27

INTERLUDE

Teryn

"How did she escape her cell?" Morkai's voice was low and calm, yet his face was twisted with fury.

I stood tall with my hands clasped behind my back. "She used her magic."

"Impossible! I was blocking her powers." Morkai seemed to say the last part more to himself than to me.

"Yes, she could tell, but her powers returned after you last summoned her. She opened the door like it was nothing."

Morkai grumbled, striking the bars of my cell with his staff. He turned toward the line of guards behind him. "Who was on guard?"

After a moment of silence, Dimetreus stepped forward. "I was, master."

Morkai stormed over to him. "How did she escape on your watch?"

"I don't know, my king."

"You were last to lock her in her cell. Did you?"

"Yes."

"Did you lock the door?"

Dimetreus swallowed hard. His eyes flashed away from Morkai and met mine for a moment. "Yes."

"Did you remain here to stand guard as you should have? Did you leave your post? Did you let her escape?" Morkai reached out and grabbed Dimetreus by the throat.

Dimetreus gasped but did not put up a fight. Again, his eyes met mine. I was suddenly struck by the color of them, a subtle green that I'd previously seen as a dull black.

"It's obvious how she got by him, considering she was invisible." I tried to keep my voice level.

Morkai turned his head to the side. "What do you mean she was invisible?"

"One moment she was in front of my cell, and the next, she was simply gone. I've seen her do it before. She can disappear without effort."

Morkai released his grasp from Dimetreus' neck and walked back toward my cell. He paced, his brow furrowed as he stroked his beard. "Perhaps it is a blessing. I don't need that kind of magic around here, interfering with my plans. I never should have spared her life. The next time I see her, I will kill her."

With that, Morkai strode from the dungeon, his guards falling in line behind him.

Once alone, I slumped to the ground and closed my eyes. The effort I'd made to remain calm in front of Morkai now unraveled in ragged breaths and tears that stung my eyelids. I thought of my family, my friends. Wherever Cora was, I hoped she was safe. I hoped Lex had safely delivered his message. I hoped my father was formulating a plan to protect our kingdom. As for myself, all I had to do was wait and hope Morkai kept me alive long enough to see the people I loved one last time.

Cora

I closed my eyes and thought of Salinda.

Her face filled my mind, every feature clear as if she were truly standing in front of me. I breathed in deeply and could smell the cook fires, the familiar aromas of steeping herbs. I could hear birdsong and the rumble of busy voices.

Where are you?

Salinda paused as she hung a piece of cloth on a line. Her eyebrows knit together, and she closed her eyes, placing a hand over her heart. Her thin mouth twitched into a smile.

I opened my eyes and returned to the present. I was mounted on Hara's back, reins warm beneath my hands. I could still hear the birds chirping amongst the trees, but they were different birds. The smells of cook fire and pungent herb were no more.

"Did you get it?" I looked at Valorre trotting next to me.

Yes. I can feel them. We are close.

My chest felt light, flooded with a joyful fluttering. I was almost home. Despite everything I'd experienced since parting ways with the Forest People, the pain of missing them was still fresh. My time at Ridine Castle renewed the loss of my first family, but nothing could compare to the family that had rescued me, cared for me, loved me. The family that had taught me the Arts and helped me understand my power.

"Valorre, do you have a family?" I was struck by the realization that Valorre had never communicated about his own home or family.

All unicorn is family.

"But what about a mother and father? The unicorns that made you? The unicorns you were born to?"

Valorre seemed to ponder for a moment. *I was born. It was long ago. I don't feel them anymore.*

"Are they still alive?"

Perhaps. Home.

"Where is home?" I knew Valorre and the other unicorns weren't native to Kero, but I hadn't thought much about where they had come from. Even Morkai seemed surprised by their sudden introduction to the land.

Home is a place very close...but very far away. Like here, but not here.

"How did you get here? Why are so many unicorns coming to Kero?"

It was not on purpose. I was home. In forest. Then I felt the pull. I had to go forward. There was something...calling. A goodness. A magic. Sorrow. I was needed. Then I stepped onto land that was not my land. The call was like memory and so was home. I was lost.

His words made my heart sink. "Are you able to go back?"

I don't know where home went. It is far away now.

"How many of your family are here in Kero? Can you feel them the way I can feel mine?"

There are many, but less than before. I can feel them. They understand Roizan now. And hunters. They understand hiding.

It was a small comfort that perhaps their numbers would remain if they were aware of the dangers around them. Still, I had no idea how many hunting parties continued their hunts. Had Morkai gotten enough of what he was after?

Thoughts of Morkai made me think of Teryn. Not even the joy of returning to the Forest People could make up for the thought of Teryn alone in his cell. I knew he'd wanted me to save myself and leave him, but had that really been the right decision? Would Morkai keep him alive to take him to Centerpointe Rock as promised? Or had I destroyed everything with my escape? *Be strong, Teryn. I'm so sorry.*

I let out a deep breath, releasing with it my dark thoughts. I focused on the memory of cook fires, dirt, and laundry lines, and filled my mind with home.

~

Larylis

I saddled my horse in the empty stable, moving as slowly and quietly as possible. I cocked my head at every noise that even remotely resembled approaching footsteps. My heart beat high in my chest, increasing tempo with every passing moment. What if she didn't get my note? What if she did and decided not to come? I looked to the open door. Still no one. Maybe it was for the best.

Just as I finished loading my saddlebags, I heard the stable door shut softly behind me. I turned and saw a cloaked figure in a peasant-style dress walking toward me. Her clothing could fool anyone, but her proud walk and sultry, swaying hips betrayed her.

"You came." I resisted the urge to run to her like an excited child.

Mareleau shook her golden hair from her hood and looked at me, her mouth twisting into a mischievous smirk. Her pace quickened and a moment later she was in my arms, our mouths hungrily meeting.

She filled my senses—the smell of her hair, the smoothness of her skin, the sound of her eager breaths as my arms pressed her closer. I would remember every second of this. It was likely the last I would ever get.

Mareleau gently pulled her lips from mine and began unhooking the clasp of her cloak. As it fell to the ground, it revealed a plain dress beneath with a very hastily laced bodice. The smirk returned to her mouth as she grabbed my hands and led me to a corner of the stable.

Together we slid down on dirt and straw, our lips again entangled as my hands slid over the loosened laces of her dress. For just one moment I paused. The woman in my arms may one day be the wife of my brother. *My brother.*

Mareleau reached her hand to my cheek. "What's wrong?"

"Nothing." I smiled and brushed my lips against hers.

"You can't fool me, Lare. Don't think about Teryn. We don't have to go too far. What we do won't hurt him."

"If he knew about any of this, it would kill him."

"I promise you, I will do whatever I can to avoid marrying him."

I sighed. There was no use thinking about it. I'd already made my choice, regardless of the circumstances. I knew what I'd gotten myself into, and I knew where I wanted to be—with her.

I swallowed my guilt, shoved thoughts of Teryn to the farthest reaches of my mind, and immersed myself in the moment. In that time and place, encircled in my arms, she was nobody's wife. She was the woman I loved, and she loved me.

Mareleau pulled me back down to her until we were again lost only in each other. An eternity wouldn't have been long enough to enjoy our time together. But the moment came when we knew we must return to breathing our own air.

I reclined on my back, catching my breath as Mareleau rested her head on my chest.

"Did you really have a poem for me, the day of the contest?" Mareleau asked.

"You mean the day you sent me away?"

Mareleau playfully nudged me in the shoulder. "Come on, I'm serious."

I laughed. It seemed so pathetic now, how I'd argued with King Verdian in front of everyone, how furious I'd been as the guards pulled me from the crowd. And how cold Mareleau had seemed to me. Now she was a warmth I would never forget. "No. I didn't write you a poem."

Mareleau wrinkled her nose at me. "I don't believe you."

"But I did write you a song."

Mareleau rolled her eyes and smiled, but when my face failed to mirror hers, her eyes grew wide. "You're not joking."

"Would you like to hear it?"

After a moment's hesitation, she nodded.

"Just don't laugh." I searched my mind for the words I had struggled so hard to write. Words I thought I'd never get to say to a tune that had never ceased playing.

> "If my lips are ever blessed with your kiss,
> I'll fall into the deepest bliss,
> And if your heart is ever my own,
> Forever will it have a home.

> My love for you will never be an ember,
> It will burn for you from now until forever,
> For one could never extinguish the fire of
>   love,
> Its eternal glow shall rise above.

> And you, my dear, are the one I adore,
> You, my love, I could hold forever more,
> You are the one I want by my side,
> You, Mareleau, are the love of my life."

"I love that, Lare." Mareleau raised her head from my chest and kissed me lightly on the lips. Her eyes glistened with a sheen of unshed tears. "I'm sorry I had you taken away. You understand now, right? That poem—that song —would have broken my heart for all to see."

"At least you finally got to hear it." I ran my hand down Mareleau's hair. "What about the letter? When I sent you a message, asking if you could love my brother? You sent him a rose. But me..."

"I never sent him that rose, I promise you. It was my mother. And my letter to you...all I can say is I'm sorry. At the time, I thought what I was writing was true—I didn't think I ever *could* be allowed to love you. I didn't think I'd ever be able to tell you the truth. Writing you that letter, rejecting you yet again when all my heart wanted to do was tell you how I felt, took everything from me for days. You don't know how hard I cried."

I swallowed the lump in my throat. "As terrible as it is to say, I suppose one good thing has come from this war."

"War." Mareleau's voice shook as she said the word. "I wish you didn't have to go. Can't we stay here forever? Or run away together?"

Her words were everything I'd ever wanted to hear. Couldn't I just say yes? "There's nothing I want more, but I made a promise to go to Tomas with Lex."

"I won't see you again, will I? Before Centerpointe Rock?"

It was uncertain whether we'd see each other again *ever*, but I left that unsaid. "You'll be on my mind and in my heart every moment from now until my death."

Mareleau rolled her eyes. "You're so dramatic."

Third bell struck the morning hour. I was scheduled to leave by fourth bell.

"When will the stable hands return?" Mareleau asked, peering toward the stable door. "How much time did you buy?"

"Enough." And with that we were again entwined, making memories with our lips.

28

FOREST PEOPLE

Cora

I made my way through the trees, feeling the nearness of my people with every step. Hara kept a graceful pace beside me, and I wondered if she would miss Valorre as much as I would.

Valorre and I had parted ways a small distance behind, and even though I'd grown fond of Hara, nothing could replace my bond with my unicorn companion. His absence would be an ache in my heart.

However, Valorre had his own mission. And I had mine.

As I stepped into the clearing of the camp, I calmly halted and raised my hands. Just as I expected, not a moment passed before my intrusion was detected.

A young man appeared before me, arrow nocked and raised. His scowling face softened as he looked at me, down to the hem of my dress, then up to the bow at my shoulder. "Who goes?"

"It's me, Cora." I couldn't recall the young man's name and doubted he would recognize me at all.

"Cora?"

I turned toward the familiar voice and saw Roije staring at me with wide eyes. "Roije!"

"Lower you bow, Eiden. Don't you remember Cora?" Eiden lowered his bow, and Roije gathered me in a bear hug. "Maiya and Salinda are going to be happy to see you. Come on."

I followed Roije into the heart of the camp, catching many curious looks as I passed by. Some were accompanied with a smile and a wave, others with a pause and a whisper.

As we approached a tent patterned with familiar fabrics, a small figure ran out with open arms. I ran to meet Salinda's embrace.

"I knew you were coming!" Salinda took my face in her hands, her eyes creased with joy as they glistened with tears. "I could feel it. You found us with your power, didn't you?"

I nodded, unable to speak, knowing my next words would shatter our happy reunion.

Nothing could get past Salinda. "But you come with dark news. I knew as much."

My heart fell with the weight of my mission. "There is something terrible happening in Lela. I must speak with the elders."

Salinda's smile remained yet it no longer reached her eyes. "Come. There will be time for us later."

"I'll take care of your horse," Roije offered.

I handed him Hara's reins and followed Salinda to the tent of the elders. Inside the tent, it was cool and dark and filled with herbal aromas that were so intense they made my head spin.

Salinda led me to the center, placing a cushion for me to sit. She took my hand, squeezing it with a smile. "Wait here. I'll gather the elders."

As I sat alone in the tent, I steeled my resolve to deliver the words I'd rather not say. My eyes grew heavy and my breathing became slow and deep. The heady aromas no longer overwhelmed my senses, and instead gave me something to focus on.

I had to focus on something. Anything but the fear.

It wasn't long before the tent began to fill with the eight elders of the Forest People. The group consisted of four female and four male leaders of the tribe. Salinda was the youngest of the group, while the oldest was Nalia, our Wise Woman. Nalia was an impossibly thin wisp of bone, white hair, and nearly translucent, brown skin. She was known to speak rarely yet smile constantly. All eight elders were respected for their wisdom, guidance, and powers in the Arts.

Salinda placed a small, clay bowl before me, its contents sending undulating plumes of aromatic smoke to fill the air. I breathed it in, steadying my nerves as the elders took their seats on the floor.

I looked at the faces surrounding me. Some were kind and smiling, some wore frowns of concern, others looked at me with annoyance. It was unusual for someone like me, a youth of the Forest People—adopted, no less—to demand an audience with the elders. And, while I'd been with them for many years, some still considered me very much an outsider.

Nalia spoke with her quiet yet steady voice. "Great Spirit, we honor you."

The remaining elders each spoke in turn.

"We look to your many faces."

"Mother Moon of life and land."

"Father Sun of strength and power."

"The air of life."

"The land that feeds us."

"The fire that warms us."

"The water that sustains us."

Nalia nodded her head at me. "You may speak, child."

I stood and drew a long, shaking breath. "Thank you. Many of you know me as Cora. You have raised me and given me shelter, home, and family. I come to you in great need and bring with me a heavy burden. But first, let me tell you who I really am. I am Princess Coralaine, rightful heir of Kero. My kingdom is in danger."

WHISPERS SURROUNDED ME. I HAD DELIVERED MY STORY and now awaited the judgment of the elders.

Finally, one spoke. "Why should we involve ourselves in the royal matters? We never have before."

"Did you hear her?" asked another. "This isn't a royal war. This is a magic war."

Voices blended as the arguing escalated.

"He's calling himself Morkai. He's trying to become the Morkaius."

"If our old stories are true, the Morkaius cannot claim the magic without being destroyed by it."

"He has created a Roizan! A channel between his body and the magic."

I stared wide-eyed at the elders, shocked to hear them speaking so fluently about Morkai and his plans. In fact, they seemed to understand more than I did. My heart raced as I fought the urge to interrupt with a fountain of questions.

"War is not our way. We protect our own, that's all."

"We protect the land and the Arts."

"How do we even know the girl speaks truth? The Princess of Kero is supposed to be dead."

"She is one of our own! I have raised her since the age of ten," Salinda said.

"And she's been hiding a secret identity from us the entire time."

The anxiety pounded faster and faster in my chest until the voices doubled into a burning cacophony of thought and feeling. My mind reeled and sweat beaded at my brow.

"No." I didn't mean to say the word out loud. My voice was firm and steady, as if it came from somewhere outside myself. Or, rather, deep within. I let my breathing slow and felt the chaos leave my mind. The arguing came to a stall, and when I opened my eyes, the faces of the elders were fixed on mine.

"No, war is not our way," I said. "And yes, I have been hiding my identity from you, and I apologize. I thought I was protecting myself as well as you, the Forest People, my family. I wouldn't burden you with this choice if I didn't think we, as protectors of the Arts, had a responsibility to stop Morkai. Mena and Sele may be able to fight a war, but they know nothing of magic. Morkai already has great power that no Royal Force can stop. And if no one stops him, he will become more powerful than we can imagine. What then? What will become of the Arts then? What will become of us? Of the land? *Our* land?"

"The girl is right." Nalia's voice was small but powerful, carrying with it undeniable authority. "We live as we do to honor the Ancient ways of our ancestors. The Ancient Ones fought to protect the Arts, as we must do now."

Silence followed. Some elders bowed reverently, while others bore scowls with their nods of resignation.

"And so it is," Nalia said.

"And so it is," the elders echoed.

Once outside the tent, I took in the cool night air, grateful to be under the stars and breathing something other than incense.

"Cora!"

I looked toward the sound and saw Maiya running toward me. We gathered each other in our arms, squealing like children.

"I thought I'd never see you again." Maiya's voice shook as she laughed and cried all at once.

"I wasn't sure myself."

"Roije told me you come with dark tidings. So dark you had to speak with the elders immediately."

We released each other, yet kept our hands clasped. Once again, I knew I must dampen joy with the weight of my mission. "It's true. Those tidings will now spread throughout the camp like wildfire. I want to be the first to tell you. There's something you need to know about me."

Maiya nodded. "Tell me over dinner. You must eat."

We ate next to the cook fires, the bowl of soup

shaking in my hand as I spoke. After all the truth I'd shared with Teryn, then with Salinda and the elders, it was a surprise it wasn't getting any easier to divulge. I went into more detail with Maiya than I had with the elders, which only made my words heavier. She was a polite audience, only furrowing her brow when I admitted the identity I'd hidden from her for so long. Her eyes widened when I spoke of Morkai, the Roizan, and war, but never did she interrupt or cry. She'd grown stronger in the short time I'd been away.

Once there was nothing more to say, we sat in silence, finishing our meals.

"I'm not angry, you know," Maiya said. "I always knew you were hiding your past. So did Mother. It's not as big of a secret as you think."

I smiled at that. "Thank you, Maiya. You're my best friend and nearly my sister. I'd never want to hurt you. And I hated lying to you. I just didn't know what else to do."

Maiya reflected my smile. "You know, there's something I want to tell you as well, before you hear from—"

Maiya paused as Roije came up behind her and put his arms around her shoulders. He gently planted a kiss on the side of her forehead. My eyes locked with Maiya's, just as a wide grin spread across her face. Even in the light of the cook fires, I could tell she was blushing.

"I'll be home soon," Roije whispered.

Once Roije had left, Maiya and I fell into a fit of giggles.

"Home? You share a home?"

"That's what I wanted to tell you," Maiya said. "Roije

chose me as wife. I couldn't be happier. I've loved him for as long as I can remember."

"I know. I think we all knew."

Maiya sighed and stared into the fire, her eyes sparkling and her smile still firmly stretched over her face. She never looked more beautiful.

My heart was full of joy at seeing my friend so content. I carried it with me through the remainder of the evening, smiling as I bid Maiya goodnight and watched her retire into her new tent. However, my smile began to fade as I curled up beneath my own makeshift tent, alone.

It was strange being back with the Forest People. So much had changed in such a short time. Maiya had changed. I had changed. The entire land I loved had changed. Valorre was nowhere near, which brought a fresh wave of sadness.

And then there was Teryn. Teryn, alone in the cell where I had left him, kept alive only by Morkai's wicked grace. Teryn, whom I could have rescued. Teryn, who'd stood up for me to my lifeless brother. *Teryn.*

I curled into myself, pulling my blanket close around me as I wiped a tear from my cheek.

29

TOMAS

Larylis

Tomas was an abundance of rolling hills, expansive farmland, gray skies, and lightly misting rain. Throughout every moment of our speedy travels, I wore the memory of Mareleau's last kiss as a smile on my lips. Lex and I and our small retinue spoke little and moved quickly. King Carrington was expecting us but had no idea as to our purpose.

When we arrived at Lex's castle, we'd barely set foot through the gates before we were greeted by four plump, squealing, blonde girls, ranging from child to teen. They surrounded Lex, tugging at his sleeves, planting kisses, and stealing hugs.

"Did you win the Quest?" the youngest asked.

"Of course, he didn't, you oaf. He would never betray Lily," said another.

"Lily is so mad. You must see her, Lex!"

"Will father let you marry her now that you've lost?"

"How do you know he lost? He hasn't even said a word!"

"Settle down, sisters, one at a time." Lex was red-faced and smiling as he gently extricated himself from their grasp. "No, I didn't win the Quest. Yes, I still love Lily. Yes, I know she's mad, but I explained everything to her before I left. She should know better."

"Who won the Quest, then?" asked the eldest. Then, with a wrinkle of her nose, added, "Don't tell me it was Prince Helios."

Lex's face fell. "No one won the Quest. That's why I'm here. Prince Larylis and I are here to speak to Father about some...complications."

The girls responded with open mouths and worried faces until they turned their attention to me.

"And you must be Prince Larylis!" the eldest said, noticing me for the first time.

"What an honor," a younger sister said, looking at me from under her eyelashes.

After blushes and clumsy curtsies, the sisters fell back into a fit of unfettered giggles.

"Just ignore them, they're ridiculous," Lex said in an exaggerated whisper.

His sisters landed playful punches on Lex's arm while casting furtive glances my way. Having no sisters of my own, I found the interaction surprisingly heartwarming.

"Brother," came a drawling voice behind us.

"Ben." Lex nodded once as a young man approached.

Ben looked to be about four years Lex's junior with a small, lanky build and his brother's messy, dirty-blond hair and ruddy cheeks. He smirked at Lex in such a superior way that was both arrogant and juvenile. It was safe to say I immediately disliked him. "Did you lose the Quest already?"

"Don't tease him," the eldest sister said with a smile. "We've already done that plenty."

"He's brought a prince to speak to father," whispered the youngest.

Ben considered me for a moment with a raised brow.

"King Carrington is expecting us," I said. "Have any messages been left for me? I'm expecting a messenger from Norun to report to me here."

Ben shrugged. "Not that I've heard. I'll take you to Father."

"There's no need, brother. I can take the prince there myself. I'm equally responsible for what we have come to share with him today."

Ben ignored Lex and began walking ahead. "Come along."

KING CARRINGTON OF TOMAS STARED OUT THE WINDOW OF his study, back turned to me and Lex. "Why didn't you announce yourself winner of the Quest?"

Lex and I exchanged a confused glance.

"After everything I told you, that is what concerns you?" Lex said. "Not the sorcerer, not the monstrous Beast, not the magic war?"

The king waved his hand at his side. "Yes, yes. But first, I need to understand why you have failed."

"Didn't you hear? The Quest is over. We didn't capture a single unicorn. Helios is dead. Teryn is captured—"

"Which should make you the champion by default."

"King Carrington, Lex is right. The Quest has been declared forfeit. It is my understanding that Mareleau has now been promised to my brother, Prince Teryn." I tried to say the words with as little disgust as possible.

The king spun around, eyeing me with an angry frown. "That is a betrayal! My son is the fair champion, and your brother—captured and useless—has been named the betrothed?"

"Father!" Lex's voice reverberated throughout the room with a strength I never would have expected. "The Quest is over. I don't want to be the champion. And there are more critical issues at hand that you need to listen to."

King Carrington slowly turned to face his son, considering him as if he'd never quite seen him before. The anger melted from his face. "Why should we involve ourselves in a war that is not our own?"

"We're talking about a sorcerer. I've seen him. I've seen his Royal Force. I've seen an evil creature he's created with magic. Lela is our neighboring land. What's to stop him from coming here once he's conquered the three kingdoms of Lela?"

"Not to mention, he has harmed and threatened your own son," I added.

"He looks fine to me." Ben sat sprawled behind the king's desk, one leg dangling lazily over the arm of his chair. He aimlessly picked at his fingernails, as if the conversation around him was about nothing more than the weather.

Lex ignored his brother. "Mena and Sele need allies. We must help them."

King Carrington's face fell. He looked younger than my own father, with blond, shoulder length hair that hadn't a single strand of gray. His build was set some-where between his two sons, neither slim like Ben nor round like Lex. "We have avoided being conquered by Norun for this long by being small and insignificant in their eyes. We are not suited for war."

"Then it is time to get suited," I said, surprised at the confidence in my voice. "Because if Morkai invades Risa, the small and the weak will be the first to go."

Again, the king frowned at me. I was doing an excellent job at getting on his bad side. He opened his mouth to reply but was interrupted by the appearance of a messenger in Mena's livery.

"I am to report to Prince Larylis." The messenger gasped through ragged breaths, the scroll in his hand shaking slightly.

"What is it?" I asked.

He handed the note to me. I felt the blood leave my face as I read it. *Your offer of alliance is a lie and a joke. We know about the murderous Prince Teryn. Prince Helios will be avenged.*

"Norun will not be joining our alliance." My mouth felt dry as I handed the note to the king.

King Carrington rubbed the pale stubble at his chin as he read the note. Lex went to his father, reading over his shoulder with wide eyes.

"I could have told you they'd deny an alliance," Lex said. "But to call Teryn a murderer? The sorcerer's Beast killed him! I mean, that and his own stupidity."

"The original rider returned with this note in hand and an arrow through his ribs," the messenger said. "He also reported that Norun is preparing for war."

"They are going to invade Tomas!" Ben said, springing to his feet.

"No, they are joining Morkai, you dimwit." Lex narrowed his eyes at his brother before turning his attention to his father. "You see, Father? Now Morkai has the power of Norun at his side. We must help them."

Ben leapt in front of the king, pushing Lex out of the way. "Don't listen to him. We can't leave. The best thing we can do is add to the fortifications at our borders. We will be safe if we stay here."

"You know nothing, Ben."

"I know more than you about protecting our kingdom! I built a wall!"

Lex's eyes bulged, jaw clenched tight as he took a step toward Ben. "No, you postured around like a peacock with your nose in the air while our people slaved away at building our wall. I should have been the one to do it, I'll admit that. But this time I'm not going to sit and do nothing. This is not the time to be small, insignificant Tomas. This is the time to fight."

Ben's mouth hung open as he struggled for words. I wondered how Lex resisted the urge to send his fist into Ben's jaw.

The king gently brushed his younger son aside and put his hands on Lex's shoulders. "What can we do? Even if we fight, what kind of difference could we possibly make?"

"I don't know," Lex said. "I'm scared. I don't want to do this any more than you do. But I know we have to try."

The king closed his eyes and hung his head. "Prince Larylis. You may report that we will join our forces with yours at Centerpointe Rock."

30

ANCESTORS

Cora

I carefully unwrapped the cloth from the two horns, swallowing the bile that rose in my throat. The horns sat exposed in my lap, reminding me of everything I'd seen and experienced in the weeks behind me. Everything I'd fought for. Everything I'd lost. My hands unconsciously rested on my abdomen, reminding me of my forever-empty womb. I closed my eyes and moved my hand to the horns.

Darkness and pain rippled through me, filling my mind with terror and suffering. I breathed it in. I breathed it out. Blood. Rage. Starvation. Defeat. The dark magic that flowed from the horns enveloped me in a prickling shroud, suffocating the air. I felt the hair on my arms stand up, skin crawling, gut roiling.

Breathe in. Breathe out. It was all I could do not to toss the horns away from me. I turned my focus away from the dark magic, ignoring its writhing presence as I mourned the two lives lost for the horns that lay before me, honoring their sacrifices and gentle spirits. The darkness revolted, squeezing tighter around me.

I thought of Valorre, and through him I felt a connection to the other unicorns. I knew their pain. I knew their goodness. The sorrow in my heart was replaced with love. *Breathe in. Breathe out.* The darkness faltered, loosened. With every breath, I blew it away until I felt nothing but a calm, pure energy radiating beneath my palms.

I opened my eyes and saw Salinda watching me. I set the horns aside, tucking them under the hem of my dress and patted a space on the ground next to me.

"What is this project you have?" Salinda asked.

I blushed, embarrassed that I had been caught in the middle of my task. I wasn't even sure what I was trying to accomplish. "It's just a little something. Not a big deal."

"You can tell me, Cora. I can see it is a big deal to you."

Reluctantly, I pulled the horns from under my dress and showed Salinda. "I managed to save these from being consumed by the Roizan. At first, I thought I would destroy them. But then I decided the deaths of the unicorns shouldn't go to waste. I thought maybe I would carve them, but they are unbelievably dense. Do you happen to know how?"

"You simply have to ask."

I furrowed my brow and tilted my head to the side. "Then how?"

"Not me. You ask the horns. Ask their spirits. They will oblige."

I felt a small smile spread over my lips, though it didn't go far.

"What bothers you? So much sadness, my dear one."

I bit my lower lip. "It's just...there's so much uncertainty. I still can't believe what's happening. So many people that I love have already been hurt by Morkai. I hate to think how many more will be lost to him in battle."

"Many more will die, this is true. But we must not focus on that. We must only focus on what we can do right now."

"I wish I could do *more*." I kicked at a rock in front of me. "More for the people I care about. If I'd been more powerful, I could have saved my parents. If I'd been quicker to act, I would have saved Teryn. And now I'm bringing my family into battle when I really just want to protect you all."

"You are always so concerned with others," Salinda said. "This is a noble thing, and a gift. As an empath, you will always feel what others feel and absorb their pain as deeply. That same gift allows you to connect to animals, nature, even inanimate objects. It allows you to disappear, to blend, to work with the elements you touch and think about. But your greatest power lies in your greatest challenge."

"What is my greatest challenge?"

"Think about it, Cora. When has your power been the strongest? The clearest? The most surprising?"

I thought of my unplanned attack on Morkai in the field, of the fire that had burned within me as my powers returned. Where had that come from? I'd simply been protecting myself.

Then it dawned on me. I was protecting *myself*.

Salinda nodded as I met her eyes. "You will always try to protect others. That is your natural way. But every time you conquer your challenge, when you use your power for *you*, you unlock more and more of your potential. This in turn makes you stronger in everything you do. Even in helping others."

"Does every practitioner of the Arts face a special challenge to grow their power?"

"Every one of us. Empath. Oracle. Narcuss. Some of our challenges are more difficult to uncover, as not all of us have a power so easily defined. And I don't need to have met Morkai to know he's a narcuss."

"What is the power and challenge of a narcuss?"

"A narcuss can control and manipulate the people and objects around him. He can project what he wants others to see and feel. He is entirely focused on self-protection, self-advancement, and personal power. A narcuss takes power for personal gain. Can you guess what his challenge would be?"

It wasn't difficult. "The challenge of a narcuss lies in using power selflessly. Morkai is so powerful, yet I can't believe he has ever done a selfless thing in his life. If he hasn't gained power through overcoming his challenge, how has he become so strong?"

"Perhaps he isn't as strong as you think," Salinda said. "Strength and power are not the same. When it comes to the Arts, power is something that can be gained or lost. It can be learned. It can be forgotten. But strength is something innate that becomes forever part of you as you grow. Strength in your Art can never be taken away. Morkai is powerful, but it comes from his use of death-magic. He has taught himself to be a necromage through knowledge and practice alone, without the strengthening that comes from conquering his challenge as a narcuss.

Yes, his power is frightening, but a power like that, untempered by challenge, will always have a weakness."

I couldn't believe how much Salinda and the elders knew about Morkai and his power. All the time I'd spent searching for answers when they were home all along. I just didn't have the right questions then.

"Morkai told me he is of Ancient blood and the rightful heir to Lela as King of Magic," I said. "I remember the elders mentioned something about a *Morkaius*. What does that mean?"

"This *Morkai* isn't the first to claim the title. The name simply means King of Magic. The last man like Morkai wanted to become *Morkaius*, High King of Magic. He wanted to rule all of the Ancient Realm and take control of the magic for himself. Sound familiar? Maybe this Morkai is carrying the legacy of an Ancient ancestor as well."

I didn't like the idea that Morkai had any rightful blood running through his veins. "Who is this Ancient Morkaius? Was he a true heir to Lela?"

Salinda looked thoughtful, as if trying to find the right words to say. "It is said a bastard son of the Elvan queen sought to overthrow the rightful heir and rule the Ancient Realm. Being the eldest, he claimed he was the true heir. With a human army behind him, he invaded the Elvan palace. This is where the significance of Centerpointe Rock comes in. It isn't simply a rock marking the center of the three kingdoms. It is a weathered remnant of the once-mighty palace that stood at the center of the Ancient Realm. He destroyed it in attempt to claim his throne, leaving nothing but ruins behind.

"What happened after isn't known to us. We believe

this Ancient usurper was destroyed when he became Morkaius and took control of the magic. It is understood that he who contains the Ancient magic for himself can only be destroyed by it."

"Morkai must have known about this," I said. "Which is why he created the Roizan. He created a channel so he can access the magic a little at a time without being destroyed by it. But wouldn't the Roizan be destroyed by it as well?"

"That is uncertain," Salinda said. "A Roizan is a thing of dark magic, created by death, fed by death, more object than creature. Morkai must know the strength of his Roizan to rely on it so heavily."

The Roizan was already powerful, and Morkai's increased abilities when near the Roizan were infinitely more frightening. How much more terrible would the two become if Morkai became Morkaius? I could only hope we would never find out.

"How does Morkai control people? He has an army that blindly follows his demands. And my brother...how does he do that?" I asked.

"Ask yourself this, Cora. What makes you lose control? What would make your mind easy to conquer?"

I needed no time to answer. "Fear. He creates an intense fear in those he wants to control."

"That's my guess as well. A fearful mind shatters the connection between body and spirit. I believe he uses that as a window into the person, using his power as a necromage to keep the separation in place. He then uses his power as a narcuss to control them."

I thought about my brother. "Do you think there's any

coming back from Morkai's control? Can a broken mind and disconnected spirit return to wholeness?"

Salinda's face was full of sympathy. "That I don't know, dear one."

I lowered my head. After all my brother had done, I couldn't help but hope he was still in there somewhere, that he would somehow return.

"I'm very proud of you," Salinda said as she stood. "You have become so powerful in facing your past. But you are not only powerful. You are also strong. Something Morkai will never be able to match." With that, she gave my shoulder a light squeeze and left me to my quiet contemplations.

I took up the horns and my carving knife. Again, I closed my eyes and connected to the horns, relieved that the darkness hadn't returned to them. I thought about the bloodthirsty Roizan and Morkai's terrible power. I thought about everyone I'd lost and everyone I loved who was still alive. Then I thought of myself. I thought of everything that had been taken from me and how much I still had to live for.

I asked the horns, *Will you help me?*

31

WAR

Larylis

"We are here." My father placed a stone eagle on the map, over the line representing the border between Mena and Sele—just outside the valley surrounding Centerpointe Rock. Alongside Mena's eagle, he set a stone rose for Sele, and a stone sun for Tomas. "The sorcerer has agreed to meet our forces at the Rock at sunrise on the morrow. If he presents Teryn unharmed, I will bargain for his release in exchange for myself. I will continue to negotiate with him to try and put an end to this nonsense. However, if Morkai wants a war, that is what we will give him."

I searched the faces of the men encircling the table—King Verdian, King Carrington, the councilmen, the officers, and Lex—hoping someone had come up with a better plan to keep my father out of harm's way. Yet every face looked as bleak as my hopes.

"What if he tries to kill you?" It was probably the hundredth time I'd asked, yet I still hadn't heard a satisfying answer.

"I will promise him that I intend to surrender if the tides turn in his favor during battle. This promise should be incentive to keep me alive long enough for my Royal Guard to succeed in their rescue."

I wanted to argue. There were still a dozen or so unanswerable questions on my tongue—*what if the sorcerer refuses my father's promise? What if he won't trade Teryn for my father in the first place? What if he kills my brother, like he says he will if we don't immediately surrender? What if...we lose?* But for the sake of not sounding like a child, I kept my questions hidden alongside the tiny spark of hope I held.

"The Red Force, the strongest and most heavily armored, will lead the charge against the wraiths." King Verdian moved three red-painted stone pieces, one of each sigil, onto the field.

"The Red?" I looked from Verdian to my father. "Shouldn't it be the Black?"

"The weakest force against demonic wraiths?" Verdian shot me a glare.

"Not the weakest. The fastest. The lithe."

"We need strength and armor to protect against dark magic."

"No, we need speed and cunning."

"I agree with Larylis." Lex flushed as Verdian turned his venomous gaze his way. He cleared his throat. "I saw them fight. It is terrifying that they cannot be permanently killed, but they did not seem particularly strong. When I saw the demonstration, the wraiths seemed to fight with repetition. They almost seemed confused by what they were doing. Speed could confuse them even more. Maybe they will grow weaker the more they are struck down."

"That's a huge risk to take on a hunch," King Verdian said.

My father turned to Verdian. "However, if the wraiths are the lesser threat, we would be making a grave mistake by wasting our strongest force on them."

King Verdian threw his hands in the air. "Nothing is certain when we are fighting against magic."

"My son's word is all we have to use against the sorcerer," King Carrington said. "Now, I'm not used to dividing my army in these Lelaen traditions, but I fully understand the wisdom behind it, and I think my son does too. If he says we use the Black Force, we should do it."

The three kings exchanged glances.

Verdian gave a resigned nod of approval. "Lela help us all."

"I'll lead the Black Force." Silence followed my words, and once they'd been spoken, I knew there was no taking them back.

My father's jaw shifted back and forth before he finally said, "No, son, you need to stay behind. I won't have both my heirs in danger."

"This is no time to leave anyone behind. We all must fight to defend our land. I'm fast. I've trained with the Black. They should have a royal leader fighting with them."

"If Teryn dies, you're all Mena has."

"Then Mena should have a man worth following."

"It's too dangerous. You're not—"

"Strong enough? Isn't that why you had me train with the Black in the first place, to make strengths of my weaknesses? Has it ever occurred to you that I might be good? You're pleased when you hear Teryn passes as a tolerable fighter with the Red, but have you ever bothered to hear how I fare with the Black?"

The hurt on my father's face almost gave me pause.

"I'm not the sickly *runt prince* I was when I was six." I eyed each man on Verdian's council, letting my glare linger on Mareleau's two uncles a moment longer than the rest. "I'm not going to let our land fall into chaos without doing my part to defend it."

"I understand, my son." Father's lips twitched with a faint smile, and I thought I recognized pride in his expression. It was a look I'd seen him reserve most often for Teryn. "But if I...and Teryn both—"

"If it should come to that, I will retreat. But first, I will fight."

～

Cora

I stood between the trees at the top of a hill overlooking the valley of Centerpointe Rock. Across the valley atop the opposite hill, I could see the faint light of fires where the allied forces of the three armies camped. The sky was dark from the newness of the moon, lit only by the expanse of stars. The old rock in the center of the valley looked harmless—nothing like an ancient ruin from a forgotten war. Nothing like a place where blood would be spilled.

In the morning, there would be war. In the morning, I would watch the Forest People put their lives in danger. I would put *my* life in danger. I would see if Teryn still lived as Morkai had promised. I would have my chance to avenge my first family.

I leaned against the rough bark of the tree behind me, breathing in the smell of the aromatic pine. Waiting. My hand idly went to the hilt of the dagger at my waist. I unsheathed it, placing it gently over my palm as I watched the pure-white blade catch the starlight.

I sensed movement in the distance, and a moment later I felt a warmth in my heart that could only mean one thing. *Valorre.*

Silently, he stepped out of the brush and came to my side. I sheathed my dagger and wrapped my arms around his thick neck as he nuzzled me in the shoulder. Tears streamed down my cheeks.

Were you able to succeed at your mission? I asked him.

It is done.

I felt the tension and fear leave my shoulders with every breath as I buried my face into Valorre's smooth, white coat. There was hope.

Valorre and I stood side by side in silence until my eyes began to grow heavy.

Sleep. I'll guard. Valorre stood in front of me, blocking my view of the valley.

I wanted to argue, but sleep was far too tempting to avoid. I laid down at the base of a tree and wrapped myself in my cloak. Sleep quickly overtook me, and I dreamed. I dreamed of blood and blades and a field of darkness punctuated by glowing white lights. In the middle of the field was Morkai and the Roizan, staring hungrily at the chaos around them. Morkai raised his staff and struck the ground, sending a ripple of power outward onto the field of war. Everything in the valley, the darkness, the light, rose into the air in tiny flakes of ash. When the ash settled on the ground, the field was empty.

I WOKE WITH A COLD CERTAINTY THAT DANGER WAS NEAR. Valorre confirmed this with his twitching ears and trembling legs as I stood and joined him to look over the valley once again. The sky was beginning to blush with the first light of day, and the air was cool and damp. Not a single birdsong whistled from the trees or soared over the hilltops. Silence.

Morkai comes, Valorre said.

A light misting of fog danced over the valley in places. My eyes searched every inch of the field and hills and between every tree for a sign of danger. With a prickling of the skin at the back of my neck, my eyes moved to the base of a nearby hill. I watched, unblinking for countless moments.

My heart raced. I held my breath.

A subtle red fog began to creep onto the field. I blinked to ensure I was truly seeing what I thought I saw. Before long, the evidence was clear. The fog rolled in thicker, bolder, undeniably tinged with red, sending the gray mist to scurry from the valley floor.

A sound echoed through the valley, a deep, reverberating pounding. Slowly but steadily the sound grew. The red fog spread until it blanketed the entire field. I looked back to the base of the hill. The pounding stopped.

A black figure emerged, walking onto the field with deliberate steps.

The Roizan followed.

32

CENTERPOINTE ROCK

Teryn

The red fog swirled around my ankles, reaching my knees in places as I walked onto the field. Bound at the wrists with Dimetreus firmly guiding me by the shoulder, I could do nothing more than follow Morkai. The looming hide of the Roizan blocked all view of anything ahead.

My skin crawled with the thought of the immense armed force crowding behind me. Would my father's army be at the Rock, standing behind him? Would they be even a fraction of what followed me?

My heart raced the further we went into the valley. I knew we must be nearing the Rock. Nearing my fate.

A flash of stone caught my eye in the space between Morkai and the Roizan. I craned my neck to get a clearer look of the Rock. It wasn't nearly as foreboding as I'd imagined it to be. In my head, I'd pictured a black, jagged crag with sharp edges, charred like Morkai's staff. But the

Rock before us was a weathered gray, spanning the length of about a dozen men shoulder-to-shoulder, and appeared to be equally as wide. It was only waist-high with a relatively flat surface.

Morkai slowed his pace and turned to me. "Come."

Dimetreus pushed me forward. I stumbled to Morkai's side, catching my footing as I took in the view beyond the Rock. At the other edge of the field, a mass of soldiers gathered. An array of banners waved over their heads, displaying three different sigils—a white rose on a gold background, a gray eagle on a blue background, and a yellow sun on a green background. Their numbers spanned from one side of the valley to the other. There was no telling how far back the forces went, but from what I could tell, there were more men than I had hoped.

Morkai led me to stand in front of the Rock, and three figures emerged from the other side and began to approach us. As they came nearer, I saw it was my father surrounded by two guards.

I choked back tears that seared my throat as my father's face became clear. My body strained to remain upright, fighting against my desire to run to him and crumble in his arms like a boy. No, I would keep my composure, no matter how small I felt at that moment.

Father stopped a few paces away, and his eyes locked with mine. I didn't need a mirror to know what he saw. I was filthy, poorly fed, and terrified. Pity, worry, and something like disgust passed over Father's face, followed by a mask of calm as his eyes went to Morkai.

"Sorcerer." He said the word as if it tasted of bile.

"King Arlous. How nice to see you. I have presented your son unharmed. Have you considered my terms?"

"I have, but before we discuss anything, I require a change of hostage. You will take me in Teryn's stead."

Morkai's face remained impassive as he eyed my father with a hungry intensity. "Agreed."

Father turned and nodded at one of the guards, who in turn stepped forward and took me by the arm.

My life had been spared. I'd known Father would never surrender, and I'd known he would do whatever he could to keep me alive. But no matter how many ways I'd imagined the meeting at Centerpointe Rock, I'd never pictured it ending in anything but my death. Morkai's words had been branded on my every thought. *Surrender or Teryn dies.*

Yet I was alive. For now.

I pulled away from the guard and turned back to my father as he and Morkai climbed upon the Rock. I opened my mouth several times, but no words would come. What did I want to say to him? I'd spent weeks imagining what my last words to him would be. And even though it looked like I'd live to breathe another breath, it still seemed imperative that I say something.

Sensing my halt in progress, Father looked my way. "Go, son."

The guard pulled me forward once again. When we reached the gathered forces, King Verdian held out his arm for me to take my place at his side. The guard cut my bindings and began outfitting me in armor. Every moment between tightening straps and securing plates, I fixed my eyes on Centerpointe Rock.

My Father and Morkai stood facing each other atop the Rock, too distant to hear as they spoke. Dimetreus and my father's guard stood on the field below at opposite sides of the Rock. Behind them loomed Morkai's army. His indigo blue banners, bearing either his own black moon sigil or the red crown of Norun, went as far back as I could see. I swallowed hard. His force was certainly larger than ours.

"What is going to happen?" My voice came out like a croak as I strapped my sword to my hip.

Verdian kept his voice low as he said, "Your father will negotiate. If the sorcerer refuses any terms for peace, Arlous will agree to battle on the condition that Morkai keeps him alive during the fight. We have a special squad waiting to rescue him."

As I stood under the weight of the armor, I found I was still shaking from the shock of being alive. At least it was a comfort to know there was a plan in place to protect my father. Even if that plan was war.

The inaudible conversation between Morkai and my father continued. I tried to read their faces to gauge how the negotiations fared, but both wore equally unreadable expressions. Morkai's hands were steepled at his chest while my father's were calmly at his side.

The conversation appeared to stop as Morkai turned his back to my father, looking pensive as he brought a hand to his chin and stroked his beard. My father turned his head toward me, and I could almost make out a reassuring smile.

As Father turned back to face Morkai, a quick flash of the sorcerer's arm brought a dagger's blade across my father's throat.

Morkai stepped back and watched with calm as Father brought his hand to the bleeding gash. Father's guard drew his sword and sprang forward. As he leapt atop the Rock, Morkai raised his staff and thrust it toward the guard. The guard fell to the ground, dead.

My father continued to struggle with his gaping wound as Morkai once again faced him. Father fell to his knees as Morkai placed a hand on his shoulder. He began to shake. His hands fell from his neck and dropped to his side as blood continued to spill forth. Then Father went still. Morkai released his shoulder and took a step back, smiling as Father fell limp upon the rock.

There was no sound. There was no feeling. I remained in place, blinking at nothing as bodies raced past me.

33

BATTLE

Larylis

One moment. I had one moment to accept that my father was dead before the horns blew, signaling war. I felt like the breath had been pulled from my lungs. My heart felt like it would burst from my chest, and my legs threatened to give way beneath me. However, I had a sworn duty to perform. In that duty I would avenge my father.

I pulled the black mask over my face as did the others behind me. I turned to them, a sea of men in dark clothing, faces covered in masks that revealed a set of blinking eyes at front with painted eyes at the back. I wasn't sure if we looked comical or terrifying, but one thing was certain; we did not look ordinary. Ordinary would get us killed by the wraiths.

"You know our target!" I raised my voice over the din of madness that surrounded us. Arrows soared overhead. The Red Force was already well underway. "Seek out the wraiths. Confuse them. Kill them. Do not stop until your last breath."

The masked men shouted their agreement.

"For King Arlous!"

The Black Force echoed my words.

"For my father," I said to myself. And with that we charged ahead, straight into the chaos of blood and flashing steel.

Teryn

My cheek stung as I blinked. Sound came rushing to my ears, a cacophony of battle cries, the screech of metal on metal, and the sound of someone shouting in my face. I looked in front of me, and a blur of colors sharpened until Lex's face became clear.

"Snap out of it!" Lex raised his hand toward my face again.

"I'm here." My voice sounded far away.

Lex let out a breath. "Thank the Gods. I saw you standing there like an idiot. You're going to get shot or stabbed standing here in the open. We need to get out there."

"So we can get shot or stabbed?"

One side of Lex's mouth lifted into a sad smile. "Exactly."

I looked Lex up and down, outfitted in plates of armor painted red. "You're Red Force too?"

"Well, I'm certainly not fast. Or much of an archer. So yeah, Red it is."

I nodded and assessed my own red armor. How much red could I add to it before my own blood spilled from beneath its plates?

Lex put a hand on my shoulder. "I'm sorry about your father."

"Thanks, Lex."

"We should go. Are you ready?"

I hadn't expected to live, much less fight, and I was in no physical condition to do so. But that didn't matter. I looked to the Rock where Morkai still stood, pointing his staff, shouting, smiling. Vengeance was calling. "Yes. Let's go."

Cora

Arrows rained down from the trees into the valley below. The Forest People archers showered Morkai's men with their deadly aim as the sorcerer's army raced to meet the charge from the other side. I nocked an arrow, pulled it to my cheek, and released it with a *thrum* and a *whoosh*. Then another. And another. It was hardly enough to put a dent in Morkai's numbers, but it was something.

As the opposing forces merged together and the clash of swords and armor rang out, the archers held back. Our warriors ran down the hillside and into the fray. How quickly blood began to flow. I swallowed the lump in my throat and resisted the urge to look away.

Nalia passed behind me, and her song-like chanting sent a wave of calm through my body. I couldn't under-stand the Ancient tongue she chanted in, but I understood the intention behind her invocations. *Protection. Strength. Victory. Peace.*

I closed my eyes and breathed in Nalia's words. Breathing out, my senses sharpened. I found Morkai atop the Rock. He was pointing his staff into the roiling sea of men, this way and that. The Roizan stomped over to Morkai and stood next to the Rock as Morkai continued pointing his staff in seemingly purposeless directions. *What are you up to?*

I remembered the way Morkai had shown me his power at Ridine, how he destroyed an entire field of wraiths with one blow from his palms. I expected him to do the same here at any moment. My breath caught each time he pointed his staff. Yet I knew he wouldn't risk killing his own men with such a reckless use of power. Or would he?

My eyes searched the valley for some clue to Morkai's motives. All I saw was a field dotted with figures in different colors—black and red from the Royal Forces, indigo blue from Morkai's men, a few specks of brown from the Forest People, and a grayish blur from the wraiths. All were mixed together in a garish, grizzly painting.

Then the painting began to change. The gray slowly began to draw away from the others, condensing closer and closer together until they filled the field just left of the hill I stood upon. From the Rock, Morkai pointed his staff directly at them.

Figures in black charged the wraiths from all sides of the field until it became a swirling dance of black and gray. Morkai's staff glowed red.

My heart raced, and a chill spread from the back of

my neck down to my arms. I understood his plan. It was now time to enact my own. I looked to Valorre who stood at my side, and not a single thought was needed to convey what we would do next. I pulled myself onto his back and closed my eyes. As I breathed out, I released the glamour, letting it slip from Valorre and the entire hillside. "Now!"

We stormed down the hill, Valorre's pounding hooves echoed by nearly a hundred others following behind us. Unicorns in all colors of white, brown, black, and gray charged into the valley. As expected, the Roizan sprang from Morkai's side, leaping after the flashes of color that sped by him, tempting him one way and another throughout the field.

Morkai stared after his frantic Roizan. My eyes narrowed as I charged for the sorcerer. Bow in hand, I steadied my breathing, my thoughts, my heart, and pulled an arrow from my quiver—my one and only white-tipped arrow with white fletching on the end. One of two gifts from the stolen unicorn horns.

I nocked the arrow and pulled the bowstring back. Morkai met my eyes, smiling a devious smile. He raised his staff and pointed it toward me. I continued to charge ahead. Ready. Aim.

I froze. A figure climbed upon the Rock behind Morkai, sword drawn. Teryn ran at the sorcerer. Morkai turned toward him and stepped gracefully out of Teryn's reach, and in the same move, plunged his dagger into Teryn's side between two plates of armor.

Grief clawed at my heart as I watched Teryn grip his side and fall from the Rock. With a strangled cry, I released the arrow. It struck Morkai's shoulder, although from the look on his face, you'd think he'd simply been stung by a bee. With a frown of mild annoyance, he pulled the arrow from his shoulder with ease and tossed it to the ground. As we neared the Rock, I slid from Valorre's back. Fire filled my body, rising from my toes to my torso, through my arms, and down my fingertips. I raised my palms toward Morkai and sent him flying off the Rock.

I had no idea where the sorcerer landed, but he was not my concern at that moment. It was Teryn I was looking for. I found him at the base of the Rock, lying in the muddy grass, gripping his side as blood flowed between his fingers. I knelt by him, tears streaming from my eyes as I gently removed the thick plates of armor—armor that had not protected him.

Teryn winced as he looked up at me. "Cora," he managed to gasp.

"I'm here. Stay here too, you hear me?" My calm voice was a mask over my frayed nerves. "Just breathe." I grabbed the hem of my cloak and cut a long strip of cloth with Teryn's dagger. Gingerly, I wrapped it around Teryn's torso, forcing him to lift his body as little as possible. I would have given anything for a healer's pouch and powers at that moment. I would trade my empathy, my power, my curse, just to make sure Teryn was going to live.

"We need to get you to a healer," I said.

"People are dying all around us. I don't expect to be any luckier than the rest."

I looked around at the field busy with bloodshed. Swords clashed. Arrows soared. The unicorns sprinted past me with dizzying speed as the Roizan panted after one and then another, sending the ground rumbling with every step.

Teryn was right—people were dying. Many were. But I wanted Teryn to live. I put my hands over his wound and felt something flow through me. It wasn't the fire of power coursing through my veins. It was something else. Something warm and peaceful and flowing. Something I'd never felt before. Something that touched my heart.

"Cora!" Teryn's eyes were wide with terror, shocking me out of my daze.

I turned around to see Morkai's shadow looming over me and felt a sharp pain as he pulled me up by my hair. His staff was quickly hooked around my neck, cutting off my breathing as I clawed at his arm.

"Let her go."

Morkai whirled around, still gripping me tightly, as we faced Dimetreus. My brother's sword was drawn, and his eyes were narrowed with a piercing fury.

"Traitor." Morkai's voice was a venomous hiss. "You serve me, Dimetreus. This girl is nothing to you."

Dimetreus shook his head. "I don't know much about what has happened to me over the years, but I do know that is my sister. And I am the rightful king."

"You abdicated to me."

"The man who abdicated to you doesn't exist."

"I thought we were friends, Dimetreus." Morkai's voice held the slightest rasp.

Dimetreus let out a bark of a laugh. "You can't *create* friends with sorcery."

"I should have killed you."

"You should have. Now let her go."

Morkai lowered his staff just long enough to replace it

with a dagger held in the other hand. I felt the sharp, cold edge press into my flesh. "Lower your sword or she dies."

"Don't do anything he tells you, Dimetreus," I said, moving as little as possible.

My brother's eyes flashed from me to Morkai. He lowered his sword and dropped it to the ground. "Let her go."

Morkai released me. Without a moment of hesitation, he sent his dagger spinning end over end toward my brother.

"Dimi!" Before I could see where the blade stuck, Morkai spun me around to face him. One arm pulled my waist against him, while his hand wrapped around my throat and pressed my neck back, forcing me to look him in the eye.

"I will destroy everything you love," Morkai whispered.

I felt the fire rise within me once again. I let it flow, filling me from head to toe. This time the fire was joined by the warmth I had felt with Teryn. The fire and warmth tickled my flesh, ready to burst from every fingertip, every toe, and every eyelash, freckle, and hair.

"Everything I love is part of me," I said through strangled breaths. "And you will not destroy *me*." I let the fire burst from me, from all around my body. Not enough to send Morkai far, just enough to push him away, giving me time to unsheathe my dagger and plunge its shining white blade into his gut. He shouted in surprise as I twisted it further, deeper.

I stepped away and we eyed each other. Morkai's face flashed with shock, confusion, and then anger. His eyes narrowed, and he opened his lips with a snarl. He looked down at the hilt protruding from his gut. A dark pattern was quickly spreading from the wound, coloring the midnight blue of his robes a red-tinted black. He gripped the hilt and pulled it free, the white blade covered in a sheen of red.

"You'll have to try harder than that, Coralaine." Even though Morkai's voice still held its steady coldness, it was weaker than before. His face was red with fury, and for the first time, he looked at me with something he never had before. Hate.

I backed away as Morkai came toward me, my dagger still in his hand. Over his shoulder, I saw a flash of white. Valorre raced toward me, eyes wild as the Roizan followed close behind. The ground rumbled, jarring my footing. I ignored Morkai's progress and focused on Valorre instead, closing my eyes as I cloaked his horn beneath my glamour. I opened my eyes in time to see the Roizan pause, sniffing the air as it looked this way and that. Valorre came to a halt behind me.

Morkai turned around to face his blood-red creature. "Yes, come to me!" Morkai held his staff toward me as he summoned the Roizan with his other hand. The Roizan obeyed, charging forward with a renewed fury. Morkai flashed a wicked grin my way and erupted with laughter. "You're finished, Coralaine."

The Roizan opened its mouth over the hand that still held the white-bladed dagger and snapped its teeth shut. Morkai's face twisted as he let out a blood-curdling cry. His staff fell to the ground as he reached for his other arm, trying to pull it from between the Roizan's teeth. He shouted, he begged, he screamed for it to let go, but it was as if the Roizan had gone blind, ravenous for more of the horn-blade. Morkai's relentless pleas were stifled as the Roizan opened its mouth again, this time snapping its teeth over Morkai's head. Morkai's body quivered and convulsed until the Roizan moved on to consume his torso, then legs.

I watched unblinking with a combination of terror and morbid satisfaction as Morkai, my enemy, the man who killed my parents, was finally destroyed, replaced with a pool of bloodstained grass.

34

VICTORY

Larylis

A strangled cry rang out behind me, startling me as I fought my wraith opponent. The cry was not that of injury or a grunt of strength. It was neither a battle cry, nor a shout of vengeance and rage. It wasn't the yelp of terrified awe that had escaped my lips when I'd seen unicorns flood the field. Instead it was a wail of torment and anguish. My opponent turned toward the cry with a look of curiosity. I used the distraction to thrust my sword through his gray body. Sweat dripped into my eyes as the wraith fell.

I wiped my brow and looked out at the bloody field around me, littered with bodies and cluttered with men still active in battle, wondering if they were as tired as I was. Nearby, men in red faced men from Norun in Morkai's blue, while the Black Force dashed between a group of wraiths, cutting them down one after the other.

Although the task seemed endless, Lex and I had

been right to suggest the Black Force fight the wraiths. The wraiths were easily confused, easily distracted, and prone to rising slower and slower after each new death. Many had already wandered off the field and disappeared, seemingly disinterested in continuing the farce. Yet, a few others seemed tireless.

I looked down at my own relentless opponent, just beginning to rise again, and cut his throat before he could even stand. Dark gray blood spilled from the gash in his neck, which I knew would begin to repair itself within moments.

Another anguished cry.

This time, it came from nearby. I turned in time to see a man in blue fall to his knees, throw his helmet at the grass, then cry into his palms. His opponent, a Red, stepped back and stared wide-eyed at the man.

Similar cries echoed throughout the field, flooding the valley with tormented wails. I watched as men in blue raised their hands in surrender, eyes darting wildly as if they didn't understand their surroundings. A moment later, our horns announced the death of the enemy, quickly followed by an unfamiliar anthem at the other end of the field. It must have signaled retreat for Morkai's forces, as those who did not surrender—most of them bearing the red crown sigil of Norun—began running for the other edge of the field.

I turned back toward my fallen opponent, expecting him to rise, but the wraith was gone. And so were all the others.

～

Cora

I raced to my brother's side. The hilt of Morkai's dagger protruded from beneath his collarbone. His face was pale as he tried to stand.

"Dimetreus, lay still. I'll get you a healer."

Dimetreus shook off my caution and planted his feet beneath trembling legs. "I'm fine. I've been through worse, trust me." He looked out at the chaos of the field, the retreating army, the hands raised in surrender, the swords still clashing, the Forest People and unicorns racing back up the hillside, the Roizan pawing the grass, sniffing the blood of its master. "I still don't quite understand what I'm seeing. I haven't understood since the day you came to Ridine. It's like I've been slowly waking from one nightmare into a new one."

My throat tightened as I looked up at his thin, tired face, the dark circles surrounding his eyes—eyes that were no longer black and unseeing. They were vibrant green like they had been when he was Dimi, the brother I loved. I resisted a shiver of repulsion as I placed my hand in his. Flashes of his dead eyes, his cold voice, and his stern hand went through my mind. I breathed the memories away. "I'll be here, Dimi. I can help you remember who you really are."

A flicker of a smile tugged at Dimetreus' lips, although it quickly turned to a grimace. His free hand reached toward the dagger, wincing as he placed his palm on his chest below it.

"The Forest People healers can help you. Or the royal physicians."

"Don't worry about me, Coralaine. I told you, I'll be fine. There are many worse injured than I."

I looked toward Centerpointe Rock and felt the blood leave my face as I thought about Teryn. "Dimetreus, I have to—"

"Go," he said. "I'm fine."

I ran to the other side of the Rock where I'd last seen Teryn. He wasn't there. I circled the Rock, looking everywhere as tears burned my eyes.

"Cora."

I turned and found him standing a small distance away, his side still wrapped with the cloth I'd tied around him. Next to him stood a man in black clothing who had Teryn's features, arm draped over his shoulder. Both men's eyes were rimmed with red and the air between them was thick with a combination of sorrow, tenderness, and a subtle awkward strain. I hid my previous distress as I calmly walked over to them, resisting the urge to greet Teryn with a relieved embrace. It was all I could do not to bubble over with excitement at finding him alive.

"Cora, this is my brother, Prince Larylis."

Larylis nodded my way, a sad smile on his lips. "Lex told me much about you, and I'm sure Teryn will tell me more. Now that I finally have him back and alive."

"I'm really glad to find him alive as well," I said. Teryn and I locked eyes, and I opened my mouth to say more, but no words seemed to match what I wanted to say. What *did* I want to say? How could I express all the feelings swirling inside me as I looked at him? He too remained silent, a questioning expression on his face.

A screeching bellow rang throughout the valley. I jumped, and the three of us looked toward the Roizan as it howled and thrashed, foaming at the mouth and turning the bloodstained grass to mud beneath its hooves. Then it stilled. The Roizan's giant head drooped as if suddenly heavy. Its eyes closed, its hindquarters quavered. As it fell to the ground with a rumbling *thud*, its skin began to blacken and char. Even the white horns protruding from its body turned the color of charcoal.

Not sure what I was doing or why, I took a step forward, then another.

"Cora, where are you going?" Teryn called. "Don't go near that thing."

I ignored him and moved toward the moaning, whimpering Roizan, watching as the blackness spread over its body more and more until fiery veins of red began to glow from within. The Roizan slowly opened its maw, and I paused. Its eyes grew heavy as if it were tired, then it released a deep moan. With that breath, the body of the Roizan fell into a pile of ash. Tendrils of smoke caught the wind and began to drift the ash away.

My breath quickened as I approached the ash, then prodded it with my toe. Nothing. I sighed with relief and took a step back, nearly tripping as my heel caught on something in the grass. I looked down. Beneath my foot lay a large, purple crystal next to another pile of ash. A rush of fear passed over me as I stared at the crystal, recognizing it as belonging to Morkai's charred staff. Why hadn't the crystal burned away with the rest?

After a moment of hesitation, I reached down and picked it up. The way my stomach flipped as I felt the cold surface against my palm reminded me of the two horns I'd taken. I expected to sense darkness immediately, yet that wasn't what I felt. There was a weight and a sorrow, but something else I couldn't identify...

A hand fell softly on my shoulder. "What are you doing?" Teryn asked.

I shoved the crystal into an inner pocket of my cloak. Whatever it was, it had belonged to Morkai and would need to be destroyed. I turned to Teryn. "I just wanted to be sure he's gone. I almost expected Morkai to pop up out of the ash."

"Me too. But he's really gone. It's over."

I looked past Teryn to the field beyond, where bodies —those of man, horse, and unicorn alike—were being gathered for burial, and wondered if war was ever truly over. Hostages were taken from the surrendered, men pursued the retreating enemy, and the last glimpse of a unicorn disappeared beyond the tree line. However, one unicorn remained behind.

I smiled as Valorre came up beside me. I placed my hand on his neck and scanned his body for injuries. Although his white coat was speckled with mud and blood, he appeared to be free of any serious wound.

"So, Lex's story was true." Larylis said as he joined us. His voice was so different from Teryn's, despite their similar faces. "You are the unicorn girl."

"She is," Teryn said with a weak smile. "She's also the Princess of—"

Teryn was interrupted by a shout. "That's the traitor! Seize him!"

A stout, gray-haired man in red armor stomped toward my brother, sword drawn. Dimetreus met the man with no resistance, raising his arms in surrender as he was surrounded and bound by the guards.

My feet flew beneath me as I ran to my brother and began pushing at the guards to get to his side. "No! He's injured! Please, don't hurt him."

"Who are you?" The man in red grabbed me by the arm and pulled me toward him. His face sparked a familiarity, but I couldn't place the name.

"King Verdian!" Teryn shouted as he limped to us. "Your Majesty, that's Cora. Please let her go."

"What does she want with the traitor?" Verdian narrowed his eyes at Teryn. Now that I had a name for the face, I remembered who he was. Even in my youth, the King of Sele had always seemed fierce.

"King Dimetreus is my brother!"

"King? He's no king in Lela. He betrayed our land and his own kingdom. Are you a traitor too?"

"Your Majesty, she is Princess Coralaine of Kero," Teryn said. "I'm sure Lex told you about her. Cora is the reason we discovered Morkai's plot."

"Lex never mentioned she was Princess of Kero, a dead girl brought back to life. What kind of sorcery is this?"

"She was never dead, Your Majesty. Let her explain."

"She can explain during questioning. Take her and the traitor with the other hostages."

Fire flooded my body as guards took me by the arms and bound my wrists behind my back. I felt the fire flow down through my hands, heating my palms, and I knew it would take no effort to send the men reeling from me. Yet I held it in and breathed deeply. *These men are not the enemy.*

"I will go with you, and so will my brother. But you must treat his wounds and hear us fairly." I was surprised at the calm in my voice, every word as smooth as honey as it slipped from my lips on waves of fire.

King Verdian held my eyes. I refused to waver beneath his glare.

"Your Majesty, I'm begging you to listen to her." Teryn's voice shook. "She's my friend. I owe her my life. I...care about her."

Teryn's words made my heart quicken, yet I kept my composure steady.

Finally, Verdian released my gaze. "Very well. Take the traitor and get him to a surgeon. Take the girl but keep her separate from the rest of the hostages. Give her a private cell when we reach Verlot."

"Treat her well," Teryn added. "And don't hurt her."

Verdian gave Teryn a scolding glare, but his face softened when his eyes fell on the bandage wrapped around his side. "Someone get Prince Teryn to a surgeon as well."

The king stomped away, his final order sending the guards into a frenzy of movement. Dimetreus and I were prodded forward as Teryn was quickly surrounded by a flurry of healing hands. I craned my neck to watch him, and our eyes locked until I was pulled out of sight. Then I searched for a hint of white.

Valorre was nowhere to be seen.

Good. Stay safe.

I'm never far, he said. *I go where you go.*

His words filled me with warmth. I carried it with me as I marched, head held high, toward my fate.

35

FATE

Cora

My cell was private, but that was its only favorable amenity. It was dark, cramped, cold, and had the smell of dirt and dying things. I could hear cries and shouts from further down the dungeon hall at all hours of day and night. They could have been the cries of my own brother dying from an infected wound, for all I knew.

After three days of questioning by a team of unknown men who stood in shadow alongside a young scribe, my patience was wearing thin. I'd done everything to cooperate and explain what I knew, yet every question I asked went unanswered. I had to know how my brother fared, and I was beginning to consider alternate means to get those answers.

My palms flooded with heat as I imagined using my power to slip through the bars. I knew I could do it. They would have nothing in place to stop me. Verlot seemed to be a place of no magical understanding, and no one—unless Teryn had mentioned it—had any clue to the extent of my powers. I could be free of this place within moments.

Yet, without my cooperation, what would they do to my brother? What would come of Kero?

No. I must stay. For now.

I let out a resigned sigh and rested my back against a wall, trying to remember if it was day or night. The bells that marked the hour didn't reach the dungeons. Time was lost as easily as it had been in the dungeons of Ridine. I shivered at the memory and closed my eyes, determined to think something else, *anything* else.

The sound of feet coming down the hall distracted me from my thoughts, and I sat up eagerly. Perhaps it was someone who was ready to answer my questions for once. A figure carrying a lantern stopped in front of my door and swung it open.

"Come with me," Orin said.

My breath caught in my throat as I scrambled to the farthest corner of the cell, my heart racing fast enough to burst. "You're dead!"

"Silly Coralaine." The voice came from behind Orin, a cold hiss that chilled my blood and bone. I tried to activate the fire within me, but it had been extinguished by my fear. Slow footsteps came nearer and nearer as I opened my mouth in a silent scream. Morkai stepped into the light of the lantern, smiling. "I'll never die."

Someone shook me by the shoulder. I opened my eyes, blinking into the face of a guard. The nightmares that seized my mind each time I drifted off to sleep were by far the worst amenity Verlot's dungeon offered.

"Come with me," the guard repeated, no longer bearing Orin's voice. I shuddered and tried to steady my breathing. Once I had my wits about me, I followed the guard from my cell, surprised that I was being released without bindings.

He led me beyond a door and into a narrow hall that seemed endless as it wove this way and that, up thin, creaking staircases, down more windowless corridors, breaking off in separate directions here and there. After three days stuck in a cell, it was hard to keep up with the guard without finding myself short of breath. Finally, he opened an unseen door into a room spilling blinding light.

I stepped inside, blinking at the daylight flooding through the elegantly curtained windows and illuminating intricate designs on the tapestries that covered the walls. In the middle of the room stood an immense, four-poster bed that was larger than anything I'd ever seen at Ridine Castle. The posts were of a thick, dark wood carved with flowers and trailing vines, and draped with a gauzy, white canopy. The bedding looked so plush with its countless pillows and thick blankets, I could have cried just imagining sleeping in it. The remaining furnishings in the room—a lounge, a table with two chairs, a wardrobe, a vanity—paled in comparison.

"Is this her?" A wisp of a girl stood from one of the chairs and walked toward me, hands folded at her waist and a shy smile on her pale, youthful face.

"It is," the guard said. "She is not to leave this room until she looks presentable. Have her bathed and dressed, then have the guards take her to the king's study."

The girl gave a small curtsy, and the guard left

through two heavy doors at the other end of the room. I looked back toward where we'd entered and saw nothing suggesting there had been a door.

"Servants' hall." The girl walked to the wall and pulled aside a tapestry. "You aren't to go in there, though. It was just so you weren't seen in the palace until you are cleaned."

"Yes, Lela forbid anyone in the palace be made aware the conditions the Princess of Kero was held prisoner in."

The girl giggled, ignoring the malice in my voice. "Are you truly the dead princess?"

"I was never dead. Just...elsewhere."

"I've heard so many rumors. I can't wait to hear the truth. I'm so honored Mareleau chose me to be your chambermaid." The girl paused. "She doesn't like me much. I try not to talk, so I don't irritate her."

I felt the tenseness release from my shoulders as the girl's innocence prompted a small smile from me. "What's your name?"

"Lurel," she said with a curtsy. "Now, let's get you looking like a princess again."

I felt every bit the princess as I walked down the halls of Verlot Palace, two guards flanking each side. My hair had been brushed in rolling waves of brown with four rows of braids running from my temples and sides of my head to meet in the middle at the back. My lips and cheeks were stained a rosy hue, and I was dressed in the most elegant gown I had ever seen.

The dress Morkai had made me wear at Ridine was

commoner's garb compared to what I wore now—an exquisite gown in emerald green and gold brocade, cinched so tight at my waist that I had no other option than to stand tall, taking slow steps. The only threat the dress posed was its length. According to Lurel, the gown had belonged to Mareleau three years prior, and she had since grown out of it. Even three years ago, it seemed Mareleau had been taller than I was now. Lurel did her best to hem the front so only the back trailed behind me. Still, the thought of tripping on the gown made every step that much slower.

Heads turned my way and curious eyes stared shamelessly as I passed on our way to King Verdian's study. Once we reached the large, double-doors, I took a deep breath and stepped into the room. Verdian stood behind his desk, and a regal-looking woman sat in a chair beside it.

"Welcome, Princess Coralaine," the woman said. It was the first time I'd been addressed as a princess since I'd been at Verlot. "I'm Queen Bethaeny, mother of Prince Teryn, who has done a great deal on your behalf. He has been tireless in arguing your case and bargaining for the release of your brother."

I felt heat rise to my cheeks, which I hid as I sank into a deep curtsy. "I appreciate everything he is doing, and for your willingness to listen."

"Have you been treated well?"

I paused, wondering how much honesty was treasured in this new world I'd been thrust into. "I find my most recent accommodations treat me well."

Queen Bethaeny gave me an apologetic smile. "You must forgive us our need for the lengthy questioning."

"After what we've been through, we were not willing to take any chances," Verdian said. "Lives have been lost. We need to do what is best for Lela."

"And what have you decided?" I asked.

Verdian stepped in front of his desk, leaning against it as he crossed his arms and fixed me beneath his gaze. "First, you must know what is at stake. Even though Teryn has assured us Dimetreus was under Morkai's control and not acting of his own accord, he's been seen as a traitor by everyone in Lela. It would be no difficult task for me to seize Kero, divide the kingdom in two, and place it under the control of Sele and Mena. If you and your brother fail to agree to our terms, we will enact this plan, and you will remain hostages here. Any resistance from you as hostages, and you will both be executed."

I clenched my jaw and fought the anger that threatened to spew forth. "What are your terms?"

This time, Queen Bethaeny spoke. "Your brother will be allowed to resume his place as King of Kero, but his council and heads of both staff and military will be selected by King Verdian from men of Sele and Mena. Dimetreus has already agreed to this."

I let out a sigh of relief. That didn't sound too bad.

"But we need something from you too," Bethaeny said. "We have had a difficult time deciding whether to trust you, considering all reports name you deceased. But we want to trust you and need to find a way to secure that trust. That has been the focus of Teryn's biggest fight. He has spoken highly of you. I can tell he trusts you and is fond of you. He seems willing to do anything to guarantee your safety and position as princess."

Again, heat rose to my cheeks, but for different

reasons this time. I couldn't help but smile at the thought
of Teryn working so hard for me...or the thought of Teryn
at all. He'd long been on my mind during my stay in the
dungeon. How was he? Had his wound healed? My heart
begged me to ask, but I remained quiet as Bethaeny
spoke again.

"Therefore, I have agreed to arrange a marriage
between you and my son. Dimetreus will make him his
heir, and rule will pass to the two of you and your children upon Dimetreus' death or abdication."

"If Dimetreus is deemed incapable of the crown by his
council, he will be forced to abdicate immediately,"
Verdian added.

"Dimetreus has agreed to these terms as well but has
left the final choice for you to make." Queen Bethaeny
folded her hands and awaited my response.

My eyes flashed from Verdian to Bethaeny, my mind
reeling as I tried to sort through what they'd said. If I
wanted to save my kingdom, I would have to marry.

I would have to marry *Teryn*.

This time the heat flooded more than my cheeks. My
entire body filled with warmth as something unfamiliar
fluttered in my heart. Calm fell over me, and my feelings
became clear, as unexpected as they were. Teryn had
become my friend in the short time we'd known each
other. But if I was being honest with myself, he'd become
so much more than that without me even realizing it. Not
until now.

I was nowhere near ready for marriage, but with
Teryn, it wouldn't be so bad, would it? I knew he would
be patient with me. He'd give me time. He'd allow our
relationship to grow naturally, no matter what we were

forced to do. My lips pressed tight to suppress my grin. Marrying Teryn would be far better than not bad. I...*wanted* it to happen. The realization made my heart flip in my chest. "When would we need to marry?"

"My husband is dead, so his rule must pass to Teryn as soon as possible," Bethaeny said. "Teryn will be coronated within days after his marriage to Princess Mareleau, who will then be coronated as queen. You and Larylis will marry immediately after."

My heart froze. "Me...and Larylis?"

"Yes." The queen's face softened when my eyes grew wide. "You didn't think..."

I shook my head. My breath quickened, lungs feeling as if they were being squeezed tight. Waves of noise flooded my mind with thoughts, words, feelings. It seemed like every person in the palace were suddenly in my head all at once. I closed my eyes over my swimming vision and collapsed to my knees.

"Oh dear. Help her!" I heard the queen shout over the noise in my head.

A pair of guards grasped my arms, keeping me upright as their thoughts and words pounded into my temples. I took a deep breath and let it out slowly, fighting the anxiety crushing my chest, pressing the noise from my mind. Once the cacophony receded, I was left with nothing but my own thoughts. And shame. A deep, flooding shame that made me wish I was invisible. I stood and brushed off my dress.

"Forgive me, Your Majesties." My voice sounded weak and distant. "I haven't eaten enough, and I am overwhelmed. Please allow me to excuse myself and consider your terms."

"Of course." Verdian's face shifted between annoyance and concern beneath a furrowed brow.

I sank into a slow, deep curtsy, then left the study.

I did not feel like a princess as I walked back toward my room. The halls were a blur of color and sound as I tore through the halls, furiously wiping the tears from my cheeks. Passers-by stopped and stared, eyebrows raised as they whispered amongst themselves. They no longer looked at me with admiration and awe, but I didn't care. What did it matter now? I wasn't a beautiful princess like Mareleau. I was nothing more than a pawn.

"Cora. Cora, wait. Cora!"

I ignored the calling of my name until Teryn stood directly in front of me, taking me by the shoulders. "Cora, are you all right? I saw you rush out of the study, then my mother said you almost fainted."

I looked into his face, and my tears poured over my cheeks like molten streams. "Did you know?"

Teryn's brow furrowed. "Did I know what?"

"That they promised me to your brother. They say you fought for me, but did you fight for me on that?"

Teryn's expression darkened, but he said nothing.

I shook my head. "Everything else I can understand. But your brother? How could you allow such a thing? Why would you want that?"

"It wasn't my...it was the only way—"

"It wasn't the only way! There was another, yet you obviously found it distasteful."

"What do you mean?"

"I was so stupid. I can't believe I thought..." I knew my voice sounded childish, which filled me with even more shame. What was happening to me?

"Cora, I don't understand. What could I have done? Why are you angry with me?"

I shook free from his grasp and brushed him aside. The guards scrambled to keep up with me as I stormed ahead. I took one look at Teryn's fallen face staring after me, yet I felt nothing but anger.

"I thought she meant you." I wasn't sure if he'd heard me, and part of me hoped he hadn't. My head whipped forward as I blinked my eyes dry, my every step fueled by rage as—dress be damned—I picked up speed and ran back to my room.

36

SACRIFICE

Teryn

Cora's words echoed through my head. The memory of her angry eyes pierced my heart as I returned to the study.

"Good of you to rejoin us." King Verdian's voice held an unmistakable bite. "Can we start now?"

My eyes remained unfocused as I took my seat. I met my mother's smile, then stole a glance at Mareleau, who sat with her arms crossed, refusing to meet my eyes. Next to me sat Larylis, sinking low in his chair, shoulders so tense they looked to be one with his neck. Queen Helena stood tall next to Verdian behind the desk, her glowing smile and sparkling eyes seeking to shine their radiance on everyone in turn.

"As I was saying, Larylis," Mother said. "We've made the offer to Princess Coralaine, and she is taking some time to think about it. Despite our initial reservations, this is a very advantageous match for you. It would place you as future King of Kero."

Larylis nodded, yet his eyes wouldn't budge from their fixation on King Verdian's desk.

"Which brings us to our most important topic." My mother turned her attention to me. "Your coronation as king. Once we return to Mena, we will arrange for the ceremony. Before we leave, we will secure your marriage to Mareleau so we can celebrate her coronation as queen as well."

My stomach churned, and I had to force my head to nod, feeling as if it suddenly held the weight of the world. This was not how I'd once imagined my marriage to Mareleau would go. In fact, as I looked at her, lips pursed and eyes glaring into the opposite wall, I couldn't fathom what had prompted my attraction to her in the first place. She was cold. Unknowable. A stranger to me. What had I been thinking? How could I have ever convinced myself I loved this woman?

"The two of you can sign the agreement now, and we will have the ceremony tonight." King Verdian spread the contract over his desk and held out a quill.

I felt as heavy as lead in my chair. Nothing could make me stand. Nothing.

"No."

All eyes turned to Mareleau. Had the word, so strong and forceful, come from her?

Verdian shot his daughter a ferocious glare. "Excuse me?"

"I'm not marrying Teryn," Mareleau said, her voice calm yet with an undeniable air of finality.

"Don't be silly," Queen Helena cooed. She waved a

hand at my mother, whose lips trembled as she stared wide-eyed at Mareleau. "Ignore her, she doesn't mean it."

"I do mean it." Mareleau stood and stepped toward her parents. "I want to marry Larylis, and he wants to marry me."

"That's absurd!" Verdian pounded his fist on the desk.

"No, *this* is absurd. All my life you've told me I need to marry a crown prince. Teryn, specifically, for the good of Lela. You said Larylis could never be king, yet you have no problem with him being heir to the King of Kero. Why can't he be *my* king? If Dimetreus can make his sister's husband his heir, why can't you make Larylis yours?"

King Verdian's face flushed. He opened his mouth but was quieted by the gentle hand of his wife.

"Your uncles will never follow Larylis." Helena's voice was smooth as silk. "You know this. They would argue and fight and overthrow your rule to take as their own. However, they would have no choice but to follow Teryn, a crown prince made king in every right."

"This makes no sense." Mareleau threw her hands in the air, then turned to me. "Teryn, I don't want to marry you. I want to marry your brother. I love him. I don't love you. That makes sense, doesn't it?"

I was speechless, torn between shock and giddy laughter as I looked from her to my brother, still hunched in his seat.

Frustrated with my lack of reply, Mareleau shook her head in annoyance and returned to face her mother. "You know what makes even more sense? I missed my moon cycle. I'm pregnant with Larylis' child. There is no better reason to allow us to be together as we wish."

This time, there was no laughter bubbling inside me, only shock.

Larylis bolted upright in his seat. "Teryn, we never...I swear...I wouldn't—"

"We don't have to hide anymore." Mareleau's eyes bored into Larylis, crystal blue daggers so sharp, even I could feel them.

"But we..." Larylis stared back, his face growing pale as she held his eyes without falter. Finally, he nodded and turned to me. "I'm sorry. What she says is true. I never meant to betray you, but...I love her. You've always known this."

Shame and guilt mingled with my surprise over this turn of events, sending my stomach into a roiling mess. The blood left my face. He was right; I *had* known. I just never believed him. The tumultuous array of emotions vying for control coalesced into a deep anger at myself. How could I have let this happen? I went after a woman I didn't love, a woman who didn't love me back. A woman who'd loved my brother all along. I was so stupid.

I stared at the floor, unable to keep the rage from my face.

"I'm sorry," Larylis said, misreading my expression. I wished I could explain, wished I could meet his eyes. He wasn't at fault here. I was. I just couldn't find the words to admit it.

I felt as if I were being crushed by the weight of my guilt until a flicker of peace wound its way through my regret, whispering something I couldn't ignore. It was a small thing, but it was true. If I hadn't done what I'd done, if I hadn't gone on the Quest, I never would have met Cora. We never would have learned everything we learned. We never would have defeated Morkai.

With this knowledge, I was able to release my anger, my shame, my humiliation, and focus on what was in front of me. I'd made a mistake, but it could be undone. I knew what I had to do.

"How could you do this, Mareleau?" Queen Helena's words shook me from my thoughts. She lost her unworldly grace as her face turned nearly purple, hands clenching into fists at her sides.

"You have ruined yourself!" King Verdian roared, then stormed toward Mareleau.

I jumped to my feet and stood between them, Larylis leaping to my side. Keeping my eyes locked on the king, I waved a hand at my brother to return to his seat. "Your Majesty, please calm down."

Verdian's chest heaved as his eyes slid from his daughter to me. He took a step away from Mareleau. "You're her only hope now, Prince Teryn. You'll be doing both our kingdoms a great honor if you will take this spoiled, ruined wretch of a girl for your wife."

"Did you not hear me?" Mareleau's voice quaked through clenched teeth. "I love Larylis. I'm pregnant with *his* child."

"And if Teryn agrees to marry you, no one need know of your shame." King Verdian passed a palm over his face, then let it rest on his chin. His voice had grown calm, empty. Hopeless. "Otherwise, you are ruined. Your uncles will fight for the throne."

Tears streamed down Mareleau's cheeks. "You are insensible!"

"No, my daughter, you are. You care more about your

selfish desires than the security of your kingdom. If Teryn won't have you, no one will." Verdian looked from Mareleau to Larylis. "The two of you have likely doomed our kingdom and should be executed for treason."

My mother stood, rushing toward him. "You can't mean that! You're talking about my son!"

Voices raised as everyone but me began shouting, drowning out any sense of audible words. I stepped forward and took Mareleau's hand, pulling her away from the others. The arguing subsided to an uncomfortable stillness when she faced me, fury in her eyes as she met mine.

It was all up to me now. "Don't worry, I can fix this."

She narrowed her eyes at me, lips peeling back from her teeth as she pulled her hands from mine. "I don't want your help."

"But you need it."

"Don't do this." Her words shifted from fierce to panicked. "Don't marry me. Please, please, please." I was stricken by the terror in her face, the plea in her words as she slid to her knees in a wail of defeat.

I turned away from her. "Mother, I have an announcement to make. King Verdian, please bear witness, as this is an official decree. I am denouncing my claim as crown prince. I abdicate to Prince Larylis, effective immediately."

Mother put a hand to her mouth. "Why in Lela would you do such a thing?"

Verdian shook his head. "No...no..."

"Do you mean that?" I turned to find Mareleau, tears glistening on her cheeks as she wrung her hands. "You will give the crown to Larylis?"

I nodded. "Without a doubt."

"No," Verdian said.

Mareleau rose to her feet and shot her father a glare. "You can't tell him no, Father. He has a right to abdicate if he chooses."

"Oh, no you don't," Verdian shook his head, veins pulsing at his temples. "You don't get out of this so easily. You really think I'm going to let the two of you," he pointed from Mareleau to Larylis, "go from condemned traitors to king and queen?"

"You were willing to let Teryn marry me, condemned traitor as I am. Why can't Larylis marry me, the mother of his child? It's the clear solution."

"The clear solution is to take off your head! And Larylis' too!"

Anger surged through me. "What I said is final, King Verdian. I abdicate. I will gather Mena's councilmen at once to make it official. Whatever you choose to do, Larylis is now crown prince. Are you really planning to condemn the future king of your closest ally?"

Verdian sighed, the redness receding from his face. He rubbed his chin and turned away from us, walking toward the window. "No, I cannot condemn Mena's crown prince."

"Then what Mareleau said is true. Letting her marry Larylis is the clear solution. We just fought a war. Let there be peace between us, at least."

Larylis came to my side, his voice pitched low. "I appreciate what you're doing for me, but you don't have to do this. I don't deserve the crown."

Verdian mumbled his agreement as he stared out the window.

I took my brother by the shoulder, finally able to meet his eyes. "I'm not only doing this for you. I'm doing this for me too. You are just as worthy of the crown as I am. You led the Black Force against the wraiths. You negotiated an alliance with Tomas. You made sure Lex's message from Morkai was delivered with haste. You are worthy, and if Father were here, he'd say the same thing."

My eyes moved to my mother. Her lips pulled into a sad smile, and she gave me a subtle nod.

Helena took a step toward her husband. "No matter what she has done, Mareleau is our daughter. She is still our only hope for an heir."

Verdian scowled at Helena, then closed his eyes. When he opened them, they locked on Mareleau. "Yet again, you get your way." His expression held so much malice, it was hard to believe it was all directed at his daughter.

Mareleau took slow steps to Larylis' side, then laced her fingers through his. She met her father's gaze with defiance.

Verdian threw his hands in the air. "Fine. Let the traitors marry."

Relief washed over me, echoing in Larylis' sigh and Mareleau's squeal as she wrapped her arms around my brother's neck. The sight of them together, their smiles and tears of joy, lifted a weight from my shoulders. I'd done it. I'd fixed my mistake. Yet, there was still something else I needed to take care of.

"Now that that has been settled," I said, "I have one more thing to discuss. It's about Princess Coralaine."

~

Cora

"What do those bells mean?" I asked Lurel. The bells resounded, too many to count, louder than anything that would have marked the hour.

Lurel looked up from her place beside me on the lounge, head cocked to the side. An excited smile stretched over her face. "I'll find out, Your Highness." She skipped out the doors before I could say another word.

I went to the window overlooking the garden and saw figures below pause their strolling along the paths, their composure excited as they exchanged words with their companions. I closed my eyes and extended my power past the glass of the window, past the shrubs, and onto the garden path.

Before I could catch a word, my doors flew open. With an irritated sigh, I turned toward Lurel, who was prancing into the room and squealing with excitement.

"Princess Mareleau has been married!"

"Oh?" My voice came out like a croak. "To...Prince Teryn?"

Lurel shrugged. "Who else? It was a secret wedding, I just heard from one of the guards! How romantic is that? She and the prince will soon return to Dermaine for their coronation. There is a celebration dinner tonight in the great hall, followed by the procession to the wedding chamber. Would you like to go? I can have you re-dressed in no time. Your hair still looks lovely, so hardly a moment's work is needed there."

I swallowed a lump in my throat and pulled my robe tight around my shift. "No thank you, Lurel. I'm not feeling well. But you should enjoy the festivities."

Lurel's brow furrowed. "If you aren't feeling well, I will stay. I'll get you whatever you need—"

"Don't worry about me." I forced a smile. "I'm tired and would prefer to be alone to rest. Be excused and send my congratulations to the happy couple."

"As you wish, princess." Lurel grinned and fell into a deep curtsy.

Once she left, I reeled back toward the window and pounded my fist on the wall beside it. The air in the room felt too thick to breathe, and I wished I was anywhere but within the stifling palace walls.

Why was I so angry? Hadn't I known Teryn would eventually marry Mareleau? Had I really been so stupid to think he'd choose me over her, or that our friendship meant the same thing to him that it did to me? I wanted to scream, to curse myself for realizing my feelings too late. Yet, if I *had* realized them sooner...would it have mattered? Embarrassment brought a flood of heat to my cheeks as I remembered what I'd shouted at him in the hall. *I thought she meant you.*

Had he heard me? For the love of Lela, I hoped not. Then again, why should I care? *What is wrong with me right now? Of course I shouldn't care! Since when do I care about boys or love or romance?*

I let out a shuddering breath. *Since I met Teryn.*

I slid down in a heap and leaned my head against the wall, wondering why I ever agreed to come to Verlot in the first place. Perhaps I should have fought the guards on the battlefield. I could have stolen away with Dimetreus to the Forest People. I could have left this mess behind.

But no matter how tempting those thoughts were, I

knew why I'd chosen to come here, why I'd endured the questioning and imprisonment. I came to Verlot to get my kingdom back. It may have been a broken kingdom, but it was *mine*. And there was still so much work to do. Morkai's body was gone, but I couldn't help feeling that his shadow lingered on. It hid in every corner of my mind, taunting me, reminding me of the hurt he'd caused me, my friends, and my people. Knowing what I did about Morkai, he wouldn't have died without leaving a trail of even more danger in his absence.

This is far from over.

I let out a heavy sigh, knowing I'd already made my choice and there was no going back. I'd taken the risk to reclaim my kingdom, to return Dimetreus to his throne. To begin to right the wrongs Morkai had inflicted. Now I would see it through, no matter the cost.

Even if I have to marry Teryn's brother.

I closed my eyes and let the tears flow.

37

RENEWAL

Cora

Eighth bell rang, and I still hadn't moved from my spot on the floor against the wall. I opened my eyes and found daylight had vanished. I stood and stretched my limbs, cramped from sitting so long, then made my way to the lantern on the table. Once lit, it filled the room with a soft glow. My eyes felt heavy, sore from tears, yet my heart was at peace.

I pushed away a stray thought that threatened to shatter that peace—Teryn and Mareleau proceeding to their wedding chamber—and instead thought of Valorre. I smiled, imagining how quickly I would see him once freed from this prison. All I had to do was sign a marriage contract. I could feel Valorre's closeness, just beyond the palace walls, waiting amongst the trees.

A sound from behind startled me from pleasant thoughts of freedom. I whirled around, bringing the light of the lantern toward a rustling tapestry. A moment later, the unseen door opened, and into the lantern light stepped Teryn.

I gasped. Anger, hatred, and confusion followed. *Breathe.* My heart pounded, yet I forced the fury away. "What are you doing here? Shouldn't you be at the festivities?" *Or in your wedding bed.*

"I...had to see you," Teryn said.

I tried to think of something clever to say. Something hurtful. Yet, my eyes fell on the hidden door, still slightly ajar behind the tapestry. "Why did you come through the servants' hall?"

"You're still considered a hostage. The guards posted at your door would never let me in without permission from King Verdian. Besides, it wouldn't be proper for you to be seen receiving a male visitor at this hour."

I raised an eyebrow. "So, you thought it would be more proper to sneak into my room?"

A hesitant smile played at the corner of his lips, sending a ripple of irritation through me.

"How did you know about the servants' hall in the first place?" I asked.

"Mareleau told me about it. She told me how to get here."

The irritation grew from a ripple to a wave. "Why in Lela would your wife send you sneaking into another woman's room on your wedding night?" Teryn laughed, making my hands clench into fists. "It's not funny!"

"Mareleau is not my wife."

My jaw dropped as I tried to form words from my frazzled thoughts. "What? But I heard she—"

"She's married to Larylis, the new Crown Prince of Mena, and soon-to-be king."

"But...why? How is this possible?"

"I renounced my claim as crown prince so Larylis could wed Mareleau." Teryn shook his head, smiling as if he found his words funny. "It's crazy to hear myself say it out loud. I never would have imagined it would turn out this way."

"I still don't understand."

"It's a long story, and it's not what I came here for." His tone was gentle, and there was a pleading quality to his expression.

I set down the lantern and took a step toward him. The anger that had roared through my veins had extinguished, leaving me trembling in its wake. Hope threatened to ignite within me, but I breathed it away, keeping it a mere ember inside my heart. "Then why did you come?"

He took a deep breath, as if nervous. "With the newest developments, I was able to renegotiate your terms to reclaim your title. I wanted you to hear it from me first. I never want to cause you pain again, or for you to be surprised or hurt by anything I do on your behalf. So I will share the terms with you now, and if you don't agree, I will counter them before you even hear another word of them."

I bit my lip, heart racing. "What are the new terms?"

Teryn led us to my lounge, extending his arm for me to sit, then pulled a chair across from me. He clasped his hands, elbows propped on his knees as he leaned forward. "Now that Mareleau and Larylis are wed, King Verdian and my mother have agreed for me to marry you."

I opened my mouth, but no words came forth.

He seemed to take my silence as reluctance, rushing to add, "We don't even have to marry at once. They have agreed to let us wait a year for you to settle into your title, and for your brother to strengthen his kingdom."

Hope continued to burn, begging to transform into excitement, yet I still couldn't give in. Teryn was whom I wanted, and he was here, asking for my hand. He wasn't going to marry Mareleau after all. But wasn't I still Teryn's second choice? Could I live with that?

"I am committed to my cause," I said, keeping my voice level. "I will do whatever it takes to get my kingdom back, but I won't take pity from you, if that's what this is about. I'm sure this isn't ideal for you, considering you lost Mareleau—"

"I never loved Mareleau," Teryn said, shifting to the edge of his seat. "Even you could see that. When I returned here, I thought marrying her was my duty, a promise I had to keep. You have no idea how relieved I was when I found a way out. When I found a way to be... with you. This isn't about pity. This is about *us*. It's about everything we've been through together, good and bad, and never wanting to let you go from this point on. I want this. I hope you do too."

The ember of hope became an inferno flooding my chest, radiating down to my fingertips and toes, heating my cheeks. I opened my mouth, but again found myself speechless.

Teryn searched my face, worry creasing his forehead. "But if this isn't what you want—"

I leaned forward and pressed my fingers to his lips, quieting him. Tears swam in my eyes as my lips pulled into a smile. "I do. I want this."

Teryn's grin stretched across his face, hazel eyes shining in the light of the lantern. My fingertips felt warm where they pressed against his lips. I pulled them away, but my eyes remained where my fingers had been.

Teryn lifted a hand, then brushed it along my cheek, as if exploring the touch of our flesh. The trail of his fingers burned me in a way I'd never felt before, and I had to suppress a delighted shudder. "I don't know every-thing about you yet," Teryn said, "but I want to. I do know you're fierce and strong and beautiful. I know you're my friend. I know I want you to be more than that."

His hand came to a pause at my jaw, and he ran his thumb over my bottom lip. I leaned into the touch. "So do I."

He leaned closer, brow raised, a sly smile playing on his lips. "Does that mean you agree to the terms?"

I answered him with a kiss.

ABOUT THE AUTHOR

Tessonja Odette is fantasy author living in Seattle with her family, her pets, and ample amounts of chocolate. When she isn't writing, she's watching cat videos, petting dogs, having dance parties in the kitchen with her daughter, or pursuing her many creative hobbies. Read more about Tessonja at www.tessonjaodette.com

Made in the USA
Columbia, SC
10 August 2021

43356125R00200